REINING DEVOTION

CHAOTIC REIN
BOOK 2

HALEY JENNER

Editor: ellie mclove @ My Brother's Editor
Cover Design: Ellie McLove
Cover Artist: Fernando Ferreiro
Original Photographer: Jessica Wikstrom
Model: Jorgen Andreassen

This book is intended for those 18 years and older. It contains content of an adult nature.

"No one is ever the villain of their own story."
Cassandra Clare, *Lady Midnight*

Firstly, to those who have, at any point in their lives, felt unworthy.
Can we tell you a secret?
Your value is limitless. You are worthy.

Last, but definitely not least… to Viv, for the choking belly laughs at midnight. We love you. Please don't break up with us, no matter how much we pressure you to love us back ;)

Warning:
This book contains sensitive topics that may upset or offend readers.

Trigger / Content Warnings

Please note that while Reining Devotion has been written as a standalone, it is the conclusion of our Chaotic Rein duet. For the full effect of the story, reading Tangled Love prior will enrich the experience of this book.

To keep up-to-date with our new books, sign up for our newsletter at www.authorhaleyjenner.com

CHAPTER ONE

ROCCO

My shoulder pushes back with the power of the gun, jumping away from the bullet propelling forward in slow motion. It flies through the air with the soft sound of silence, the catch of every breath in the room wrapping around my spine like poison.

Only this time, she doesn't move.

There are no quick-moving feet to shift her body in front of mine.

No selfless act of love.

Because this time, I'm on the other side of the room. My feet planted in the very spot Marcus' were.

I am him. He is me. We're one and the same, and she can't protect me from that reality.

I will myself to scream, to yell at her to move. But my mouth remains comfortably closed, watching on in expectation.

My warped perception has me believe I could reach out and take it back. Catch the lead bullet in my hand and keep it there forever. In a place that could never cause her harm.

Except I don't. I watch my perfect aim penetrate my aunt's skull. The center of her forehead pierced by *my* bullet.

The heartache in her eyes flashes like fireworks. Bright blues of sadness. Apple greens of terror. Pulsating reds of rage. A rainbow of regret blinds me. The emotional explosion has been pushed aside by her acceptance. She knew this would be her end. She knew her death would be my doing, her blood forever staining my hands.

I wake with a shout. My apology balanced on the tip of my bleeding tongue, the acquiescence in Mira's eyes tattooed into the forefront of my mind. A place it will stay for eternity.

My heart pounds against my breastbone. It begs me with every tortured beat for escape against the agony of living within me. I can't say the feeling isn't mutual. If I could rip it from my chest cavity, I would. I'd squeeze the organ forcing me to continue living until it stuttered in my palm. I'd watch it bleed, and I'd smile, knowing that my agony was finally over. I'd die in peace. Which is more than I deserve, but I'd take it anyway.

I push against my chest, hand open, massaging my hateful heart into calm.

Awake, I can direct my thoughts away from the ghosts of my past.

I can pretend that it was Marcus that killed Mira. That my quest for vengeance wasn't what powered that final bullet.

I can pretend that I'm not coated with the blood of responsibility. If I'd only listened to her, I know her life would have been spared.

I can pretend that she doesn't regret giving her life to save mine.

They're all tiny lies that flutter through my conscience with force. They live on the precipice of life and death every day. Waiting patiently for a hint of weakness that will let them shrivel up into nothing, leaving me with nothing but the bitter taste of the truth. If that moment doesn't come in the light of day, my lies relish the night when they can finally leave. The truth is too potent to overcome when I have no choice but to sleep. With the deeper crevices of my mind open, a tsunami of reality crashes through me, making me face the real world once again.

Bile rushes up my throat, the acidic reminder of my worst failures burning my insides. I swallow it back down, knowing I deserve the pain.

I often wonder how long I can survive like this. My mind is hellbent on killing me, on rotting me from the inside out. Poetic, isn't it? Murdering myself with guilt. The only solace I can take from that notion is that it will be a horribly slow way to die.

CHAPTER TWO

ROCCO

ONCE UPON A TIME, I thought my mom and dad were invincible. *Kane and Lila Shay*. They were my very own superheroes. *Immortal*. Two people I believed would stay by my side forever.

What encourages us to believe that our parents will never leave? Possibly their constant reassurance that no matter what you do or who you are, they'll love you. Their affection comes without judgment, without condition. It's resolute. Add that to the fact that love is the most powerful commodity in this world, and there you have it, invincibility.

What a load of shit.

I was trained for sixteen years to believe that life was good. That it was fair. That I was loved unconditionally. My belief system wasn't gradually twisted into the hate inside my heart today. On the contrary, it was ripped from me with so much violence it's surprising I ever regained the ability to stand on my own again. I was pushed, unwillingly, into survival mode. I was forced to pick myself up after my heart, spirit, and mind had been broken down until all that was left was the rotting taste of rejection and disappointment.

My life irrevocably changed the day Marcus Dempsey and Sarah Rein decided my mother needed to die. It set off a timeline of events that seemed to plunge me farther into the depths of hell. I'm not gonna lie, from that moment, I went gladly. I dug my way into the very purgatory I now live in and taught myself *this* was real life. The pain I live within. *This* is what life actually feels like. Not the fairy tale my mother gifted me for sixteen years. No, that was designed to ensure I felt life's agony in all its glory. The nightmare that was always meant to be.

"Marcus is dead," I tell her. "Dominic killed him. Imagine that, a Rein saving a Shay."

My mother's gravestone mocks me, staring back at me in eerie silence. I shift uncomfortably at the bite of wind rushing over my skin. Moving forward, I rearrange the white roses resting against the stale gray headstone.

"Maybe you know that, or maybe not. I'd bet my life that he isn't with you. In heaven, or wherever the afterlife has taken you."

My cell buzzes in my pocket, but I ignore the persistent vibration against my thigh. "I'm trying to find some semblance of peace in the fact that he's gone. That's what I wanted. *Revenge. Retribution.* It's what I hurt everyone I love searching for. Don't get me wrong." My voice picks up. "I'm happy as fuck that piece of shit is dead. I'm just not sure that in the end, it was worth everything we lost." The regret in my tone is potent, and I cough to clear my throat.

The last few months play like a constant loop in my head. A horror film I'd prefer to forget. One I played a leading fucking role in. Only I wasn't the hero or the villain. I was the fucking idiotic errand boy. Too stupid to see the bigger picture, still powerful enough to cause catastrophic damage.

"Park's good." I change the subject. "Happy. His woman is good people. You'd never believe she was related to Marcus. I guess in the end, it's nurture over nature, probably why I never stood a chance." I exhale heavily at the melancholy in my voice. "You'd like her. A lot." A bark of laughter escapes my lips, and I sigh loudly. "She's a lot like you. Kind. Happy. Thoughtful. All sunshine and rainbows."

I could imagine her smiling at that. Her white teeth on show, her gray eyes dancing in joy. My chin wobbles involuntarily, pissing me off.

"How did I not see it?" Head tipped back, I let the piercing temperature of raindrops fall against my face. Hoping like hell they camouflage the tears pooling in my eyes. "It was right in front of my eyes this whole time. *Right. Fucking. There.*"

I wait patiently for her to speak to me, but of course, there's nothing but the sound of the wind whipping along my eardrums. "How did Kane not see it? How did your fucking *husband* not see his closest friend was responsible for *everything*?"

Turning my head to scan the empty cemetery, my eyes fall along the rows of stones similar to my mother's. Flowers are scattered amongst them; some are fresh while others that have been left to rot into the earth. How many people have done what I'm doing right now? How many men and women have had to sit at the gravestone of a loved one and apologize for failing them so irrefutably?

"I imagine she's with you." My voice cracks and I scrub my hands roughly along my face. "That's what I'm hoping anyway. That hope is the only thing keeping me breathing right now."

Coughing to clear my throat, I growl, blinking to let my tears mingle with the rain touching my cheeks. "I'm so fucking sorry, Mom. Tell her I'm sorry, would you? I know it means shit, but *please*, tell her I'm sorry." I suck in a desperate breath, trying to control the emotion wracking through my body but failing. Miserably. An agonized cry falls from my mouth, and I rip at the grass surrounding me. "*Fuck.*"

I toss the blades of grass to the side. "I can't even blame this fucked up mess on Marcus. In the end, I was exactly who he wanted me to be. Who he knew I was."

I wipe at the final tears, standing abruptly, needing to be as far away from the suffocating guilt as possible. "I'm sorry he was right."

I turn away and hightail it the fuck out of the cemetery. Head down, hands stuffed in the pockets of my jeans, I feel decidedly worse than when I arrived.

It's done.

She now knows for certain.

My mother knows I'm the monster responsible for her sister's death. It may not have been my bullet like my dreams want me to believe, but I made sure those dominoes fell.

Lila Shay now knows that the evil that lived inside Marcus also resides in her oldest son. We may not be related by blood, but I was Marcus' spawn. He made sure of that. Worse, I let that sick son-of-a-

5

bitch mold me into the villain I can't deny that I am. I'm unbalanced. Unfeeling. I seek out violence and hate. I'm the devil, and I deserve a fate worse than the fiery depths of hell.

My car shakes with the force with which I slam the door, working to deny entry to the hollow feeling fighting to find entrance into my space. Inhaling heavily, my lungs fill with the soft scent of the ground I was sitting on seconds ago. The leather of my seat creaks under my ass. My foot clamps down on my clutch. My hand itching to throw the car into gear and feel its power beneath me.

It revs to life at my demand, drowning out the sound of my heart. Glancing toward my mom's resting place once more, I make a silent prayer, begging for her forgiveness. Slamming the car into gear, it rages beneath me, the exhaust firing like a gun, finally letting me escape the oppressing pain of my mind.

I wasn't ballsy enough to visit Mira. I'm a fucking coward. Mom would forgive me; I know that. Maybe that's wishful thinking, but my mom saw the good in everything, in every*one.* Her love would be with me. But Mira, I all but pulled that trigger myself. How could she *ever* forgive me? I don't deserve it, and I'll never ask for it. She can hate me. It's nothing I don't already feel for myself.

I zig-zag through the cemetery, arching my back to retrieve my phone from the back pocket of my pants. Eyes moving between my screen and the road, I hit the recall button.

"Roc." Raid's voice echoes through the car's Bluetooth.

"Tell me you have something." I ignore pleasantries.

His sigh filters through the car speakers, and I clutch my steering wheel in agitation. "Sarah Rein is a tricky bitch. She's off the grid. I have a lead, it's not solid, but I'll look into it and see what comes of it. Rein's looking for her too."

My tongue drags along the line of my teeth. "I know. I want her before he finds her."

"I'll do what I can, but he has more manpower at his disposal. Good chance that won't be a possibility."

I growl deep in my throat. "Unacceptable."

Sarah Rein deserves the same bloody ending as Marcus. One I'll be happy to oblige her. They lived by the same sword. They're gonna fucking die by it too.

I can't trust that Dominic Rein has the stomach to kill his wife, and if he *is* too weak, he needs to step the fuck aside.

"Word on the other thing I had you look into?"

Raid goes quiet for a loaded second, and I punch my steering wheel, fury coursing through my body.

"Roc, I've been searching. High and low. She's gone. I don't know how... but it's like she doesn't exist, and there's no record of—"

"Keep looking." I end the call without letting him finish his sentence.

"Fuck!"

I push my foot against the pedal harder, my car roaring louder. The feeling calms me in the same way it fires me. The speed soothing, the sound waking the beast clawing to escape.

THE TASTE of metal dances along my taste buds, stirring the sleeping barbarian inside me. My eye socket throbs from the force of the fist that landed against it only moments ago. It'll bruise up, shade my face blue, maybe purple—a picture of defeat, of coming up second best.

A falsehood.

I smirk at the sweat-soaked fucker in front of me. Height mirroring mine, tattoos cover every slender line of his frame. I have an easy sixty pounds of muscle on him, and his mistake is his assumption that my size makes me sluggish.

The loud cheer of the derelicts surrounding the makeshift ring thumps lowly, a drum of expectation in their vulture-like eyes.

The snap of my jaw cracks through the space, head whipping to the side in a jar so powerful my head pounds.

Control. A perception.

To the outside world, I look as though I'm powerless. That I'm beaten. I haven't landed a single punch. *Yet.*

The man opposite me smiles with premature victory swarming in his eyes.

Idiot.

This fuckwit has lost his control all because of his inflated ego. He's underestimated me. I let him land a few right hooks, and now his confidence is greater than it should be.

Control. A power of influence. Over another person, a situation, one's self. It's all *perception.*

I control this motherfucker. He walked right into my game. I'm about to dominate this situation. Readying myself to make a split-second decision as to whether he lives or dies.

I'm *always* in control of myself. I gave in to the pain I needed as punishment for failing *again.* Now I've had enough. I'm ready to go home.

My opponent lands one last violent jab to my eye socket, and I feel the skin split over my eyebrow the moment his knuckles connect. The warm trickle of blood slides down my face like a waterfall.

I grin.

It gives him pause. I watch understanding dawn upon him like a ray of sunshine. It pumps my blood harder through my veins. It makes my dick hard.

Power.

With a simple look, this asshole knows he's about to be fucked.

No lube, motherfucker.

My knuckles connect with a resounding *crack,* loud enough to quiet the crowd and echo through the dank space. I don't let him fall, landing a forceful jab to his ribs before my fist slices across his face again.

The feel of bones breaking beneath my fist quells the tsunami crashing inside me. It offers me a sliver of peace with every grunt of pain I inflict. Lost to the mayhem in my mind, my fists hammer over and over again, only pausing to let the power of my kick to take over.

"It's done, Shay," a voice bellows in my ears, arms hooked under my shoulders to drag me off.

I could take this asshole too, but I don't. It'd be too easy. Shaking him off, I smile down at my handiwork. The guy's face is unrecognizable; swollen facial tissue, split skin, and pools of fresh and congealed blood covering every slice of flesh.

Spitting a mouthful of blood to the ground, I jump from the ring, walking away without another word.

I don't bother showering; sweat, blood, and grime coat my skin like a filthy moisturizer. I yank my shirt over my head with little finesse, my body groaning in protest. I relish the pain, taking comfort in my discomfort.

I collect my cash at the door, pissed-off glances aimed my way as I stuff the bills into my pants without counting them. I don't fight for the money. I'd do it for free. Hell, I'd pay for the fucking privilege. But I'm not gonna lie, watching the hate spike in the eyes of these slimy fuckers... it's a bonus. Winking at the asshole who handed me my winnings, I smirk, knowing damn well he bet against me.

Dickhead.

"Gonna get yourself killed one day, Shay."

"Like to see 'em try." I sling my duffle over my shoulder, walking through the door and into the cold night air.

"Face needs stitches," he yells after me.

He's not wrong. The split on my eyebrow won't stop bleeding. The warmth of my idiotic need to feel pain scoring along my skin quicker than I can mop it up.

"FUCK, ROC," Parker grates as I walk through the door.

I'd long since removed my shirt, balled it in my fist, and pressed it against my face to soak up my blood.

"It's fine," I lie. "Just a little cut. Nothing a bit of tape won't fix."

His girl stands a few feet behind him, a grimace on her pretty face. "Doesn't look fine."

"Why are you here anyway?"

Parker shrugs, unperturbed by the sting in my tone. He steps into my space, grabbing my shirt to pull it from my eyebrow. "Codi's sister told us to make ourselves scarce for a few hours," he answers distractedly, worry lining his face. "Apparently, we're too loud when we fuck."

I smile, the gesture forcing more blood to spill from the open wound. "It's true," I grunt.

"You need a doctor." Codi ignores us both, the shade on her cheeks highlighting her embarrassment like a neon sign.

My brother's fiancée used to be as innocent as they come. Who even knew twenty-five-year-old virgins still existed? Especially ones as hot as Codi Rein. Park is doing his best to corrupt her, though. Not that she's protesting. It's sickening.

"I'm fine." I push Parker's hand away, stepping back.

"Parker," she pushes, ignoring me.

"She's not wrong, Roc." He steps forward again. "I don't think tape is going to cut it."

I sigh. "Doctors and hospitals ask questions. It's a paper cut. Just chill. I'm going to bed."

They stare at me for a beat.

"I'm calling Ryn."

"Like fuck you are," I argue.

Codi nudges Parker.

"Dude," he combats. "I'm either driving you to the hospital to have someone stitch your face, or Codi's calling her sister."

Whipped.

"No, and *fuck* no." I move away. "Don't let me hear you fuck. Do it quietly. I've got a headache."

I walk into my bathroom, stripping down to nothing. Stepping into the rain of the shower, my skin breaks out in goosebumps, the water like ice. It soothes my muscles and irritates my skin all at once. It only takes a second longer to warm up, a loud groan falling from my mouth in relief.

Letting the warm water run over my face, I wince at the pulse of pain it causes. I watch the water—stained the color of rust—swirl down the drain only to be replaced seconds later.

I wash quickly, needing to get off my feet and sit down before I fall. The room spins as I step from the shower, the effects of too many knocks to the head catching up with me. Towel tucked around my waist, I move into my room, pausing at the brunette perched upon my bed.

"Heard you needed assistance."

"Parker," I growl loudly enough for him to hear me.

"He's chicken shit. He and Codi hid in his room as soon as they let me in. It seems they think you're unstable. Don't know what would've given them that idea," she ponders sarcastically.

"I'm fine."

"I beg to differ. You're wearing blood like a sash. I'll stitch your face, and *then* you can go on pretending you're inhuman and don't require medical attention."

"Why are you here?" I ask skeptically.

There's no love lost between the oldest Rein sister and me. I'd bet my left nut that she abhors my very existence. Not that I blame her, I'm reading the same fucking page.

She stands as I sit, her fingers poking at the broken skin without pause. "Codi asked me to come."

"And here I thought you'd grown a soft spot."

She snorts. "Let me be clear. I don't want to be here. If I had my way, I wouldn't be. I don't like you. Frankly, I despise you. Codi called me panicked," she explains absentmindedly. "I thought she was hurt. I could hardly go home without stitching your stupid face."

"You could have," I argue.

Her eyes focused on the split in my eyebrow, don't blink and her fingers work seamlessly to stitch my skin. She doesn't speak.

I cough out a laugh, shaking my head. I'm in shock. My mind is working tirelessly in an attempt to reconcile my current circumstance.

Camryn Rein is in my bedroom, helping *me*.

She scowls when I move, her deep blue eyes settling on me in irritation. "Stay still, Hercules."

"Calling me a god?" I whisper.

A soft blush heats her neck, skin darkening in awkward patches of embarrassment.

That gentle look of discomfort brings me joy. As pretty as she is, Camryn holds a shield of frigidity that deters her appeal. Shaking that shield tenderizes her, offering me the upper hand in this tug-of-war of animosity we're playing.

"Maybe the god of stupidity," she rebuts. "How did this happen anyway? How did the other guy get one up on you? You don't seem like someone who'd get knocked around."

I shrug, making her glower once again.

"I'm about to poke you in the eye with this needle. *Stop. Moving.*"

I roll my eyes. "You wouldn't understand if I told you," I offer.

Stepping back, she smiles at her handiwork. "You don't know me, which means you don't know whether I'd understand. Don't generalize me by your misguided opinion of who you *think* I am."

I blink.

"All fixed. Try to keep it dry. I'll come back in a few days to check on it and remove the stitches. In the meantime, try not to let anyone else beat you up."

With that, she's gone, and I pop a few Tylenol. I drop to my bed, feet still planted on the floor, welcoming the few hours of unconsciousness I'll manage.

CHAPTER THREE

CAMRYN

My skin tingles with the pain of his touch. The soft caress of his fingers along my naked thigh. A touch that, in another world and another life, I'd crave. One that I'd arch into, pleasure coursing along my over-sensitive skin.

Not here, though. Not in this life, and definitely not with him.

Eyes clamped shut, I fight for the control my mind so desperately seeks. I beg my strength to prevail. To show itself when I need it most.

Tears sting my eyes as I pray my body doesn't shake. That the fear that quickens the already racing beat of my heart doesn't make itself known. He likes my fear. It excites and encourages him.

A calloused palm moves up to my breast. Pinching my nipple, a growl of pleasure vibrates against my neck. Bile rushes up my throat. The power I was seeking flees, as it always does, abandoning me in my time of need. Leaving me nothing but a feeble pawn in the sick and twisted game he likes to play.

Straining through my panic, power having deserted me, I search for the next best thing.

Numbness.

I exhale heavily through my nose, pushing everything invading my subconscious away.

I'm not here.

He's not here.
I am nothing.
I am no one.
I feel nothing.
I don't *exist.*

My body relaxes into nothing as I repeat this silent mantra over and over. Willing myself to believe, for it to overtake me. To deliver me into nothingness. If for no other reason than to let me survive another day. Because tomorrow, *maybe* tomorrow, I'll find the strength to pull away.

He *tsks* softly against my ear, his chuckle cutting into my search for detachment with a serrated blade of reality.

"Come back to me, Kitty Kat."

A choked cry involuntarily breaks through my lips, encouraging a wide grin to split along his face. I can't see it. Maybe that's worse, the *feel* of his smirk dragging along the column of my neck.

"That's better," he praises, his hands moving roughly along my body.

Hovering over me, his dark eyes connect with mine. A promise of persecution staring back at me, the menace dancing within the black pools cutting off my ability to breathe. The fear in my eyes excites him —the evidence hardening against my thigh.

I shudder in disgust.

He yanks at my sleep shorts roughly. My thick, stuttered sobs crack into the shadows, begging him to stop. It infuriates him in the same way it turns him on.

"I own you, Camryn. *Me,*" he snarls. "So be a good little whore and open your fucking legs. Give me what belongs to me."

I close my eyes, squeezing them shut as a mechanism to shut him out. But I do as he asks, hating myself more and more with every second that passes.

He's right. He owns me. I'm an object. Nothing but an empty shell of the person I used to be. I don't exist in this world. Not without him. I'm his puppet. One he controls. One he manipulates. One he *hurts.*

I should leave. *Run.* But in the very depths of my shattered soul, I know I'm not just scared; I'm petrified. He'll kill me. He's promised me that much.

It wasn't always this way. I wasn't the weak human he's molded me into, just like he wasn't always the monster that now haunts me day and night. Not outwardly, anyway. Deep down, he was likely always this person. He hid it well enough to make me fall in love with him. He loved me once. Treated me like a queen. The fall was hard. A slap to the face so forceful it left a bruise. It dropped me to my knees until I realized this was where he always wanted to stand. *Over me.*

"Open your fucking eyes."

I hate this part the most. The violation of my body I can handle. I can shut myself off from the physical damage he wounds me with. But the eye contact, the open window to my soul, he knows that fucks with me the most. He knows it breaks me apart. It violates my mind more than his body entering mine ever could. He pushes me to witness my own humiliation. He commands me to concede to his power, knowing he'll *always* have this over me. And I hate it.

I wake with a loud shout, my skin covered in the panic of my nightmare. The fiery, cold touch of sweat clings to my skin in recollection.

His eyes waver in front of my face, and I shake my head, working to rid his image in the harsh reality of consciousness. My room is dark, the ghosts of my past threatening me from every shadowed corner. Crawling across my bed in haste, my lamp crashes to the ground in my rush to turn it on. Discarding it, I jump from my bed, tripping as I search for the light switch. Swallowing against my want to be sick, my eyes race around my room for the demons I know won't be there.

No. That would be too easy. I could fight then. I could call the police. My monsters are smarter, they stay firmly trapped inside my skull. Haunting me in sleep, and in consciousness. They attack from all angles, and I can't escape them.

Convinced I'm alone in the physical space of my room, I focus on my breathing, settling the sobs echoing around me, mocking my weakness. Scratching at my skin, I will the pain to stop. I can still feel his weight on top of me, his body inside mine. I gag, the tears on my skin stinging like fire.

Rushing to my bathroom, I empty the limited contents of my stomach, heaving with my need to expel him from my body. My body shakes. I move to the shower, turning the faucet on as hot as I can manage without causing third-degree burns. I let the scalding water rush over me, burning away his touch. I scrub at my body, scouring away a layer of skin I could've sworn he'd touched.

It's not enough. Not even close.

Wet, naked, and with the shower still running, I stumble toward the vanity, slipping as I go. I pull at the drawers roughly, searching for the only thing I know will bring me the seconds of reprieve I crave so badly.

The small gray blade shines in the dim light. Touching my thumb pad to the edge, I feel the sharp bite of its power. Dropping onto the toilet, the blade hits my upper thigh before my eyes do, and finally, after being choked with agony, I find my power. I take away the pain he caused by creating my own.

My warm, wet skin splits open with ease. The red pool of blood falls along my leg, letting me take my first full breath since falling asleep last night.

THROWING two Tylenol down my throat, I swallow them with the bitterness of my coffee. My leg stings as I move around the kitchen, and I work to cover the pain without limping. It's still dark out, and Codi won't be up for a few more hours, but I don't need her asking any questions. It's easier this way.

She knows about the nightmares but not how I overcome them. She wouldn't understand, and I couldn't stomach her judgment or pity. All that's important is that I've pushed my nightmare down, at least for today. That knowledge courses relief through my body. The soft, pulsating pain I caused letting me feel in control.

Adding another sugar to my coffee, I tidy the kitchen, wiping at the counter for likely the fourth time. I like cleanliness. I crave order. It helps with the Rubik's Cube inside my head.

Satisfied the kitchen is as sterile as I can achieve, I move toward the living area. I've made it two steps when a soft moan filters out from the direction of Codi's room.

Motherfucker.

The rough rumble of Parker's voice is loud enough that I'm now an unwilling audience to *all the things* he wants to do to my sister.

I exaggerate a gag. They don't quit. *Ever*. Morning, noon, and night. They're at it. I'm exhausted, and I'm not even involved. But, Jesus, the things I've heard...

Making myself scarce, I move back toward my bedroom, cursing the need to reenter the space I was scurrying to escape only minutes ago. Settled on my bed, I sip my coffee in silence, focusing on the heavy pulse of pain gifted by the cut along my thigh.

It's not deep. Not enough to need stitches. I've perfected the art. Small scratch-like scars decorate my upper thighs. Invisible to everyone but me. A flashing neon sign for my self-worth. I'm tainted inside. My soul blackened and broken.

Cutting. I see it all the time working in A and E. Mostly teenage girls, the odd adolescent boy. Never a woman in her thirties. I'm sure other adult men and women partake in the trauma of self-harm. It's just not *as* common.

Emotional trauma is severe enough to cause excruciating pain. I've learned that over the years. It's a harsh lesson to have shoved down your throat. There are days I'm sure it'll kill me. It halts my breath. It tightens my chest. My entire body tenses. I sweat. I shake. Rationally, I know it's my anxiety. Panic attacks convincing me I'm about to die. Irrationally, I see no light at the end of the tunnel. The small slice into my skin helps me manage all that. The *physical* pain numbs my emotional pain when it's too heavy a burden to carry.

Today, I blame Rocco. The unwelcome necessity of coming face-to-face with him a few nights ago. Alone, I can admit that I have something in common with a psychopath. He welcomed the pain of my needle piercing his skin, and in that messed-up moment, I *understood* him. It offered him a reprieve from the distorted thoughts twisting him up inside.

Rocco Shay is guarded. Painstakingly cautious. His face is nothing but a hollow void. You'd be stupid to attempt to read him. But he wasn't strong enough to hold on to his mask at that singular juncture. It slipped, because, for a split second, he was free. And for the first time in years, I didn't feel alone.

How fucking stupid is that? I felt a kinship with Rocco fucking Shay. The man who, blinded by his need for revenge, aimed his murderous sights on Codi. If that's not a clear outcry at the bleakness of my existence, I don't know what would be. The man who had wanted to kill my baby sister is the first person I know who would *understand* me.

Good God.

I shake my head, ridding myself of the hideous thought.

Sustenance. I'm shaky after a too-hot shower and blood loss. I shift off my bed with purpose, hoping like fuck Parker and Codi have finished ruining my morning.

"Morning," Parker greets as I move into the kitchen, the sound of Codi's shower echoing through our apartment.

"Hey. D'you make more coffee?" I glance around at the mess he's made, my forehead creasing in irritation.

Hands lifted in surrender, he smirks. "I'll clean it up. Promise. Refill?"

I nod skeptically, moving my mug toward him.

I watch him fill my mug, his inked skin on display. "I find it hard to look at you after I hear the shit you say to my sister when you're fucking."

He raises an eyebrow, adding cream and sugar without prompting. Who would've thought? Parker Shay, domesticated by my sunshine and rainbow sister.

"Was gonna talk to you actually"—he slides my mug over—"that comment probably isn't gonna help my cause, but I was wondering if you'd have an issue with me officially moving in?"

I can't hide my shock. "Codi didn't mention you guys were discussing shacking up."

Parker lifts a single shoulder, sipping his coffee. "We're engaged," he tells me unnecessarily. "We spend every night together. I just wanna make our living arrangements official."

I nod gently, my mouth chasing my coffee.

"I haven't spoken to Codi about it yet. I didn't want her to be excited by the prospect if you weren't on board. Would cause unnecessary drama."

This guy went from being stuffed full of hate and violence, raging a misguided war for revenge with his brother... to this. A man standing in my kitchen, knowing how I take my coffee and checking in on my feelings before telling my sister he wants to move in.

"It always shocks me when you're considerate. Seems out of place when judging you by the way you look."

He laughs. "Make a habit of judging people by the way they look?"

A smile pulls at my lips. "Anyone that says they don't have assumptions about someone based on their appearance is lying."

"So?" he prompts. "All honesty, Ryn, I'm fucking exhausted. Ruin is hectic at the moment, and your sister is insatiable—"

"Please don't." I hold up my hand, cutting him off.

He grins, the gesture saying too many things I don't need to hear. "Having to continually duck into the loft to grab more of my shit each day is wearing thin," he continues. "Codi'll come to the loft but hates it. The memories are too much for her, so we always leave soon after."

His thoughts drift into a place of darkness. He's placed the need to be away from his loft on Codi, but I know it'd haunt him, too.

"As long as you keep the volume of your fucking down," I concede to this request. "It's disgusting."

He offers nothing but a nod, the gesture full of appreciation.

"I'll clean this in a bit." He turns, walking backward out of the kitchen. "I'm gonna go tell Codi."

I grimace. "I'm already regretting my decision," I call after him.

CHAPTER FOUR

ROCCO

I FROWN at the screen of my cell, my body heaving with the air my lungs are attempting to catch.

I feel alive, body dripping, muscles aching, blood pumping through my veins, readying my body to fight.

ROCCO

Whatever you're selling... I'm good

I wipe the sweat off my face with a towel, watching three reply dots dance on my screen.

UNKNOWN

I'd be happy to let your stitches stay in your face, grow an infection and give you septicemia, but Codi would give me grief, and drama isn't my jam.

Camryn Rein is a pain in my ass.

Case in point, she just fucked with my workout.

More than that, it's just *her.* Judgmental and angry eyes always watching me in scorn. It's, at a minimum, annoying. At its worst, it reinforces the hate I hold for myself. I need little encouragement there.

It shames me to admit, and I'd never do it aloud, but Camryn Rein holds a power over me few others do. Not that she'd know it, and I plan to keep it that way until I'm buried six feet under. But she does. It dangles in front of my face in a nightmare come to life.

I remember her pretty blue eyes watching me in pity as I begged her to save my aunt. The tenderness in how she handled me—knowing it was all my fault—when she told me she couldn't.

The way she blinked in sadness, watching my grief unabashedly. Accepting the broken version of who I was even after I'd threatened her sister's life.

She saw me at the weakest point of my life, and that simple fact spreads unease through me like poison ivy. My weakness is real. Most would argue against that statement, but it's true. It's small. But it's there, and it scares the living fuck out of me. It's the sliver of my soul I show to no one. Why would I? Weakness only offers your enemies a hand-drawn map of how to undermine you. It's your defeat handed over on a silver platter. Everything that is most important to you is offered like a gift you've tied neatly with the bow of your surrender.

I recall how she gently cleaned the blood off Mira's face in mourning. The care she took in doing so. I hated being grateful for her at that moment. I hated that she kept her cool as I fell down a tunnel of unimaginable grief.

Camryn Rein is the ultimate reminder of one of the worst moments of my life. And she's now my greatest foe, whether she knows it or not.

Opening the door, I lean against it in silence, forcing my thoughts to wash away, refusing to let her see my inner turmoil.

Attitude oozes from her small frame; forced scowl, popped hip, not complete without a singular brow lifted in distaste.

Her eyes track my naked torso, skating along the divots of muscle twitching from use. They widen as they duck down to the band of my gray sweats, her will strong enough to stop them from dropping to my crotch. My cock is thickening by the second, a direct result of the blood pumping through my veins from my workout and not the snarky bitch standing at my door.

21

"You going to let me in? Or are you going to make me smell your sweaty ass for longer than necessary?"

Lies. That flash of want in her eyes was enough to tell me that she may hate me, but she wouldn't be averse to licking the sweat from my torso either.

I step from the door without speaking. She isn't welcome, and it's best she knows that from the get-go.

Stepping in after me, her feet pause as her stare falls to the very spot Mira took her last breath. Looking at the floor, you couldn't tell life was stolen in that same place. It's like brand new, scrubbed clean of any visible reminders. But her eyes fall to the spot in horror, as though Mira's body remains, lifeless and bloodied.

"Let's get this done. Bathroom or kitchen?" I pull her from her haunted thoughts.

"Couch is fine." She moves toward it, offering Mira's ghost a wide berth.

She notices I do the same, her eyes blinking in sadness before she turns away.

"I could'a had a doctor do this." I drop to the couch, waiting impatiently for her to hurry up and leave my home.

"Would you have?" she challenges.

"No," I answer honestly. "Easy enough to just pull 'em out myself."

She exhales heavily, her minty breath hitting me in the face. "You're so... *ugh*... I don't even have words."

"Handsome. Charming. Addictive."

She stops, dropping her hands to her side, a grimace on her face. "Please stop."

I attempt to hide my smirk but fail.

Shaking her head, she steps closer to me. "Stay still," she murmurs.

She smells good. Sweet citrus mixed with coffee, the sugary bitterness of her scent not at all different from her personality.

I frown, annoyed that I noticed.

Her hands are soft and gentle in the way they move along my skin. A slight tug, a quiet snip, a gentle pull, and she drops the discarded suture into an open tissue beside me. She does this until all the stitches are removed, not speaking a single word.

Dabbing the wound with a strong-smelling antiseptic, I watch her eyes narrow over the injury. "It's healed well," she says, pleased with her handiwork. "I'll pop some adhesive strips across it to keep it from reopening. You'll need to replace them. I'll leave you some."

She waits for my nod of confirmation, which I offer in one quick movement.

"They come off by themselves, don't rip at them," she instructs. "Keep the wound clean." She steps back. "And dry. So, like, this"—she gestures to my body—"is a no. Just chill out on the excessive physical exertion for a few days. No swimming either."

I nod again, letting her know I've heard her.

"Dominic having any luck finding the cunt you affectionately call mom?"

Her hands pause halfway inside her bag. "I didn't realize he was looking for her," she lies, zipping her bag up.

I scowl, the adhesive strip stuck to my face pulling with the movement.

Deceit is the most damaging of all sins. The act of misrepresenting is as lethal as murder, for the simple fact that *everyone* has the stomach for it. Give me a single person who hasn't lied, cheated, or distorted the truth, and you'd be guilty of that exact crime. A simple lie can be the sole cause of catastrophe. It's the very tip of a pyramid that breaks everything beneath it. Pain, suffering, and heartache are all casualties of an untruth unraveling. It takes no prisoners, maiming everyone in its path.

I narrow my eyes, and she straightens her shoulders, meeting my scornful gaze.

We both know she's lying, and she's caught between holding onto her lie and letting it go.

"Not that I know of," she eventually answers with a reluctant sigh. "But that means less than nothing. He wouldn't tell me if he were. You'd have a better chance of getting information like that from him."

I stand.

"Are you looking for her, too?"

I consider ignoring her, showing her out without another word. I might hate lying, but I'm not against refusing to engage.

"Yes." I shock myself by speaking.

It's her turn to nod, a quick up and down movement as she moves toward my door without instruction. "What will you do when you find her?"

Camryn is no stranger to grief, to pain, to the fucked up reality this world has to offer. It's worn like a shield. A giant barbed wire fence warning people to back the fuck off.

"Best you don't know."

A dismissive shrug. "Make her pay," she shocks me by saying, her hand to the door. "Sarah never gave us a second thought," she explains unnecessarily. "She couldn't give two fucks about Codi or me. She's as good as dead to me anyway."

Pausing at my front door, she eyes me cautiously. "I hate you," she confesses emotionlessly. "But I hope you find her before my dad does. He has too much goodness inside of him. I hope that I'm right in assuming you have none."

I pick up my phone as she closes the door softly behind her, unperturbed by her opinion of me. She's right—no point denying it to her or myself.

"Roc," Raid greets.

"Tell me you found her?"

"Sarah?" he clarifies, and I grunt in affirmation, pissed off at needing to spell it out.

"Dude. She's a fucking ghost. Who knew the drunk wife of a career criminal would be so in the know?"

"Bitch is smarter than everyone gives her credit for," I grit out. "She was fucking Marcus for decades, hid his kid... she was part of a plan to kill my mother, and *no* one had a fucking clue."

Raid sits quietly at the end of the line.

"What about the others?"

"Roc, I'm sorry... she doesn't exist."

I inhale deeply through my nostrils. "What the fuck do I pay you for?"

He attempts to speak, but I cut him off.

"Two fucking jobs. You've come up empty-handed on both."

"Sorry, man. Not through a lack of trying. I promise you that."

I roll my eyes. "Promises mean shit. I've had plenty of people promise me shit in my life, Raid, and you know what they've done with them? They've stomped on every fucking one. Promises are

24

nothing but a collection of empty words that mean nothing to me. You're fired."

I hang up, throwing my cell onto the first surface I see.

Fist clenched, I yell into the empty loft, muscles pulsing with the need to be pushed to their limits.

I haven't felt this useless in life since my mom was killed. I'm flailing. I'm drowning in my failings again, and I'll be damned if I let it continue.

My life is about structure. Determination. Master discipline and control, and you can walk through the fucking depths of hell to grab your end goal with both fucking hands. Lose it, and you're like every other fucker walking this planet. *Aimless.*

I have the means. I have the power. Yet, the two people I *need* to find, the two people who shouldn't have the first fucking idea of how to disappear, are like the fucking wind. They've outsmarted me. They've played me like a fool, and I plan on ripping their jugular from their naked throats for the inconvenience.

Grabbing my cell, I flick through my contacts.

ROCCO

Put me on the schedule

CARMICHAEL

Throw three rounds and you're in.

The weasel is working to win back his losses after betting against me last week.

ROCCO

Whatever. Actually give me a fight this time.
Not some wannabe.

He responds, but I ignore it, heading to my room to change. Rein didn't say *not* to partake. She said chill out. This *is* how I chill out. Through pain and dominance. Through violence and release.

"BRUISING IS ONLY JUST GOIN' down, Shay. Are you sure you're up to this? Hate for you to lose me any money tonight because you can't pull it back."

I flip Carmichael off as I shove past him, his bony body flying back against the wall.

The guy is the worst kind of scum. All greasy slicked back hair, acne-scarred face. He'd weigh a hundred-pound soaking wet, teeth missing, skin scabbed up from his incessant scratching.

The guy is a junkie through and through. It seeps from him like a neon sign. Bleeding in desperation and soaked in deceit.

If there's one thing my dad taught me before he died—violence and hatred aside—you can never trust a junkie. They lie. They cheat. They'd step on their own mother to secure their next hit.

Carmichael Woods is no exception. Tattered jeans, a shirt that's likely older than he is, and a leather jacket I have no doubt he stole; he's made far too much money through me over the years. He knows I'm a sure bet. But you'd be forgiven for assuming he's homeless. The truth is, he likely is. Every cent that falls into his pocket finds its way up his nose or into his veins.

"Four rounds," he calls after me.

My feet pause, neck twisting to look at him. "You said three."

His scrawny shoulders lift, an ugly grin showing off his gappy smile. "Things change."

I walk away without so much as a glance.

Ass planted on the cold metal of one of the change room benches, I sigh in relief. There's something therapeutic about the festering stench of blood and sweat. It's like a kiss of anticipation. It seeps into your lungs like a vow.

Freedom.

So fucking close.

Chaos and pain. The stinging relief of a fist against your skin. Splitting it open to let the suffocating sense of failure seep out in rivers of blood.

The deafening crack of knuckles kissing bone jarring you enough to rid you of any coherent thought. If you're lucky enough, sometimes a bone will break, gifting you the freedom from your demons for that little bit longer.

My uncle taught me the salvation physical affliction could offer. Not intentionally, of course. But after Mom died, I was *drowning*. My heart was broken. My soul was destroyed. My life had all but up and left me without a fucking direction.

Then Marcus hit me, and for that split second in time, my heart didn't ache. I forgot it existed. Every depressive thought was replaced by the sweet agony Marcus' fists rained down on me.

I craved it.

Physical pain; that I could manage.

Emotional pain; that needed to be healed in a way I will never understand.

"You're up," Carmichael shouts into the room, the sound of his feet moving away as quickly as they came.

Standing, I roll my shoulders, shifting from foot to foot in a pre-game dance that builds my adrenaline. Cracking my neck one way and then the other, I run my tongue over my teeth.

One full inhale into my lungs, and I move from the stench of defeat and victory, mixed together so potently, it's likely neither *actually* exist, not in this world.

"LOST ME A LOT OF MONEY, SHAY."

Carmichael steps out from behind my car.

Opening my door, I throw my duffle inside, never taking my eyes off the fucker. "You should know better than to bet against me."

"You said you'd give me *four* rounds." He steps forward, spit flying from his mouth as he yells.

I raise an eyebrow. "I said three, and I have somewhere to be."

I hear footsteps sound behind me, but I don't let myself turn around. "Don't make an enemy outta me, asshole."

He lets me see the glint of his knife held tightly in his hand by his side—a silver spark glowing in the gleam of the streetlight.

I can't tell how many of his cronies have stepped up behind me, but I'm not stupid enough to turn my back on a fucking junkie. Especially one seething over the loss of tonight's fix.

"You pissed a lot of people off tonight." He steps closer again, making it known he has a fucking death wish.

"Nah, fuckface, that was you. Now put your butter knife away and move the fuck on," I growl.

He laughs just as the barrel of a gun pushes against my spine.

I blink slowly in irritation. More at myself than anything. I had to know the dickhead would do something unhinged after fucking him the way I did.

"Big, bad Rocco Shay knows he's about to see Mommy again."

My eyes flash open. "Bring up my mother again, cunt. I dare you." I bare my teeth, a threatening growl cutting across the night air.

Shoulders pushing back, my fists opening and closing in anticipation, I have no doubt I look like a wild animal. Feral and unmanageable.

He steps back in fear.

"Wise decision," I snarl, right as the fucker at my back lifts his gun, whipping it across the back of my head.

"Fuck," I spit out, grabbing my head.

Carmichael takes the opportunity with my reflexes slowed by the bright yellow dots dancing in my eyesight. I hear his feet shuffle forward, the tip of his knife sliding into my abdomen like a hot knife into butter.

Smooth.

In and out in one quick burst.

I reach for him, but the dickhead with the gun, dissatisfied with his first attempt, whacks the butt of his gun against the back of my head once more.

I stumble against my car, one hand clutching my side, the other my head.

Carmichael is off before I can even consider running after him, my body dropping to the asphalt, eyes falling in and out of focus.

I yell out after them, promising their slow and painful deaths, but the words are nothing but a jumble of gibberish.

CHAPTER FIVE

CAMRYN

"CAMRYN," my dad warns, and I turn to scowl at him.

"*No*," I argue. "When did our family become so entwined with the Shays?"

Parker clears his throat.

"No disrespect to you, Parker, but your relationship with my sister has nothing to do with me."

"Parker is my family, Ryn, which means Rocco is too. As my sister, I'm asking you to help," Codi pleads, and I hate that she's playing on my loyalty to her. Can't she see it's *because* of my loyalty to her that I refuse to help?

"Are we all just forgetting that he tried to have Codi *killed*? That he charged Parker with *shooting* her. All because he refused to see what was *right* in front of him. Did I miss the family meeting where it was decided that we'd all move past this..." I'm yelling. My voice breaks like brittle glass and shards stab our already tender wounds.

My dad clears his throat. "Camryn, sweetheart—"

"*Don't* use that voice on me," I cut him off. "You all may have forgiven him, but I haven't."

"The circumstances—"

"I get his pain," I concede angrily. "I'm not denying him that. But if Kane Shay killed you." I gesture to my dad standing in his office, the

29

epitome of calm. "Would I have conspired with Codi to take Parker's life?"

"Of course not," Codi argues. "But that's because we were raised with love. Rocco was molded in hate."

I sigh. "You're asking me to do something I don't want to do. I've stitched his face once. That was my good deed."

"He's really hurt, Ryn." Codi's purple eyes are filled with tears, panic twisting her features.

"Because he fights for fun," I contend.

"You'll have him die because you want to hold a grudge?"

There's little I hate more than being manipulated, which is precisely what my sister is doing right now—playing on my conscience, on an oath I'd taken eagerly.

I step back in shock. "That's not fair. All I'm saying is that he should go to a hospital."

"Questions will be asked," my dad answers.

I laugh sardonically, irritated that they won't let this go. "Nothing you can't clear up for him."

"Watch your tone, Camryn," he warns, and it's the first time I've ever heard my dad speak to me with such authority, with such demand. "No one is asking you to befriend him, Camryn," he continues more gently. "All I'm asking of you is to care for his injuries until he's well enough to go back home."

I open my mouth to say no, my words catching in my throat as Parker steps forward.

I don't know if his imposing nature has worn off, the love of my sister quietening the demons that stir within him. Or if I'm just so used to his presence, I can no longer see the darkness.

"You found it in yourself to forgive me," he speaks quietly. "I'm not asking you to do the same for Roc. I'm just asking you to help me save the only family I have left."

I swallow my animosity.

"He's all I've got left, Ryn. *Please.*"

My eyes close in defeat.

"Thank you," he whispers, reading my reluctant acceptance.

"You manipulated me to get your way," I bite out. "Save your thank you. Where is he?"

"Your old room," Codi mumbles.

"You have got to be fucking kidding me." I storm past her, moving toward the staircase with purpose.

This was the last thing I wanted or *needed*. Avoiding Rocco Shay has quickly become my number one priority. I don't want to know him. I don't want to fall down a hopeless hole of pity because of the life he's been forced to live. I sure as shit don't want to *understand* him or the way his fucking mess of a mind works.

Our similarities have become like cancer, growing steadily within me. Small moments of accord I felt creeping inside me the last time we spoke, spreading like a wildfire I needed to extinguish. The threat of destruction and devastation in finding camaraderie with someone like Rocco Shay is all too real.

I throw my door open with an excessive force of anger. The handle hits the plaster with a crack that shakes the wall.

Rocco lies on my bed, a towel held weakly against his side. The usual tan of his skin has faded, replaced by a shade paler than white. His breathing is quick and sharp, his body attempting to pull oxygen in at a rate too quickly. Eyes closed over, his eyelids flutter open. He tries a smile when he sees me, but it barely forms before it's replaced with a pained grimace. He coughs, all of his features twisting in agony before he passes out again.

"*Fuck*," I worry.

"What can I do?" I hear the restrained panic in Parker's voice.

"Towels," I instruct. "There's also a medical bag in my closet." I point to the corner of my old room.

I move closer to Rocco, my fingers gripping his wrist to feel his pulse.

"Cold," Rocco breathes out.

"You're burning up," I tell him, watching Parker return with my bag.

Dropping to my knees, I pull at the towel pushed against his side. The pristine white of the material is forever lost, now stained red with the blood leaking from his body.

"Hold this here." I stand, moving aside to let Parker move into my position.

I rush into the ensuite of my childhood bedroom, not recognizing myself in my reflection, in the crazed look of fear that is staring back at me. I've stitched countless patients and seen more blood than a vampire, but never like this. Never with the pressure of my family weighing on my shoulders, daring me to fuck it up so they can attribute blame.

Hair tied up, hands disinfected, I move swiftly back into the room. Parker lets me move into his space, shifting easily as I push him aside. Retrieving a new towel, I dump the blood-soaked one onto the floor. "It looks surface," I offer, taking a closer look. "He likely would've been dead if it wasn't. The knife has nicked at the muscle, though. I'll need to suture that first."

I pause briefly. "Do you know his blood type?"

Parker nods as I look at him.

"Good. Speak to Dominic, and ask him to call in a favor. Get some sent over, just in case."

He doesn't look at me again before rushing from the room.

"You are gonna be the fucking death of me, Shay. You're lucky someone loves you," I murmur. "I probably would've let you die."

"Do it," he chokes out, and I'm human enough to admit that I feel a little guilty he heard me. More, a little taken aback by the confidence in his request. He'd be happy enough to die right now. To take his final breath and be done with the heinous world he's been both born into and crafted for himself.

"Sorry, pal. You don't get to do that to Parker."

"Better off without me," he grunts, a soft groan following the anguish in his words.

"You may think that, but he doesn't, and this may shock you, but I trust him more than I do you."

A burst of air shoots from his nostrils, an *almost* laugh that makes me grin.

"Dominic's on it." Parker breaks up our private therapy session, rushing back into the room.

"Come." I usher him over unnecessarily. "Shine the light of your cell onto the wound. Let's get our god of stupidity all sewn up."

"Thank you, Ryn," Parker whispers.

The words echo around the room like a tornado, swirling in and out of my ears like a thick barrel of wind, demanding I hear them. My throat closes over at the distress in his tone, at the complete and utter desperation.

Looking at Parker Shay, you'd be forgiven for making your assumptions. Tall and broad, tattoos peek along the thick line of his neck. They drip down his arms, wrapping his hands in various colors. His eyes shine in hostility to those who don't know him, the set line of his jaw communicating the same. But if you dig deeper and take the time to *know* him, it's easy enough to recognize the scared and uncertain boy he once was.

I don't acknowledge his thank you, not trusting my throat to open up enough to let my words release evenly. I would be expected to tell him he's welcome. *Of course*, I'd help. But he knows the truth. We both know he backed me into a corner, a pitchfork of expectation and burden aimed at my heart. He, Codi, and my father forced my hand, and I refuse to push away my resentment toward them for that.

I let my thoughts wander away, focusing on the broken tissue and blood in front of me. I lose myself in repairing muscle, in sewing together Rocco's skin.

His body is an ode to violence. Muscles like stone, skin marred with scars of battles fought. Fresh ones like warning signs of a warrior still standing. Others are old enough to twist at your heart, knowing they were gained in adolescence.

He falls in and out of consciousness as I work, mumbling incoherently, grunting in pain involuntarily.

"Did he tell you what happened?"

Parker's eyes fall against my profile. "No. A guy we know through the club found him. He'd been knocked out, copped a nice blow to the back of the head."

I glance up at him. "Pull his eyelid up for me," I instruct.

He does so without delay.

I lean in. "Not dilated," I murmur.

"Back of his head just looks like a surface wound," he offers. "It had stopped bleeding by the time he'd woken up."

"No other signs of a nasty concussion?" I refocus on my hand, indicating Parker move the light back to where I'm working. I concentrate on the needle, watching it slide through Rocco's skin without issue.

"Mac said he was walking okay, aside from the limp from the knife wound. Told him Carmichael was a dead man, so, coherent enough to throw out threats."

"Carmichael?"

I feel Parker shrug beside me, anger bristling under his not-so-calm exterior. "No idea. Mac said he'd found him outside some dive where illegal fights pop up from time to time."

"Sleep is probably good for him then," I offer. "He hasn't vomited or slurred his words?"

"Nah," Parker offers, hand resting on his brother's leg.

A comfortable silence settles between us, me working, Parker watching on in interest.

"I don't think I ever apologized to you for the shit Rocco and I started."

I pause for a beat, clearing my throat on a roll of my shoulders.

"I've apologized to Codi a million times over, a few less to Dominic, but never to you."

My eyebrows pull together, working to push away his ill-timed apology. "You have their forgiveness. You don't need mine."

"That's where you're wrong," he mumbles. "It's nice having a family again, Ryn. Roc and I forgot what it felt like."

I frown. "Bullshit," I lash out. "You had one another, and you had Mira."

He nods, unbothered by my show of anger. "That's true, but we were too caught up in our pain to appreciate it all. Codi healed those wounds for me. She taught me that life would continue no matter how shitty and painful it was. The sun'll still rise in the east, and you'll breathe for another day."

A heavy exhale drifts across my shoulder.

"I should've learned all this from my mom's death. Better late than never, though, hey? Until your heart stops... there's always a new fucking day."

My heart spasms in my chest, and I stop what I'm doing to look him in the eye. I can't determine if what he said was truthful, if it was his new philosophy, or if it goes deeper. Was it aimed at me or, more likely, an excuse for his older brother?

"My brother hasn't found a way to heal his wounds," he explains.

"His sun never rises, Ryn. It's *all* fucking dark. Most of the time, he's ready to give up, and Mira only lives in our memories now."

He clears his throat, the thickness in his voice giving way with the forced cough. "What I'm trying to say is that you guys are my family, so I'm sorry for threatening your people. Not lying when I say it's a guilt I'll carry forever."

"All finished," I announce louder than necessary, unsure how to respond. "I'm going to clean up. My Dad's contact should come through with some fluids and blood soon enough."

He remains quiet, moving into the space I sat to rest his hands atop his brothers.

"You're forgiven." I stop, turning on my foot to look at him. "Only because, in a *small* way, I saw you as a victim in this fucked up situation. I saw the conflict in your eyes. I *felt* it. It's always been obvious to me that *you* didn't set anything in motion." I pause, letting a soft breath go before speaking again. "It was all Rocco. I saw how you wanted to move away from everything in your past; the hurt, the anger, the hostility. Rocco wanted to watch it grow. He took the person he was supposed to protect and forced him into a corner he had no hope of escaping. You're forgiven because the moment you were finally set free from your father and uncle, you fell into the trap of someone just as dangerous. Maybe even more so because you trusted him to know what was best for you."

I look at his brother, unconscious, his chest's steady rise and fall comforting me. I don't need to communicate that Rocco will never have my forgiveness. He's as poisonous and damaging as Sarah and Marcus were. Their fates are aligned, and I don't wish for them to be pleasant.

CHAPTER SIX

CAMRYN

I WALK into the dining room, stomach grumbling in anticipation. Having just finished a twenty-hour shift, I've survived on little but stale coffee and a bran muffin from the hospital cafeteria.

Barf.

I'm famished and as close to an extra on *The Walking Dead* as I've ever been.

"You look awful."

I blink at Codi. "Thank you." I place a hand on my heart. "That's *so* sweet."

"She always looks like that."

I turn to Rocco. The color in his face has returned, making him look a *little* healthier than he did a few days ago. "Ventured from your prison, I see. Emerging like Gollum, just us creepy and unwelcome."

He laughs, face twisting in discomfort the shake in his body causes.

I want to ask him about his pain levels and how his wound looks, but that would look like I care. Which I don't. I did my part, and making him comfortable is of no interest or concern to me.

Parker greets me on a lazy wave, one I return with just as much enthusiasm.

"Why are you even here?" I bite out, sliding into my seat directly opposite Rocco, irritated at how uncomfortable I feel in my father's home.

"Your father invited me," he answers stonily, a shrug to his left shoulder. "I didn't have much of a choice in the matter."

This family has officially lost it. Codi and my father have accepted Rocco Shay into our fold like a long-lost relative. *I* feel like an outsider. The three musketeers have been officially severed, ripped apart. We're no longer an impenetrable wall. We've evolved into a cheesy family of five, and I'm the only one who seems to find an issue with that.

Rein and Shay have always been two sides of a bitter and nasty war. Opposing factions fighting for dominance. Now Codi and Parker have seemingly extinguished the bad blood with an unplanned union that has cleansed old wounds. And I'm supposed to accept it with a smile.

I couldn't care less about the conflict of our fathers once upon a time. But Rocco pulled that feud into our lives with his plan to take my sister's life. He took on Kane and Dominic's misguided hostility and quest for revenge, almost drowning us all. We made it through by the skin of our teeth.

Well, some of us.

I think of Mira. The collateral damage in a war she wanted no part in. A stranger that now haunts my dreams. My heart is aching for a woman that I didn't know.

I replay how she stepped forward to save the life of someone who some would argue didn't deserve it. The confidence in her decision as she did it.

Is he grateful?

I stare at him in an attempt to find answers.

Did it cause him pain to know that, in the end, she decided that his life was worth more than hers? Or is it forgotten? Has he just moved on with little to no remorse that Mira paid the ultimate price to save him?

"Thinking about hurting me, Rein?" Rocco breaks through my thoughts, his voice just another reminder of the betrayal we'll forever be tied to.

I'm angered that I let my face openly play out my thoughts for him to see.

"Yeah." I roll my eyes. "I saved your stupid life just to kill you when you least expect it. *Please*. Ill-thought-out plans of murder are more your jam."

I catch the look of regret that flashes in his eyes, and I want to grin in triumph.

"*Camryn*," Codi admonishes.

"What?" I argue arrogantly. "He started it. Accusing me of hate and violence *after* I did him a solid. Don't tell me you're afraid of little old me?" I tease, turning back to our unwelcome guest.

His eyes bore into mine, fire, and hate burning his retinas. "Only that your pitiful existence will rub off on me."

"I'm pitiful?" My voice raises without permission. "*I'm pitiful?*"

He raises a single eyebrow. "You dress like you're homeless and not in a fashionable way. I question your hygiene. You work to repel human contact. I don't know if it's on purpose or just incidental. You're single and likely haven't been fucked in years... if *ever*. You hate pretty much everyone and everything. You're a hermit. You work, and that's it. And I don't even know why you do that. You obviously don't spend your money on anything. I think you're a nurse because you enjoy human suffering."

I swallow the emotion caught in my throat. The pain in the words he uncaringly stabbed me with.

"Roc, man, chill." It's Parker's turn to scorn his sibling, but like me, Rocco only shrugs, not concerned with how his words maim.

"Want to hurt me now?" he whispers, leaning forward in challenge.

"What's your obsession with me causing you pain?" I snap. "You want to kneel and be spanked like a naughty boy?"

He laughs at me—a thick roll of laughter echoing across the room.

"You're paranoid," I accuse. "Probably because you've fucked too many people over in your life. Case in point." I point at Codi and Parker. "Maybe they asked me to fix you because they know how much I despise your existence. Maybe they were hoping I'd let you die."

"Jesus, Camryn," Codi yells. "Rocco, we do not think that. Why are you being so horrible?"

"Not paranoid," Rocco murmurs, ignoring my sister's assurance. "Cautious."

I move my gaze to Codi, watching her blankly. Her perfect blonde hair falls in a curtain around her face, her purple eyes shining at me in anger. She's beautiful. Most would say unfairly so, but not me. Beauty is nothing but a curse. One that paints a target on your back. It encourages women to judge you. It entices men to see you as nothing more than an object they're free to use and play with. My sister is also too kind. It welcomes undesirable attention from others. Kindness is too often mistaken as a weakness. It's nothing but an invitation for people to take advantage of you.

"I'm being real, Codi. Not horrible," I tell her calmly. "Rocco has decided I'm aiming for his pain when I don't think of him at all. You're paranoid." I turn back to the bristling asshole sitting at my dinner table. "Not to mention psychotic. You wouldn't know kindness if it slapped you in the face. You probably kiss with your eyes open, afraid to actually enjoy life."

Silence cups my words uncomfortably, and I shift in my seat.

"Beauty, trust me, I've never had any complaints about the way I kiss." He sucks his bottom lip into his mouth, and as much as I want to, I can't pull my eyes away from the way he slowly releases it.

Leaning closer, he drops his voice. "Now," he drawls. "Let's talk about the fact that you just admitted you'd thought about kissing me."

I scowl. "No, I didn't." My eyes dart between his teasing gaze and the wet line of his lips.

I glance at Codi for support, but she looks away before I can catch her eye.

"I would never kiss you."

Rocco shrugs. "Besides the point, you've thought about it. You want me. You just don't want to admit it to yourself."

I bark out a laugh. "Add delusional."

The tip of his tongue skates along the top line of his teeth, a salacious smirk tipping along the side of his mouth.

"I'd rock your world, Rein, and you know it."

I stand abruptly. "I've lost my appetite."

"Sit." My dad walks into the room, oblivious to the lead-in conversation. "You know the rules, Camryn. Family dinner includes everyone."

"We're hardly family," I bite out.

"Contrary to your thoughts, we are. Codi and Parker are engaged, which means he and Rocco are family."

I swallow the acid in my throat. "Shouldn't Sarah be here then?"

The room turns cold, Rocco's teasing dissipating into ice and thunder. It makes me feel powerful, and I straighten my shoulders, lifting them higher in victory.

"If you know where she is," my dad offers coolly. "Please, do invite her. Until then, sit down and eat."

I glance around the table, looking at my family. "Like I said." I step back. "I've lost my appetite."

Retrieving my keys from the bowl in the entryway, I storm through the door. Embarrassed by my outburst and irritated at my family for putting me in a situation I want no part in.

"You okay?"

I whirl on Parker.

"What do you care?" I shoot back.

"I care a lot. You're important to Codi, which means you're important to me. I get that the situation is fucked up. I don't expect you to play happy families with my brother. You know that, right?"

I drop onto the bench seat outside the front door with a huff.

"If it's any consolation." He drops down beside me. "Rocco is as out of sorts by the whole scenario as you are."

"You're kidding, right? Mr. Antagonist in there."

Parker laughs, pushing his shoulder against mine playfully. "Rocco's never been dependent on anyone. Confrontation is most of what he knows, where he feels comfortable."

"Why me, though?"

His eyes focus on the ground at his feet, the muscles in his arms bulging as he rests his elbows on his knees. "I have my ideas, but telling you would be breaking the code."

"Fair enough."

"Rocco's not the easiest person to love," he admits shamefully. "Hell, he's hard to *like* most of the time. But there's a reason behind everything he puts into motion."

I consider Parker's right, but I don't want to know. More specifically, I don't want to *care*.

"As angry as you are at him for what went down, he's angrier at himself. The hate you feel for him... trust me when I tell you he feels all that for himself and more."

"I should hate you, too."

He agrees readily enough. "You should. But you know I make your sister happy, which is important to you. You forgave me because you saw past my mistakes and looked for what Codi saw in me. I know he doesn't deserve it, but if you could do that for Roc, it'd make this situation much easier."

I sit up straighter, rolling my shoulders. I open my mouth to speak, to dispute his request, to tell him I owe his brother nothing. But my words catch in my throat as Rocco's skate across us both in disinterest.

"Thinking I owe her enough," he grumbles, reluctantly admitting that he hates that he feels indebted to me in *any* way.

I take joy in how his face grimaces as he shuffles forward to lean against the wall. "I'm not interested in your forgiveness, Rein," he adds just to be a jerk.

"I'm not interested in giving it to you." My words are delivered cantankerously, his attempt at taking control by telling me he doesn't *want* my forgiveness, pissing me off more than his presence in my life.

Newsflash, asshole, it's not up for grabs.

"Save a repeat of last night, think I can head home? Save us both the horror of spending another minute in one another's company."

He's referring to his pitiful *escape* attempt. The one where he was still burning up from a fever and fainted in my dad's living room on his way *home*.

Dickhead.

Once again, I was called in to check on him. He's become the ultimate thorn in my side, one I see little hope in removing.

Rocco has accepted my family's hospitality as graciously as one would had they been chained up in the basement. I'm here saving his fucking life, begrudgingly nursing him back to health, for reasons I can't even begin to *want* to understand... and he acts like he's a prisoner.

"Free to go whenever you care to, Shay," I gripe. "You're not our fucking captive." I roll my eyes. "For the eight millionth time, my dad has insisted I help you. I'm doing that. The word you seem to have lost is *thank you*."

He scowls.

"Unfortunately, I need eyes on that wound for another few days. Save a repeat of last night," I continue. "Twenty-four hours at least to make sure that infection has subsided. Let's skip the middle-of-the-night escape fiasco. Trust me when I tell you, the moment you're healthy enough to go home, I'll make sure that's exactly where you are."

He clears his throat uncomfortably, lifting his chin an inch before ambling off toward the front door.

"He's not used to being dependent on other people, Ryn. I wish you could appreciate how hard this is for him." He stands. "It's been Rocco and me against the world our whole lives. I had him to lean on, but he had no choice but to build himself like concrete, to stop anyone from pushing us down."

I follow his lead, standing. Meeting his eyes head-on, I shake my head. "That's not entirely true," I combat. "You both had Mira. He's no impenetrable wall, Parker. He's the fucking bomb that blows it to pieces."

Pushing past him, I enter the house, not feeling in the least bit guilty at Rocco's expression as I brush past him. The asshole was eavesdropping, and it's about time someone made him see the fucking truth. Rocco Shay is a poison, offering pain and suffering to those around him, the worst of all fates gifted to his family.

CHAPTER SEVEN

ROCCO

THE SHRILL and deafening scream wakes me with a start, my body bolting upright in alarm. Disoriented, my eyelids blink against the blackness surrounding me. My side throbs, my temples pound, and my body is covered in sweat.

The house falls into an eerie silence, the sound of my heavy breaths fastening my heart's beat. My mind, foggy and still semiconscious, can't differentiate between my dreams and reality. I'd swear the sound that woke me was real, but it wouldn't be the first time my mind had tricked me into believing the terror from my nightmares was alive and kicking, ready to torment me once again.

I listen harder, my eyes finally adjusting to the darkness.

Rein.

The last few days flood my memory bank like a movie on fast forward. Camryn stitching me up. Me telling her she should've let me die. Attempting to leave in the middle of the night. Fainting and having to be hauled back into Camryn Rein's bed. My body burning up so bad I was certain Dominic Rein had chosen to take his revenge. Forcing his daughter to help me, only to set me on fire while I slept.

The scream happens again. The hysterical sound piercing the still night. It's a hell of a lot more haunting in full consciousness, being forced to bear blind witness to something that agonizing for another human being.

I scramble out of bed, ripping at the damp sheets to find my footing. Soft sobs echo through the tenebrous house, my skin crawling with the despondency in the sound.

I limp toward the stairs, hand brushing the wall to guide me through the unfamiliar surroundings. I struggle through my descent, my body protesting violently with every staggered step. I force myself forward, the distress in the tortured cries too heavy to ignore.

My heated skin chills with every step I take. I feel as though I'm walking willingly into my own afflicted dreams.

I expected a real-life victim. Anticipated live torture to be unfolding in Dominic Rein's sitting room. What I didn't expect was Camryn Rein, caught in a nightmare so brutal, her body looks ready to break into a million pieces.

Her eyes, clenched together tightly, look ready to bleed. Her fingers, pulled into white-knuckled fists, are no doubt ripping at the skin of her palms. Her entire body twists aggressively, jerking violently against the horrors in her mind.

"*Fuck.*"

I step up to the couch, standing over her cautiously. "Camryn," I whisper loudly.

I shake her leg. She doesn't wake, her body only cowering against the feel of my hand against her skin.

It's not lost on me that I'm the only one here. The woman currently living in her own nightmare has stayed, begrudgingly, to keep an eye on me. How pitiful that I'm the only potential safe harbor she could wish for now.

My heart tightens in my chest. I can see the panic coursing through her veins. Her mind is forcing her to relive something so traumatic it haunts her in her sleep.

Rubbing a hand down my face, I pull at the hairs of my beard in frustration. Kneeling beside her, I take her hand in mine. I let my thumb rub slow circles over the soft skin. She attempts to rip it back, a pained whimper breaking from her cracked lips. I keep my grasp firm. The tears, balancing delicately at the corners of her eyes, fall, setting salty, wet tracks across her temples.

"I got you," I soothe, wanting nothing more than to pull her from the hell she's caught in. "You're safe."

Her breathing stutters.

I want to shake her. I want to wake her up immediately and ensure she doesn't have to endure any more pain. I refrain, *barely*, knowing it would only cause her further distress.

"Shut it down, beauty." I move closer to her ear, letting her feel my words against her skin. "You're safe," I repeat.

Her body jolts, her cries trickling off on a hesitant breath.

"*Safe?*" she murmurs, the disbelief in the jaded word as heartbroken as it is hopeful.

"Safe," I echo, letting her hear the fight in my quietly spoken promise.

After a drawn-out minute, her eyes open with a pop, her hand squeezing mine tight enough to make me wince. I watch her chest heave, her heart beating so violently, I swear I can see it attempt to escape her body. Short sharp breaths only exaggerate her panic, her frantic gaze skating over the room.

"Gotta fill your lungs up, beauty," I instruct. "Whatever's cutting off your ability to breathe can't touch you here. You're safe. I got you."

Her mouth opens, a thick choking sound catching itself in her throat as her desperate need to breathe suffocates her.

"*Fuck*," I spit, moving from my position on the floor.

Lifting her into a sitting position, I push in behind her, shifting her, so we're sitting flush. Her back to my front, her straight legs nestled comfortably between my bent ones. "Don't gulp it in. *Slow. Deep.* Feel me. Copy."

She stutters on a breath. Then a second. But her body eventually finds rhythm with mine. Our chests move in unison, the thick intake of air expanding our lungs and deflating with a shaky exhale.

"Good girl," I praise. "That's it. *Slow*. Take control. You're in control. *You.*"

It takes a good five minutes of repeating the motion and words over and over for her to settle. For her breathing to even out and her body to relax.

Her skin is clammy, her shirt damp with the sweat her overwrought nervous system has caused. Thick tendrils of her hair are stuck along the wet line of her neck, and I can feel the heavy thud of her heart beating in her chest.

"We good?"

Exhaling shakily, she nods quickly, the rest of her body as still as a statue.

Seconds pass before the realization of our position hits us both. Plastered against one another, there's little left for our imagination. She can feel *every* inch of me, and I feel every soft curve of her.

Another beat, and then she moves, shifting quickly out of my space and the warmth my body was offering hers.

I stand, watching her cautiously. "Gonna get you some water."

She refuses eye contact, grabbing the nearest cushion to pull it tightly against her chest. Her knuckles are white with the pressure of her hold on the cotton, taut muscles spasming in an uncontrollable form of shock.

I'm no stranger to nightmares. To the memories that haunt my dreams and rob me of the peace I desperately crave. It's taken me years, almost twenty to be exact, but I've taught myself how to overcome that oppressive panic that seizes you. That forces you to believe you're close to dying.

The way Camryn feels right now.

I can see her from the kitchen entryway, frozen in place. The quick sharp movements of her shoulders dance with every harsh breath her body pulls in.

Moving back toward her, her big blue eyes look up at me through wet lashes, her hand reaching for the glass stretched toward her.

Her hand shakes the glass involuntarily as mine pulls away, but her free hand steadies the tremor, clutching it to her lips. Her throat moves quickly to swallow the entire contents in seconds, and I silently watch on.

She hands the glass back without a word. Wiping her hand across her mouth, she removes the droplets that escaped in her haste to rehydrate.

"Why are you helping me?" she bites out.

Generalizations are the assholes of the world. They're attached to everyone you see, nothing but an avenue to pour shit on the planet. Most people look at me and decide I'm a selfish motherfucker who would step on my mother to get what I wanted. They look at the cold glint in my eyes and decide I'm unfeeling.

"I'm no stranger to being woken by past experiences that feel the need to haunt me in sleep," I reply. "And as much as you don't want to believe it, I do have a fucking heart."

"I know that," she rushes out gently.

I raise an eyebrow, a slight smirk playing at the corner of my lips.

"I'm a nurse. Everyone has a heart." She looks embarrassed. "Even the people who don't deserve to breathe."

I dip my chin in agreement, not certain that comment was directed at me, but also not entirely confident it wasn't either.

"Hearts don't determine if you're a good person or not. It's your soul."

My head moves back slightly in shock. "You work in the medical field and believe we have a soul?"

She nods. "I have to. Otherwise, I'm forced to believe we're just vessels, all capable of evil."

"You don't think you're capable of hurting someone?"

I watch the line of her throat as she swallows. "I know I am," she whispers. "And it scares me more than anything else in this world."

I let my eyes drift over her face in three blinks. My mind is trying to understand this highly complex woman.

"Let's watch a movie," I offer, unsure what else to say. "It always helps me relax back into sleep."

She nods quickly. "I just need the bathroom."

She wanders back into the living room fifteen minutes later, a slight limp in her step.

"You okay?"

She nods easily. "Jabbed my thigh against the corner of the vanity."

I watch her settle onto the couch, a grimace of discomfort on her face. "Need an ice pack?"

She shakes her head. "What movie did you choose?"

I press play, relaxing on the couch.

"*Superbad.*" She smiles. "I fucking love this movie."

Her voice is softer than I've ever heard it. Not exactly a whisper, more a hesitant murmur. It's disconcerting. Camryn Rein throws words like daggers, aiming to maim in a poor attempt to keep people at a distance.

She's shaking, tiny, almost indeterminable tremors that torment her frame as she straightens her spine, feigning calm.

Why I feel an overwhelming need to soothe her is beyond me. We're foes. But side-by-side on the sectional, I don't question myself as my hand lifts to wrap itself around hers.

A sharp intake of breath, held in for a tense three seconds before she releases it.

"Just you and me in here, Cami. Fuck the monsters in your mind. They aren't gonna go up against me."

Her hand twitches in mine, and I ready myself for her to snatch it back. But she surprises the fuck out of me, squeezing my fingers in a silent gesture of thank you instead.

She drifts off halfway through the movie, her head resting against my shoulder in slumber. I consider moving her but decide against it. She's calm and peaceful in this cycle of sleep, and I don't have it in me to take that away from her.

Stuffing a cushion behind my neck, I watch the rest of the movie, the credits rolling before it hits me. The vanity in the downstairs bathroom extends the length of the wall. Meaning there are no fucking corners for her to collide with.

She's gone by the time I stir awake hours later, the soft smell of her perfume still lingering on my shirt, and my want to comfort her again is both confusing and irritating to my psyche.

CHAPTER EIGHT

ROCCO

My feet follow the stairwell downward, thick heavy footfalls silenced by the soft carpet under my toes.

As a kid, I created an image of what the Rein mansion must have looked like. I was convinced it was built with arrogance and decorated in the same way. Reds and golds and shit that you weren't allowed to touch, couches that you were forbidden from sitting on.

It annoys me that my misguided thoughts were just another bullet point to add to my expanding list of all the ways I was wrong.

It's as homely as it fucking comes. Soft carpets, fireplaces, and pictures of the Rein girls decorating the walls. Shit, the old man still has their elementary school drawings on his fridge. It's opulent, don't get me wrong. But in a way that doesn't *scream* money. It's tasteful.

Soft music drifts from the sitting room, the quiet melody amplified by laughter. My frown comes on almost instantaneously. The scene before me is as foreign as it is uncomfortable.

Christmas decorations are spilling out of boxes. The excessive number of crates are bursting with thick wreathing, hand-crafted ornaments, holly, tinsel, and lights. You name it. It's here, spewed along their sitting room like Santa's workshop.

Parker, dressed in a ridiculous red velvet hat with a large white pom-pom hanging off the end, holds mistletoe over a giggling Codi's head, leaning in for a kiss.

"What the fuck are you wearing?" I interrupt before their lips can touch.

"Rocco!" Codi exclaims excitedly, picking up another Christmas hat as she makes toward me.

"One more step with the fucking thing..." I warn.

"You'll what?" she sasses, stupid reindeer earrings dangling from her ears.

"What's all this?" I ignore the way she calls me out.

"It's Christmas," she answers unnecessarily.

"We're adults," I retort.

Codi, having lost interest in trying to assault me with a Santa hat, moves toward the hideously large Christmas tree nestled in the corner of the room. "Parker was a bah-humbug, too, when I met him. I'll convert you," she promises.

I scowl at my brother, but he only shrugs, attempting to disguise the smile on his face.

His smile isn't smug. He'd wear that like his stupid fucking hat. Unapologetically proud. But it's not that. There's no enjoyment in my discomfort. He's attempting to hide *his* genuine happiness about a holiday we'd long since pretended never existed.

When Mom was alive, we celebrated. Much like this. Over-the-top decorations, carols, and a ridiculous and wasteful amount of gifts and food. That all died in the ass the year she was shot. Christmas was just another painful reminder of everything we'd lost. It was easier for Parker and me to shut ourselves away on a day everyone else was celebrating and pretend we were too cool for the fairytale of a jolly man in a red velvet suit.

Mira tried. Of course, she did. But we killed her need to offer us normalcy like Marcus' bullet penetrated her skull. *Brutally.*

A pain stabs me through the chest at the joy on Parker's face. A realization I've chosen to ignore for too long dawns on me in another cloud of self-hatred. He wanted this. All along, he wanted, *needed* the overblown intricacies of Christmas.

And I kept it from him.

He played along with me, shutting it all out, when in reality, even without Mom there, *this* would've let him feel close to her.

"Rocco." Dominic slaps me on the back, moving into the room, dressed much like Codi and Parker, too festive for my comfort. "Nice to see you moving around, son. Sit, relax."

I cringe at the endearment. *Son.* I'm neither. Not familial. Not a fucking child.

Oblivious to the fire raging inside me, he passes me the hat Codi had attempted to suffocate with me only moments ago. I take it reluctantly, fisting the material roughly.

It's vexatious to feel like an unwanted guest when your host insists on acting like you're family. Especially after the things I've done. The damage I've caused. I don't deserve the Rein's hospitality, yet they moved straight past forgiveness and right into an acceptance I was neither expecting nor wanting.

"I'm actually pretty shattered," I lie, dropping the hat onto the couch. "Gonna grab some more shut-eye."

The idea alone is enough to give me hives. I'm going stir fucking crazy in that room. The walls are inching closer together with each day that passes. I'd likely saw off my left arm before torturing myself with another twenty-four hours in the prison of Camryn's teenage years.

Reminders of her happy childhood amplify my nightmares. I'd leave if I felt healthy enough to do so. But I've only started to kick the fever I was certain would take my life only days ago. It makes me sick to my stomach to admit, but I'd be dead without Camryn Rein. A fact that sits like a tumor within me. Being indebted to anyone is a giant fucking red flag for me. Being beholden to a Rein. *Fuck. No.*

"Nonsense." Dominic waves me off. "You've done nothing but sleep for days. Being out of that room will do you good. Camryn's hanging lights along the front gate. You go help her."

He turns around without waiting for me to respond and I feel chided. I just got told what to do by a crime boss in a Santa hat. I blink back the irritation bristling between my shoulders, coughing out a disinterested grunt before turning on my feet.

I leave the room without delay, needing to rest my eardrums from the bleeding lyrics of some tool singing about jingling bells. A hand grasped along the banister; I pause at the first step, eyes falling on the front door. Without second-guessing myself, I move toward it. *Not* because Dominic told me to, I assure myself; but because I want to see Rein's very own angry elf stringing lights.

Much to my disappointment, she's not struggling. She's also not excelling. Her ass is planted along the curb, eyes closed, head tipped back to let the wind whip along her face.

"Most people avoid the wind."

I struggle to sit, the curb low enough to make my side scream in protest as I maneuver down beside her.

She startles at my voice. "I'm not most people."

I don't argue.

She's been avoiding me for days. Ever since I witnessed a vulnerable moment she'd offer a limb to have kept hidden. She makes Dominic bring me my meds, and when she has *no* choice but to check my wound, she refuses to speak or look me in the eye.

I'm not offended. Fuck, I'm grateful. Her cold shoulder is the greatest gift this prison has to offer.

I half expect her to stand once I've settled and run off to avoid having to converse with me.

"I wish it snowed more in December," she speaks instead. "Seattle has the shittiest weather across the country, yet, we rarely get a freaking white Christmas."

"Tragic," I gripe sarcastically. "Thought you were hanging lights."

She raises a dark brow. "We have this agreement, Dad and I. He tells me to hang the lights, which is a way to let me escape Codi and her elf-steroided-self. I sit on the curb, doing nothing, and then he does the lights himself."

I pick up a stone and skip it across the road, watching it bounce over the asphalt. "Not a fan of Christmas?"

She watches me candidly for a beat. Quiet seconds of retrospect muddled by confusion. An attempt to see inside my head, to dissect my heart. She had me pinned, or so she thought. My existence in her life has rattled her more than she cares to admit. Yet, she's too focused on her negative feelings to work out *why*.

She shakes her head. "I love Christmas. Codi is just another form of extra when it comes to decorating. For someone who shines rainbows

—and, I'm certain, still believes in unicorns—she's fucking scary when it comes to hanging ornaments."

I laugh, earning a sly smile.

"How's the injury?"

I touch my side subconsciously. "Feels good. I'm still a bit stiff, but I don't feel like I'm going to up and die anymore."

"I should say I'm glad."

"I'm more for honesty."

"Well, it sucks that I'm so good at what I do."

I bark out a rough laugh.

"Surprised you haven't attempted to escape again," she mocks me. "Obviously, we're holding you hostage, torturing you by nursing you back to health."

"You telling me if you were stuck in a bed in *my* loft, you'd stay without an argument?"

She looks positively traumatized by the thought.

"Exactly," I sigh.

Quiet settles between us, and I sigh uncomfortably. "Thank you," I murmur. "I know coming to my rescue isn't exactly high up on your Christmas list."

I watch the line of her throat bob with a thick swallow. "I didn't do it for you," she offers unapologetically. "Seeing you suffer was just an added bonus."

"Well then, you're welcome."

We sit in contented silence as the sky turns from its murky grey to the beginnings of twilight. Stars are now visible in the sky, and the temperature has dropped dramatically in the blink of an eye.

"I don't get it," I test. "Your dad. He should want me dead, but he's working his damnedest to make me feel like family. I know you owe me nothing but any idea if he plans on taking my life when he's good and ready?"

Pulling her arms around her body, shielding herself against the cold, she turns her neck, looking me over.

"That's not Dominic's M.O. If he's acting like you're forgiven, you're forgiven. If you forever let your past cloud your present, how can you expect to move forward in search of your future?"

"Poetic," I muse.

"Dad," she explains. "He's preached it all our lives. He lives by the law that you settle grievances in the moment. Hate and anger only fester, likely exaggerating a reaction that never should've been. Holding onto resentment does nothing but stop you from achieving what you're destined for."

"Smart guy."

She hugs her knees. "To Codi and my father, you are family. No matter your past sins. In this family, we don't hold your mistakes against you. Blood is blood, and that means something here."

"Even for you?"

Her eyes close, a soft flutter of her dark lashes against the ruddiness of her cheeks. "This is a hard one for me. They've welcomed in a predator who was aiming to place a bullet hole in the very back I'm supposed to *protect*."

It makes perfect sense. I'm the threat they stand united against. And yet, here I stand. In amongst them. Not a wolf hiding among the sheep. A wolf, bared, and not entirely in different attire. It's important not to forget that regardless of how hospitable Dominic Rein has been and continues to be… he's feared for a reason.

"No arguments here, beauty," I grumble. "It's whacked out to me, too."

"*Ryn*," Codi interrupts. "You do this every year. Now, Dad is going to have to do the front lights. You are such a freaking Grinch."

She storms on a huff before Camryn can respond, her stride purposely pissed off.

We watch her retreat in amusement, smiles on both our faces.

"What about you?" she asks quietly after Codi disappears. "Do you love or hate Christmas?"

I scratch my beard in discomfort. "It's just another day."

I feel her stare—the burning attention of her eyes on my profile.

"We used to celebrate," I confide when she doesn't speak. "Lila was like Codi."

I watch her blink in sadness, and I appreciate the lack of commiseration in the gesture. The situation saddens her, and that's where it ends. There's no pity or bleeding compassion in her gaze.

"When she died, there wasn't much we cared about celebrating." I take a breath, unsure why I add the next part. "I'm starting to realize maybe Parker was just going along with my rejection of everything we shared with her." Maybe it's to offer her even footing again. She involuntarily showed her vulnerability, and it made her uneasy. This small sliver of me offering it back brings us back to an even playing field. It's the least I can do, her saving my ass and all.

"I wouldn't want to celebrate if Dad had been stolen from us."

I watch her for a beat, a level of understanding passing between us.

"Something tells me you would've anyway." I pause. "For Codi."

She doesn't argue. It's the truth. Camryn Rein may be as jilted by the world as I am, but she hides it in her generosity in helping others.

I prefer to use it as my most powerful weapon. I choose to bask in the way I disappoint everyone close to me. That way, they know I'm not someone they can rely on. It's best they are comfortable in the knowledge that, in the end, I'll only fail them.

Trusting people isn't something I care to find comfort in. Now or in the future. Placing your trust in others only levels you up for failure. No matter their intention, people *will* let you down. I've learned the hard way that, intended or not, it still burns the same way.

My openness with Camryn shocks her. She no doubt pinned me as a closed book. She saw the stone wall I'd built around me and didn't for a second consider it'd be see-through. But I'm not a liar, and I'm only truthful to people I respect enough to offer any part of my psyche. The rest are undeserving of my truth, and lies are too much work to maintain. If their assumptions are good enough for them, they're good enough for me.

My respect for Camryn continues to grow with every one of our interactions. She hates me. Rightfully so. What's important is that she doesn't hide her despise, and why should she? She's honest, and I appreciate the hell out of that.

I'm truthful with her because I want the hate she feels toward me to remain. I want her to understand that her feelings toward me are right and justified. I want her to believe that I'm the monster she knows I am. It's safer that way. Because when I disappoint this family like I continually have my own, at least I won't have to be painted in her guilt like I will be Dominic and Codi's.

"I'm starved. Come on," she invites, shaking off the melancholy of our conversation. "I've kept this light charade up for long enough. Let's go eat."

My brow furrows. "How *hospitable* of you... you caught a fever out here?" I joke.

Her eyes roll dramatically. "I can hate you in civility. Even prisoners need to be fed."

"No need for that." I laugh. "I'm gonna head home tonight."

She doesn't look surprised. More than aware of how uncomfortable I've been holed up in Rein's house on the verge of death. The very people who could have taken advantage of my weakened state and sought an act of justified revenge have turned out to be my saviors. And that very significant detail makes me uncomfortable as fuck.

"I'm no longer on the precipice of death. The infection has subsided. Thinking I'll be able to hobble around my own loft while this scratch heals."

Sniffing against the cold, she nods her head in agreement.

"Let's also not kid ourselves," I continue. "I'm also guessing I've outstayed my welcome."

Her head tips side-to-side. "Only according to me."

"Well then," I smirk. "Let's say their welcome has outstayed me."

She stands, brushing the back of her jeans. She doesn't attempt to help me stand, only watching as I slowly get up.

"I'll pack you some supplies to keep the wound clean."

"Appreciate it." I follow her inside, hating myself for thinking that Camryn Rein isn't such bad company.

She pauses at the door, hand against the handle. Steeling a breath, she whirls on me. "About the other night—"

I shake my head. "Don't know what you're talking about." I ease the worry dancing in her eyes.

Her stare locks intently onto mine for seconds longer than it should be acceptable, the dark blue flecks searching for the lie in my statement. Swallowing thickly when she realizes it's not there to find, her eyes close in relief.

Not speaking another word, she steps through the door, the ice of her usual demeanor fixing back into place, the slice of vulnerability she didn't care to show me locked firmly away.

CHAPTER NINE

CAMRYN

HATE. Emotional revulsion in its purest form. It often moves hand in hand with a bitterness that is never remotely sweet.

Yet, here I am. Bent over my childhood bed, the man I despise more than anything in this world, powering inside me in the sweetest form of torture.

I don't even know how we got here. One moment we were arguing, insults laid down as we attempted to outdo one another in our provocation.

And then we were naked.

Lips clashing, fighting for dominance.

Bodies pressed together, wanting, needing more.

"You're such a bitch," he groans behind me, his generous length pulling from me almost entirely before slamming back inside.

He'll leave bruises. Blue and purple marks of frustration and lust. Fingerprints to remind me of how deep our loathing goes.

I whimper. "I hate you."

He laughs, the sound lost to the growl in his throat when I push myself back as hard as he thrusts forward. "Feeling's mutual, beauty."

We've been possessed. The adrenaline pumping through our veins in conflict morphing into arousal neither of us could resist.

The sex isn't just rough; it's brutal—a battle of wills. Power is no longer a point to prove but a victory that neither of us is willing to give away.

The thick line of his cock stretches me in a way I can't remember feeling. Broad enough to cause *just* the right amount of pain. Painful enough to have me begging for more.

A palm powers down to slap the meaty globe of my ass. His thick fingers grab hold, squeezing me savagely. "Too bad your pussy doesn't hate me." His free hand slides over my stomach, slapping my clit and making me shudder. "On the contrary, she's quite the greedy little whore. Swallowing my cock the way she is."

My pussy spasms at the vulgarity in his words.

"Camryn Rein," he muses. "My dirty, little beauty."

Something this toxic can't be healthy. The intensity is all-consuming. So addictive I'd give him my all if he demanded it.

My distaste for him is being pushed aside, overcome with passion. It's so destructively satisfying... I want to do it again.

And again.

And again.

"Harder," I command.

"Baby, I fuck you any harder, and the tip of my dick will come outta your mouth."

The visual convulses in my cunt, my walls closing in on him tight enough that he groans in *exquisite* agony.

Pulling out, he flips me without issue, his body climbing over mine, cock slamming inside me before I take a full breath.

My neck arches, my head thrown back into the mattress.

He lifts my leg, palm braced along the back of my knee, pushing it toward my chest.

I cry out.

"So deep," he grinds.

"So deep," I echo, ignoring the sting in my muscles.

Our not-so-silent loathing for one another is no longer enough. We've managed to channel every negative emotion we feel for one another into the most violently profound sex I've ever experienced.

"Tell me why you hate me."

Lip caught between my teeth, I moan when he undulates his hips.

The strong line of his pelvic bone massages my clit. "You are a reprehensible human being."

"You're conceited," he rebukes.

A bark of laughter leaves me, a needy whimper following it hungrily. "You're a Neanderthal."

"A fucking snob."

"Psychotic."

Large hands on my hips, he lifts them, thundering forward. "So fucking beautiful."

"Sinful and untouchable."

He pinches my clit softly, plucking at it with his thumb and forefinger.

The beginning of an orgasm, so *severe*, starts at my toes. My breathing stops.

He takes advantage, weight dropping on top of me to fuse his mouth to mine. Tongue plundering inside, the kiss we share is anything if not barbaric. His teeth bite into my lips, pulling at them savagely. I offer him the same. Our tongues, no longer restricted to the confines of our mouths, lick out, our intermingled taste as addictive as it is destructive.

I hate myself for finding him so stupidly attractive. I may hate him, but my body is yet to read the memo. Our attraction to one another is based solely on a foundation of contempt, and I'm intelligent enough to know that what we're doing right now is so far down a path of self-destruction, I'll be lucky to find my way back. But... consequences be damned, it feels so fucking good.

"Pussy's about to cry for me, Rein."

"Shut up."

"I can feel her," he snarls. "Throbbing. She wants to come. Should I let her?" he whispers against the hard point of my nipple.

"Fuck you, Shay."

He bites down on my nipple viciously enough to leave an imprint. I grip his shoulders, fingernails piercing his skin.

"Wrong answer."

"Got to hell."

He pays the same courtesy to my other nipple, and my entire body shudders. "Say please, Cami, or I'll pull out right now, decorate your stomach with my cum and leave you to put yourself out of your misery."

"I'd get the job done quicker." I lift my hips, searching for more.

"Wouldn't be the same, though, would it? Without my dick," he mocks me. "Come on, baby, say please."

I close my eyes tighter, ignoring his demand.

He retreats, and I cry out. "*Please.*"

I beg. I fucking plead.

"Good girl," he praises. "Now let that pussy cry for me, beauty. Soak your sheets."

I come.

Loudly.

Chaotically.

"*Ryn!*"

My eyes flash open, and my father's lounge room comes into focus.

"Are you okay?" Codi asks.

"What?" I blink away my confusion.

Parker chuckles to the side. "Baby, she was fine. I told you to leave her."

I swallow down my humiliation.

"You were having a nightmare… *I think.*"

"That was no nightmare, Sugar." Parker struggles to hold on to his laughter, and my cheeks shade.

"Fuck off, Parker," I grumble, moving to sit up.

"You fell asleep on the couch last night. We didn't want to wake you."

Palms to my eyes, I rub at them.

"Merry Christmas, Ryn."

Christmas.

Fuck.

"Go up and freshen up. I'm about to start lunch prep. Rocco should be here soon."

Rocco.

Seriously, Merry fucking Christmas to me.

Santa, all I want is for the ground to open up and swallow me. Please and thank you very much.

4

I WATCH him through the curtain, a neatly wrapped present held tightly in his hands. He reaches the door but doesn't knock. Instead, he turns on his heel, walking back toward his car.

Stopping at the hood, he shakes his head, cracking his neck side-to-side. Not the Rocco from my dream last night. This one seems almost *unsure*. Not the dominating asshole that made me come harder than I ever have done before. *In. My. Sleep.* In front of my sister and her fiancé. Embarrassment level, one jillion.

When he turns back around, there's a fierceness in his features that looks both uncertain and aggressive. Stride purposeful, he moves quickly. Three heavy knocks, all evenly spaced, are loud enough to be heard through the entire house.

I stay at the window, only the line of his back in view.

"Ryn?" Codi wanders into the room, feet moving toward the door.

She's wearing a stupid Santa apron, attempting to save her white shirt from the damage of her cooking. Thank fuck Dad is in there overseeing the disaster that is Codi cooking Christmas lunch.

"Hmm?"

"Why didn't you answer the door?"

Ah, let me see… because your future brother-in-law will read through my bitch act and know he gave me the orgasm of my life last night. Only he wasn't actually there.

I shrug, letting the curtain drop away. "He's not my guest."

She lets out a sigh of irritation. "It's Christmas Day. It'd be nice if you could be civil."

I stare at her blankly as she opens the door, her face split open in a wide grin as she wishes Rocco a Merry Christmas. Poor guy looks as uncomfortable as I feel, a tight smile forced onto his face as if someone had pulled it up with a pair of pliers. His discomfort pleases me more than it should.

His chin dips down briefly at Codi's overly enthusiastic greeting.

"Tree is over there if you want to pop that down." She gestures to the gift, but he doesn't move, only holding the box tighter.

"Rocco." I pull him from his misery. "How lovely of you to join us on this festive day." I throw in a curtsy for good measure. "We've all been eagerly awaiting your arrival. Please, do make yourself at home."

The side of his mouth twitches in amusement, but he doesn't let his grin take hold.

"Oh my God," Codi grumbles. "You're impossible."

I turn my attention to her. "Just being civil, dear sister, as per your Christmas request. Now, please excuse me as I do a quick knife count. I must ensure one doesn't find itself lodged in my back throughout the day." I fake a laugh walking toward the kitchen before Codi demands I apologize.

I hear her mumble an apology on my behalf, which only incenses me further.

"Rocco here?" Parker asks as I step into the kitchen.

He's plastered his ass to a kitchen stool, looking frightened at the mess before him.

"Hmm." I nod. "I'm going upstairs."

To die of my self-infused embarrassment, I don't add.

"Call me when we're exchanging gifts."

I kiss my dad's cheek as I walk past him, legging it up the stairs to avoid as much human contact as possible.

I pause on the threshold of my old room, the present that was held tightly in Rocco's hands now sitting on my bed.

I stare at it, trying to understand why Rocco Shay would buy me a gift.

"Won't bite." His voice tickles my ear, and I jump forward on a yelp.

"Don't sneak up on me like that."

Hands held up in surrender, he takes a large step backward, giving me space.

I eye him cautiously. "If there is a head or a sawn-off limb in that box, I'll kill you."

He laughs. "No idea what you think I get up to in my spare time, Rein. But it isn't carving up bodies. I can promise you that."

"Why would you even get me a gift? I don't like you, remember?" I dig, toying with the bow decorating the box.

Unless you're giving me orgasms in my sleep, it seems I'm impartial to that version of you.

Leaning against the door frame, he lifts his right shoulder. "Look, I'm all healed up. No need to scar your delicate morals by being in my presence longer than necessary." He ignores my statement. "Just open it."

I scowl in his direction. And he does it back.

Sighing, I rip at the bow, pulling it off with little finesse. Tearing the carefully folded paper, a plain brown box mocks me. Opening it, I half expect it to be empty.

It isn't, and I stare down at the bright red boxing gloves in titillation. A small card lays atop, and picking it up, my eyes fall over Rocco's severe and heavy scrawl.

Easier to chase away those monsters when you know how to fight.
Merry whatever
The Grinch

I smile despite myself.

"Than—" I turn back to the door, but he's gone, the space heavy without his presence.

Dropping the card onto the bed, I reach for the gloves, feeling the leather beneath my fingers. Lifting them to my face, I inhale their smell. The rich, earthy scent is addictive and overwhelming. White laces fall along the inside wrists, and dropping one back into the box; I slide my hand inside the other.

I clench my fist, listening to the crackle of the glove at my silent instruction. I force my fingers from their fist, stretching them out to feel the inner padding.

I wouldn't believe it if I weren't the one with my hand buried in the leather, but even touching the glove like this, a sense of power filters into my veins. Like the glove has melded into my hand as an added layer of protection against the world. A shield I never knew I wanted or considered needed is now present. Gifted to me by someone I had decided was lacking a functioning heart.

I hadn't considered the possibility that Rocco Shay had felt the odd camaraderie that had settled between us. Similarities that scared the fuck out of me were just as confusing for him. An unexpected kinship that has forced us out of the neat, structured lines of our individual lives.

He doesn't want to understand me. He doesn't want to feel a connection because we're both damaged.

And neither do I.

Yet, here we are.

The sides of our boxes have fallen, leaving us both exposed. And neither one of us knows what to do with that reality.

I could give the gift back.

Tell him I'd sooner saw off my arm before accepting anything from him.

He'd respect that.

I think.

I could grow the fuck up, walk downstairs, and thank him for his gift.

But that'd just make us both awkward.

I could ignore it. Pretend he didn't give them to me and accept them as a gift from... Santa.

That's a little too cunty for even me.

I yank my cell from my back pocket.

CAMRYN

Thank you

He responds almost immediately.

ROCCO

For what?

I grin. He would've accepted me being extra cunty.

Figures.

A soft knock sounds at my door, pulling me from my thoughts.

"Nice gloves," my dad greets, leaning against my doorway in a similar way Rocco was only moments before.

I nod, not exactly sure what to say.

"From?" he prods.

Tucking them back into their box, I let my shoulders lift slightly. "The Grinch."

I don't let myself read into the smirk pulling at the side of my dad's mouth.

"Seems you've already started opening your gifts, but Codi has granted us permission to the goodies under the tree."

"How kind of her," I joke, walking toward my dad.

"It's her first Christmas with Parker," he offers, an arm moving over my shoulder to bring me to his side. "She wants it to be perfect."

We shuffle through the house, Dad's cologne wrapping me in its warm embrace. His smell, it's a balm. The simplicity of his scent can ease me in a way very few other things can.

He smells like comfort and safety. Of unconditional love and those hugs only he seems to know that I need. On days when I feel as though the world is falling apart, his arm around my shoulders keeps me supported until I'm again ready to stand on my own. I've never told him that. Likely I would never need to. It seems ingrained, and he knows what I need without me vocalizing it. It's a unique talent only a caring parent can genuinely offer.

Codi smells like sugar, and how I imagine rainbows smell. Like fresh rain and sunshine all mixed into one. When clouds descend on my world, and my nightmares shroud me in darkness, she shoos them away like a quick summer shower, letting the sun break through.

I feel oddly calmed by everything packed into my family's earthy and sugary scent. Deep down, it has nothing to do with how they actually smell and more with the association with them as people. Still, I'd feel betrayed if they were to change their perfume or cologne. Like they were no longer who they were supposed to be.

I hug Codi as I walk into the sitting room, my silent apology for being a bitch earlier today. She accepts it without issue, hugging me tightly; her cheek, warmed by the fire, pressed tightly against mine.

I don't let myself consider that the smell of leather now hints at a sense of power, *my* power. I also don't let myself settle on the fact that the very smell will only ever be linked to Rocco Shay.

His presence is impossible to ignore, even in the large living room. My eyes and nostrils are assaulted on every angle by Christmas and its pitiful form of distraction. The room could be empty—a plain white space with Rocco at its center.

I work to ignore his overwhelming proximity. His silence screams at me, begging me to look at him and see him. Something bigger seems at play, demanding I look deeper to see more of who he is.

Everyone else focused on my dad opening the cufflinks Codi had bought for him; I casually glance Rocco's way. He stares back for a single blink before turning his attention to his brother and my family. Not in the least bit perturbed that I caught him staring or that I felt the need to do the same to him.

Codi and I unwrap our staple can of mace from our father. A gift we receive every year, even though neither of us has necessitated the use of it. "Thanks, Dad," I smile. "This'll come in handy for those unwanted guests you keep bestowing upon us."

I hear Rocco's chuckle, and I'm more satisfied than I should be at being able to make him laugh.

We open presents, and I recognize that deep inside, the morning feels more comfortable and natural than it has in years. With Sarah gone, Codi, Dad, and I are at ease. But worse, with Parker and Rocco taking her place, everything feels *more*.

Gifts opened, I stand, moving around the room to collect the discarded wrapping paper to occupy my hands.

I feel Rocco's gaze, the lazy and disinterested gleam in his eyes tracking my movements.

"You missed some," he mocks, lifting his foot to release the tiny piece of ripped paper he'd been holding prisoner.

I look at the half-ripped Santa face smiling up at me, my gaze moving up to Rocco, who wears a similar smile.

"It's good manners to assist when you're a guest in someone else's home. Get off your lazy ass and pick it up." I turn on my heel, stomping out of the room on a mumbled cuss word. Or five...

"I fucking hate that guy," I complain.

"But do you?" Codi saunters up behind me, moving toward the kitchen.

"What's that supposed to mean?"

She shrugs, moving toward the stove. "I see this spark when you're with him, something that you usually only show to Dad and me. To everyone else, you have this" —she twists her lips in contemplation— "don't look, speak, or touch vibe. You work to scare everyone else off."

I frown at the unintended judgment in her words.

"I'm kind of grateful for Rocco," she admits. "He seems to have brought you back to life."

"I can't stand him."

"Maybe," she sings, moving onto the oven to check the turkey. "Or maybe you lose it around him because you're not used to people seeing who you really are. It scares you," she calls me out, "which means it's real, Ryn. Whatever you feel for Rocco Shay is wreaking havoc on all those complicated feelings inside of you, and I'm not going to lie, I love watching it unfold."

I scowl in her direction, but she ignores me, tending to the lunch that is supposed to make Parker fall more in love with her. Like that's even possible.

CHAPTER TEN

ROCCO

THERE'S a bounce in Camryn's step I've never seen. Of course, that's not saying it's missing when I'm not around, but considering the way Dominic and Codi keep glancing her way with their eyebrows kissing, I think it's as new for them as it is for me.

It's stupid as shit, but I feel fucking powerful knowing I put it there. They would've tried, but they failed. It's because they won't look deep enough to see what she needs.

Power.

She's sick and fucking tired of jumping at her own shadow. She's exhausted by the monsters that creep into her dreams. She doesn't just want them to go away. She wants to fucking *destroy* them.

It was the gloves. I don't doubt it for a second. I know because I feel the same when stepping into the ring. Adrenaline pumping through your veins, your fight instinct taking over… you're invincible. You *dare* the world to come at you because you know you'll fuck every last fucker up.

It's a feeling as dangerous as it is freeing. It can make you stupid, reckless even. But it gives you something nothing else can or will. The power of freedom is too tempting to pass up. You'd bet your life on it, time and time again.

I don't second-guess myself a lot. It isn't healthy. But buying Camryn Rein a Christmas gift was an exception. I honestly have zero clue what I was thinking. It was awkward as fuck, to say the least.

I didn't need her reading into it, thinking I considered us friends.

We're not. Nor will we ever be.

We're forced acquaintances, reluctant family members. We'd both value the reality of never having to cross one another's path ever again. But, unfortunately for both of us, it seems that little dream might stay in the land of make-believe for the foreseeable future.

I was minding my business when I saw them. My eyes caught on the candy apple-colored gloves, and I knew she had to have them.

I could see her clearly in my mind's eye. Long brown hair blowing around her shoulders. Small frame dressed in tiny shorts and a tank tight enough to see her nipples. Fiery eyes and tanned skin glowing in challenge. Finished off with gloves on her fists, ready to fight. My libido got twisted up somewhere, sexualizing her in a way she'd sever my head for. But, truth be told, that only makes my dick harder.

I see something in her that I feel in myself, and even I have enough heart to realize that's fucking unacceptable. She shouldn't have to feel that way. No one like Camryn Rein should. I deserve my self-inflicted hate. No matter what haunts her at night or forces her to turn her back on the world, she doesn't or didn't warrant it. That's a fact I know to be true. So if, in the end, my one good deed for this family is to rid even a little of that for her, I'll die thinking maybe, just maybe, I did something right.

"Gloves were a genius idea," Dominic interrupts my reflection, a smile on his face that makes me believe he was reading my thoughts. "Kicking myself *I* hadn't thought of it." He ushers me away from the rest of our family—gathered around the kitchen counter, pouring mulled wine and talking shit. "There was something on her face when I caught her in her room after unboxing them... a fight to *survive* I can't recall ever seeing on her face. Thank you."

I shrug, not caring to respond.

"Something went incredibly wrong in my daughter's life," he confides, stepping into his office, expecting me to follow. "It started young; Sarah always rejected the idea of her, so she was never gifted the love of a mother. I worked a lot, so I guess, in hindsight, she also felt abandoned by me."

"Not easy for a kid," I offer neutrally.

"Hmm," he agrees, lifting a bottle of whiskey in offer.

I lift my chin in acceptance.

"We fought before she went off to college. She was done with being known for her name. *Rein.*" His eyebrows lift in sarcasm. "She wanted to carve out her place in life. I feared losing her completely if I didn't give her that."

Regret ages his face. The confidence he wears rigidly falls away in a wash of repentance.

"By giving into my daughter's demands, I failed her. Whatever happened when she went to college, too much trust had been lost for her to confide in me when she came back."

If he expects me to say anything, he doesn't let on. Happy to stare at me, letting me read his remorse like a book I'm not interested in.

"The thing that throws me about it all is that she became obsessively caught up in Codi's well-being on her return."

I raise an eyebrow, my interest piqued.

"I've searched for answers, but they don't seem to want to be found."

"Or maybe you don't really want them," I counter, accepting the glass of amber liquid he slides my way.

Leaning back in his chair, he considers my words. "Perhaps you're right, as awful as that makes me sound. Anyway" —he shakes his head— "my daughter's well-being isn't why I invited you to share a Christmas whiskey…"

The contrast between Dominic Rein and Kane Shay is striking. I've never let myself believe there was a difference. They were… *are* career criminals, not afraid to wash their hands in blood. I assumed Dominic was as unbalanced as Kane. Both have always oozed power and demand, yet Dominic is far more formidable than my father.

Kane led through fear, through threat. He forced you to see how powerful he was through menace and violence. He was unbalanced, so trust wasn't something his employees could offer him. That only cut down the effectiveness of his command.

Dominic, I'm coming to realize, leads through respect. He listens and thinks through his response. You know when you've pissed him off and how you'd go about doing so. He's *reasonable*. He leads with his mind, not his heart, which means he's in control. *Always*.

Dominic Rein refuses to let emotions cloud his judgment; for that simple fact, he's more dangerous than Kane ever was.

"I haven't found your scumbag wife," I confess, unsure what else he could want from me.

Eyes pinned to mine over the rim of his glass, he sips slowly. "I know."

Silence sits between us as he drinks slowly, and I shift uncomfortably.

"Are you planning on telling me that you're aiming for my head?"

Surely he's not brutal enough to end me on Christmas day while my brother plays happy family with his daughters.

"No."

I swallow, smart enough to be wary of the intensity of his stare. "Why am I here then?"

"Carmichael," he says, placing his empty glass gently on his desk.

My fist clenches involuntarily. "He's a dead man."

"Correct," he shocks me by saying. "It's been taken care of. My Christmas present to you."

I scowl, angered he took my revenge away from me.

He reads my reaction easily. "Rocco, one day you'll realize that when retaliation is taken out in temper and impatience, it's messy and more often than not incriminating."

"Don't patronize me," I grit out.

"I'm not," he responds calmly, unfazed by the animosity in my tone. "I'm being real, and I'm being honest. Your anger will only get you into trouble. It will take more and more away from you until you are left with nothing." He gestures toward the door, where Parker sits on the opposite side.

"You know, Rein, I had a dad once... he was a cunt. I'm not in the market for a replacement."

His gaze drops in amusement, a tight smile on his lips. "Kane also let his anger overtake his common sense," he insults. "He ended up losing his life because of it."

I shoot my whiskey back, slamming the empty glass on his desk, pushing toward his with force. It meets its mark, the glasses clinking with the potent sound of disrespect.

"I don't want that ending for you, Rocco," he implores, moving forward to rest his elbows against his desk. "You can write a different story than Kane did. You have more up here." He taps his temple. "And you recognize that you have more to live for."

He lets that sink in, watching my animosity wash away in a tsunami of feelings I can't even comprehend.

There are days when I'd tell you that I couldn't give two shits whether I lived or died. I'm not afraid of death. If an asshole with a black hood and scythe wants to come for me, good on him. I'd welcome the journey into nothing.

Then there are the days when the thought of leaving Parker leaves me cold. Not for me. In the pit of my stomach, I know he could find happiness without me if he'd let himself. The problem is, he wouldn't. My younger brother has this misconceived notion that he needs me. Maybe once upon a time, he did, but not anymore. The reality is that I won't let myself fail him again. If he thinks he needs me here by his side, I'll give him that. He's lost enough.

"Have you found Sarah?" I shift the conversation without preamble.

"No," he sighs.

"When you find her, I want in."

He contemplates me, eyes set on my face in expectation. "That's the reason I invited you here," he deliberates. "I want you to work for me, Rocco."

"*What?*"

"It doesn't take a genius to recognize that Parker isn't built for this business. He enjoys running your nightclub. He's rough but not ruthless. And my girls would likely laugh in my face if I considered them my succession plan."

He's not wrong. Camryn and Codi Rein want nothing to do with the business their father has built with his bare hands. It doesn't take intelligence to realize that.

"And, what am I?"

"Cautious. Unafraid. Callous and ferocious as required. You're willing to do the unspeakable."

I bark out an unamused laugh. "Contrary to what this family believes, I've never killed anyone. Not by my own hand," I add regretfully.

"Nor have I," Dominic combats.

His declaration shocks me. I reasoned *somewhere* along the line, Dominic had gotten his hands dirtier than he cared to. It's the way of the business. Or so I assumed.

"I didn't want a hand in my father's business. So what makes you think I'd want anything to do with yours?"

Head tipped to the side, he considers me for a moment before speaking. "Because you never agreed with his ways. You didn't want to succeed a man who brutalized you so badly."

I hate that Kane's wrath was and *is* so well known. I hate that people know he used me like a punching bag. That beating on his oldest son made him feel like a big fucking man.

Dominic is right. I didn't want anything to do with Kane Shay and a business built on deceit and betrayal. Stepping into his shoes would have gifted me a one-way ticket down to hell, effective immediately.

"I don't deal in drugs."

He tips his head to the side. "Again, nor do I."

I exhale heavily. "I don't appreciate personal matters being taken out of my hands."

"I won't let people in my circle unnecessarily put themselves in harm's way."

A rally in power struggles. Demands and warnings thrown back and forth like simple words, only they're drowned in threat.

I mirror his position. My back pressed lazily against the chair I'm perched upon, legs splayed wide. "Access to the inner sanctum has been bestowed," I muse sarcastically. "Just needed to threaten your daughter's life."

"Hiding your respect and appreciation through sarcasm won't get you far in my world, Rocco," he scolds. "*I* appreciate your honesty, your straightforwardness. But don't be a fool to make yourself look tough."

Being schooled by a crime boss isn't at the top of my Christmas list. Frankly, it's downright stupid. I don't have an army to wage war on Dominic Rein. Not that I'd care to. The man has done nothing but offer my brother and me safe harbor and forgiveness, which was far more than we deserved.

"What do you want from me?"

"Eventually, I will need a second-in-charge, someone I trust to make decisions for and with me. Someone who isn't afraid to dirty their hands or fight for my family legacy."

I feel my eyebrows pull together, shock and confusion twisting my stomach into knots. "Our families were at war for *years.*"

"*Were,*" he emphasizes. "As far as I'm concerned, that war died with your father. If you can see past his grievances to build something stronger, I can do the same."

I scratch at the back of my neck, my mouth uncomfortably dry. "Why me?"

"Loyalty can't be bought, Rocco. It's either there or it's not. You'd do everything in your incredible power to protect your brother, which means you'd also do anything to protect my daughters. You have buy-in into this family, whether you want it or not. I don't trust you because I *know* you. I trust you because of your loyalty to Parker."

I massage the bridge of my nose.

"This alliance, this partnership, whatever you wish to label it, will give you full access to my search for Sarah."

I look up slowly.

"What if our *wants* or *needs* differ?" I question.

That is, what if he wants to save his cunt of a wife, and I want to slit her throat.

"Trust me, my ending for Sarah mirrors yours."

I sit up straighter. "I'm not your bitch."

He laughs. "I can pay people to take on that role. I don't need a yes-man. I need an equal."

He pours us another whiskey, lifting his glass in salute. I retrieve mine, tapping it against his while meeting his eyes, looking for any hint he's about to double-cross me. I find none.

We tip back our glasses, swallowing the contents in one gulp.

"If we're working together now, I need help finding someone. Someone who doesn't want to be found."

He nods. "Of course."

"This is strictly between you and me. Parker can never know, am I understood?"

"Crystal," he murmurs, waiting patiently as I tell him my story.

CHAPTER ELEVEN

CAMRYN

"This is a stupid idea," I murmur, tapping the elevator button incessantly.

"The dumbest idea I've ever had," I muse, the soft sound of the bell indicating the doors are about to close like an electric shock directly at my heart.

"I'm such a loser," I groan.

I turn around, my reflection staring back at me from the elevator's wall in judgment. "He'll think I'm crazier than Codi on Christmas."

The doors open, and I consider letting them close again, ride it back down to ground level, and pretend I'd never even stepped into the building.

Easy. This never happened.

I take a tentative step out, shifting nervously on the elevator's threshold until it beeps in irritation. The sound startles me forward, and I look into the hallway, half expecting him to be waiting to send me away.

One deep breath, and I push myself forward. Step after step, one foot in front of the other until I'm standing outside his door. It looks normal enough, not the burning door of hell like I had told myself it would be. Engulfed in flames, ready to welcome me into the inferno.

I knock before I can talk myself out of it.

Like everything that Rocco Shay does, the door flies open with force. His big body bristles with the constant irritability that sits on his person like an untouchable aura.

Fuck off, it screams.

He stands on the threshold of his home, staring at me in confusion. "Rein," he greets cautiously after a loaded second.

"Shay."

We stand like that for five quickly drawn breaths. Enough time for my gaze to drink him in grudgingly. My eyes are eager to eat up *everything* before me. The way his shirt stretches invitingly over his broad chest. The muscles of his arms are thick, even in rest. The narrowed lines of his hips. The well-groomed beard that hides his scowl. The wolf-like eyes that look down on everyone like a casualty waiting to happen. All the while, my brain rolls its metaphorical eyes, calling me out on my foolishness.

My chest tightens in error. This was a mistake. I know it. I shouldn't have come. But, just as I'm about to turn and walk away without an explanation, he lets his gaze fall to my hand, candy-apple boxing gloves held tightly in my grasp.

"Something wrong with them?" he asks.

My head shakes side-to-side, quick movements that scream out I'm nervous. "No." I clear my throat.

"You don't want them?" He growls, his face twisting unhappily.

"No," I rush out. "I mean, yes. Yes, I want them."

Eyes narrowed on my face, I watch the deep swallow of his throat, the dense movement of his Adam's apple up and down. "Beauty," he sighs. "I get you don't like me, and you think I'm some fucking demon, but I can't read minds. So, tell me what you need, or I have better things to do than watch your eyes shoot daggers at me."

"Teach me to fight," I mumble hurriedly, the words twisting together in an incoherent mumble of drivel.

His blonde eyebrows reach for his hairline. "*Sorry?*"

"*Please,*" I add as an afterthought. "Please teach me how to fight."

His head shakes, and I feel my heart drop to my stomach.

"There are places you can go for that. Trainers who will be able to show you."

I blink in disappointment. "I don't want the basics, Rocco," I plead. "I don't want to spend months learning stance and blocks. I want to *fight*. I want to ball up this festering anger that weighs heavily in my gut and expel it. I want to feel my fury in every punch."

His characteristic look of boredom and venom gives way to understanding. He hates that, feeling that connection with me. I know it because I feel it too.

"I know you don't want to understand me. I don't want to understand you either. But there's something inside of you that can communicate with the demon within me."

"No."

I close my eyes.

"I saved your life," I guilt. "It's the least you can do."

That makes him smile, the gesture *almost* hidden by the beard covering the bottom half of his face. "Fuck, Rein. I never asked you to do that."

"But Parker did. I did him a solid. Don't make me use him to make you do one for me."

His smile grows. "Parker would never let me teach you to fight. You're fucking crazy if you think he would."

"You sure about that?" I test. "He and Codi want us to get along. They'd do just about anything to repair what's broken here."

I watch his smile drop away, and I replace it with one of my own.

"Willing to gamble on a maybe?" I tease. "*Or* we could continue to hate one another, and this would be our secret. No one would know."

The clock in his loft ticks by slowly, exaggerating the silence swirling around us.

"Once a week for a month," he concedes unhappily.

"Twice a week for four," I combat.

"You're fucking crazy," he gripes. "Once a week for two."

"Twice a week for four."

He looks at me like I've lost it. "Negotiation requires compromise."

I shrug. "I'm not negotiating."

"Twice a week for three."

I stretch my hand toward him. "Deal."

He takes it reluctantly, his grip tight. "If I'm training you, cut down on the sugar."

I laugh. "Fuck no. Sugar loves me in a way no one else ever will. I will not abandon him."

"Cut it down. It's not good for you."

I push past him into the loft.

"Woah." He grabs my bicep. "What do you think you're doing?"

I glance into his loft and then back to his big hand wrapped around my arm. "I'm here for my first training session, and I don't care what anyone says, anything that good can't be bad for you."

"I'm busy," he says slowly.

"Doing what?" I roll my eyes.

"Not training you."

I shrug my arm out of his grasp. "You're doing nothing but plotting the demise of the world. You may as well make yourself useful."

He lets me move into his home. "Most people are more cautious around me."

I lift a single brow. "You gonna kill me? Hurt me?"

"Maybe," he grumbles.

"Yeah, right. I don't expect you to be nice to me," I tell him honestly. "Quite frankly, *you* being nice to me *would* frighten me."

"Don't speak while you're here," he warns. "I won't let you slack. You'll likely vomit the first few times we train."

"And you think sugar is bad for me. Where's your gym?"

He points toward the back of his loft. "Let me change. Don't snoop, and don't fucking touch anything."

I turn on my heel, moving toward the space he indicated.

The loft is impeccable; sterile in its cleanliness. The smell of bleach and disinfectant assaults my nasal cavity. Not a single item is out of place. It's austere. No homely touches decorate the walls except one photo on the mantel—a worn image of him, Parker, and Lila.

I glance back to where he disappeared, considering moving closer to it to take a better look. But he warned me not to snoop.

I'm stupid enough to request Rocco Shay unleash the demons within me, best not to destroy our deal before it has even started.

I walk toward the home gym leisurely. Tucked at the very back of the apartment, it's impressive. A ceiling-to-floor mirror is tacked along the wall, two benches, and limitless weights are packed neatly into their place. A bright red punching bag hangs from the ceiling at the side, weathered and worn, giving the impression it's ridden out many a Rocco storm over its lifetime.

His heavy footfalls alert me to his approach, and I watch him in the giant mirror. His basketball shorts sit comfortably on his defined hips. His torso and chest are naked of clothing. He *bristles* with muscle—the protrusive line of his lower abdomen showy enough to make me stare. The golden tan of his skin stretches purposely over his evident strength. Molding to every muscle like latex, exposing every curve and sinewy bulge.

Camryn Rein. My dirty, little beauty.

Not today, Satanic libido. Off you fuck, to the land of over-my-dead-body.

A burst of fire is drawn over his heart, the delicately designed flames climbing diagonally up his chest to wrap along the right side of his neck. They finish just under the cut line of his jaw, dancing every time he swallows.

Rocco Shay oozes threat, he bleeds power, and anyone stupid enough to deny that can sign a one-way ticket into his wrath.

"Problem with clothing?" I test.

He takes a step closer. "Anything that constricts you is working against you. That includes this," he points to his head, "this," he taps his heart, "as well as physical restrictions like clothing and lack of training."

"Well, if you expect me to remove my shirt…"

"I'm pretty sure I asked you *not* to speak," he groans impatiently. "Your boobs are of no interest to me," he insults. "They're another restriction that will inhibit your ability to move as effectively as you need to. Before our next session, invest in a correctly fitted sports bra."

I frown. "Please stop talking about my boobs," I mutter.

"Pleasure. Now—" He steps closer, eyes tracking my body up and down in objectivity. "You shit-canned stance, but it's crucial. If your feet aren't placed correctly, you can trust you'll go down like a sack of shit. But if you're well-balanced, you're *much* harder to knock down. Are you right or left handed?"

"Left," I answer.

"Evil. I knew it," he teases. "Right shoulder facing me," he instructs. "Feet shoulder-width apart."

He watches me move into position, one swift nod of his chin when I've got it right.

"Right foot pointed at me. Bend your knees."

He kicks at my right foot gently to move it where he wants it. "Not so much with the bend. Find your comfort. Good girl."

Pussy's about to cry for me, Rein.

Jesus. I shake my head, expelling the unwelcome thoughts from my brain.

My eyes on my feet, he clicks his fingers in front of my face, forcing my gaze upward. "Eyes *always* up, understand?"

I nod.

"Tuck your chin in. Not so much." He smirks. "There. Perfect."

So fucking beautiful.

I roll my shoulders.

"Loose fists." He lifts my hands, watching them ball into fists. "Left hand by your chin." He pushes it into position, holding it there to ensure I have it. "Right hand in front of your face to protect the money."

Rocco takes a step back, assessing my form. "Feel good?"

"A little stiff," I admit.

He shrugs. "Let's hope it never feels too comfortable."

He says it more to himself than to me, and I feel ill at the hint of vulnerability in his tone.

I'm surprised at the patience in his voice as he directs me. I half expected him to set me up in front of a YouTube tutorial and be done with it. I was convinced he'd shun me or ridicule me. Instead, he's calm, almost kind, and definitely tolerant.

It's a side of him Parker has always spoken of, one I wouldn't believe existed.

"Hold the stance," he directs, moving away to the back corner of the room.

I watch his retreat in the large mirror. The muscles in his back stretch and pull with every movement he makes. I knew he was ripped, but the extent of *how* toned he is has shocked me. I'd bet he has next to zero body fat percentage.

"Do you have cheat days?" I find myself asking his reflection.

His large shoulders lift. "I don't classify them as cheat days. If I feel like eating pizza, I eat pizza. I just make sure I expend more energy working out that day."

Moving back toward me, his eyes on mine in the mirror, he shoves his hand into some form of flattened gloves.

"Are we going to fight?"

That makes him laugh, a thick roll of rough laughter skating along my skin in a way I shouldn't want a repeat of.

"Think you could take me, Rein?"

"I hate you enough to lose myself, maybe kill you," I offer.

"Which means I'd own you. Don't let emotion cloud what you know. It only helps your opponent defeat you. They're punching pads," he answers my earlier question. "It's your lucky day, oh-beautiful-enemy-of-mine. You get to hit me."

I roll my eyes. "I hardly call punching a padded glove sitting on your hand hitting you."

"Best you're gonna get." He shifts his stance in front of me, solidifying his footing.

I wait for instruction, holding my position.

"Elbows in," he says. "Punch with your right hand first, but rotate your arm as you do." He demonstrates slowly, his arm sliding forward, rotating slightly as it nears me.

I wait for him to move it back, punching pads held up at the ready.

"Your turn." He nods.

I let my arm fire out, the loud crack of my glove smacking against his.

It's a nice sound. A strong sound. One that ignites a flame inside of my stomach. A tiny fire that burns like a soft ember, begging to be stoked, to be laced with gasoline to overtake my entire self.

"Keep your eyes up," Rocco admonishes gently. "Don't look at your feet or your arm. Forward."

I swallow, pulling my arm back to jab it forward once again.

"Better," he encourages. "But remember to rotate your arm."

A small smile dances at the corner of his mouth whenever I get it right. A pride hits him, his face lighting up with accomplishment and conceit.

He's building a warrior, and it burns a similar fire inside of him like that one that burns in me.

He spends two hours with me, correcting my technique, praising my form, the fist of my glove cracking against his punching pad. My body is covered in sweat, my breath labored, and if I'm honest, like he promised, on the verge of vomiting. But I feel alive. I feel energized and capable, and I can't remember the last time I felt like this.

All the while, Rocco's barely broken a sweat.

"Drink plenty of water, rest your muscles, and make sure you stretch." He speaks as I remove my gloves, hands to his defined hips, authority dripping from his tone.

"Thursday work for you?"

He nods. "I'll text you once I've checked my other commitments."

"Try not to get killed or injured between now and then," I bite out teasingly. "This was good. I feel good. I don't want to have to stop."

"I obviously didn't work you hard enough," he mocks me.

I fight an eye roll.

"You gotta find a purpose for the fight, Camryn." He steps in my path, stopping me from leaving. "It can't be revenge or vengeance. You gotta find something for *you*."

I let his words sink in.

"What if revenge and vengeance *are* for me?"

"It's too easy to fall down a rabbit hole of hate." He shakes his head. "Fucking trust me on that. Find something meaningful for you." He points a finger at my chest. "Let fighting be positive. You'll get more out of it."

"What do you fight for?" I test. "*Fun.*"

He looks at me for a second and lets his granite walls fall away to show me the pain in his soul.

"Freedom," he finally speaks.

He turns away, walking to pack away his things. "See you Thursday," he dismisses me.

I leave his apartment with a heavy ache in my chest. I positioned myself on a path to heal myself, searching for peace I'm now ready to find. Never in my wildest imagination was I expecting to find gratitude and sympathy in my heart for Rocco Shay.

CHAPTER TWELVE

ROCCO

"Told you I didn't work you hard enough last time." I smirk, watching her dry retch into a small metal bucket by the punching bag.

Nothing like bonding over the sound of another person emptying the contents of their stomach as you watch on in eager entertainment.

Standing, Camryn flips me off, wiping her mouth with the back of her hand. Her chest rises and falls like a balloon inflating, only to deflate a second later.

"Do a hundred skip jumps" —I toss the skipping rope her way— "then we'll use the punching pads again."

Her eyes watch the rope fly in her direction, her body not moving an inch as it falls at her feet. "Working on not dying right now," she mutters. "Give a girl a second. I need water."

I saunter off without another word, retrieving two bottles of cold water from my fridge.

She's sitting on a workout bench when I approach, one knee bent, chin rested upon it as she chews her thumbnail in thought.

"I found my word," she tells me. "My focus word." She takes the bottle from me with a thankful smile.

"Hm."

"Peace," she says quietly. "My goal is peace."

I drop to the ground across from her, my knees bent, my body leaning forward. My attention is entirely hers. "In what capacity?"

She considers my question. "Not in the whole 'world-peace' type dream. Personally," she specifies. "Here." She taps her temple. "I want to stop being afraid. I want to go to sleep without freaking the fuck out that my demons will stalk me when I'm vulnerable. I want to *live* in a way that I want to. I don't want to be controlled by my past. I want to know that no matter what evil works to infiltrate my thoughts, I'm at peace enough in my mind that it doesn't matter."

"Freedom," I cough out before I've realized I've spoken. "You want freedom."

Her eyes settle on me, our stare catching and holding on for a drawn-out breath.

"Like you," she whispers, more to herself than me.

"Like me," I concur.

An understanding settles between us, one neither of us was ready to come to terms with.

Camryn Rein and I have been fighting our similarities since our paths crossed. It's useless to continue to fight it. We're the same because we're broken. We're haunted by thoughts stronger than anything either of us has come up against. I tackle mine with anger, with fury, more often than not failing. Camryn combats hers by hiding, which is as pointless as what I do with my fists. Her demons are part of her. In actuality, she's hiding *with* her greatest fears, isolated and alone, giving them more and more power as she becomes weaker.

"Just because we're the same doesn't make us friends," she implores, her eyes drilling into mine in panic.

Calm down, sweetheart.

"Wouldn't dream we were anything but enemies, beauty."

"You're not my enemy either," she declares haughtily. "That would mean I feel something for you. I don't. Not hate, not indifference. I feel nothing. To me, you are nothing."

She's arguing with herself. "Who you trying to convince?" I tease, not letting myself be cut down by her words. "Me? Or yourself. You pushed yourself into my world, not the other way around. I couldn't give a flying shit what you think of me, Rein. But don't stand under my fucking roof and disrespect me while I'm doinG you a favor."

She swallows thickly at the bite in my tone.

"You wanna be indifferent toward me," I tell her. "But you're not. No more than I am to you. You might have hate in your sad little heart for me, but you have more for yourself in there. You hate that you crave my company. You fucking despise that you're starting to believe that I am the one person in your life that might truly understand you and still enjoy being around you. I know all that because it's exactly how I feel."

Straightening her shoulders, her hand brushes her forehead, removing the thick lock of hair that has escaped her ponytail. "I don't want to be your friend." The broken whisper is full of devastation. She hates that she's found herself in this situation. Worse, she hates that she doesn't want to change it.

"Feeling's mutual, sweetheart." I stand. "I don't need friends. But how about you chill out on the forced animosity, yeah? I won't fucking tell anyone you don't hate me as much as you pretend you do." I move toward her, holding my hand out for her.

She slides the smooth line of her palm into mine, letting me pull her upright. "Promise?"

Body pressed against mine, our hands still entwined, I nod. "I don't have any friends to spill your secrets to. Now, a hundred skip jumps."

She pushes at my chest, keeping contact just a second longer than necessary. "I changed my mind. I do fucking hate you. You're evil and enjoy human suffering."

"Not gonna argue with you." I smirk at her, holding the skipping rope out for her.

Yanking it from my grasp, I'm pretty confident she calls me a cunt, the word mumbled too low for me to hear.

She's thinner than I realized. Her body is bordering on fragile. Not unhealthy by any means, but slight in stature. Her hipbones are easily noticeable in her yoga pants, and her ass is not exactly what you'd call plump but perky enough to take notice. Her wrist would easily be half that of mine, her fingers long and slender. I'd imagine her tits would be small, less than a handful. But perky, like the rest of her body.

Her dark hair would easily reach her ass if she let it free. Skin like gold, clusters of dark freckles dance across her face, begging to be traced. Eyes like the blue of a sapphire you know you can't afford, she fucking prides herself on being unattainable.

Camryn shares limited similarities to her sister. They look as incongruent as their personalities. Codi is a wet dream to come to life, her curves as sweet as the smile that graces her lips. Camryn is the sinister temptress that'd cut your throat while she fucked you, not quite a smile, more a smirk the last thing you'd happily see.

"You right?" She flicks the skipping rope in my direction, barely missing my face.

"What?" I shrug. "Like you haven't run your greedy eyes over me a time or two."

She looks embarrassed, her cheeks turning pink like a secret she doesn't want to acknowledge. "Not my fault you insist on being half naked more often than not. It's a lot not to look at," she defends her cheeks a nice shade of pink.

"I'm one hundred percent comfortable with your gawking. Feel free to look as often and as long as you like."

"Gross," she lies. "You're like a giant... *muscle.*"

Meaning, I've dragged my carnivorous eyes over your body, and I want to devour it... you.

"Descriptive," I tease.

"You repulse me," she continues, the fluster in her voice as apparent as the color in her cheeks. She's faking a level of disgust that is almost comical.

Still, it pisses me off.

"Anyone ever told you that you turn into an ultimate bitch when you're afraid someone is seeing more of you than you're comfortable with? Being attracted to someone isn't showing your soul, Camryn."

Her mouth gapes open in distress. "I am absolutely not attracted to you."

I sigh. "Well, feeling's mutual, baby," I insult, stooping to her level. "Your plan to repulse the male species is a success. You're an awful little hermit."

An absolute fucking lie. She's a fantasy I refuse to entertain. Her attitude alone enough to rush blood to my overeager cock.

Her tiny fists clench in offense. "I am not a hermit. I go out," she retorts.

"You go out to buy take-out when you don't get it delivered. Even then, you're usually dressed in your pajamas."

"Being able to go into public in my pajamas is something I call winning at life."

"Sure," I recoil. "If you also talk to rocks. You need to get out more. Live like you're in your thirties and not readying yourself for the grave."

"Bite me," she barks out.

"Be my pleasure, sweetheart." The image popping into my head like the beginning of a wet dream I don't fucking need. "Now, do the fucking skip jumps."

She takes a step backward. "If you think I'm staying here with your arrogant ass, you're mistaken. I was fucking delusional thinking you could help me. Go fuck yourself, Rocco."

My hand flies out, grabbing hold of her wrist before I can stop myself. "Are you fucking kidding me?"

I should let her go. I don't need this fucking drama in my life. If I let her walk out, I'm done, freed from my obligation to help her in any way.

"Let me go," she grinds out, yanking her arm back.

I keep my hold, pulling her closer.

"You're being ridiculous." My teeth grind as I speak. "Your little feelings got hurt, did they?"

Thunder strikes in her eyes. Thick and nasty spikes of fury that are aimed directly at me. "Take. Your. Hands. Off. Me."

I step into her space, our bodies now flush, my hand tightening around the delicate line of her wrist. "You throw words like daggers, not giving a flying fuck who they hit, but god-fucking-forbid you're on the receiving end of those same sharp knives."

Her nostrils flare.

"You can tell me I'm vicious, more evil than the fucking devil himself. You can come into my fucking home and tell me I disgust you. But I can't do it back?"

The fight leaves her body, her eyes blinking in shame.

"You have no right to throw a tantrum for something you've insisted on building our relationship on. You know you're no troll, Camryn. Don't let what other people say affect how you think of yourself. People rarely say what they actually mean. Look in their eyes. Listen to that truth."

Sliding her wrist from my easing grasp, she straightens her spine.

"Look in my eyes. Do I think you're a disgusting hermit? Am I repulsed by you?"

Her blue eyes bore into mine, reading what I'm silently screaming at her.

"No."

"Exactly. The same way I know, I don't disgust you as much as you wish I did. The same way I know your eyes aren't tracking my body because there's a lot to look at. Own your feelings, Camryn. They're the most real fucking thing we have to offer this broken world."

She bends to pick up the discarded skipping rope. "I'll do fifty."

"A hundred. Then stretch. I'll make us lunch."

Her eyebrows kiss in the middle, her head moving backward, her chin touching her neck unattractively.

I shrug. "Only way I can be sure you won't gorge yourself on shitty food when you leave here."

"You are cruel."

"Never argued that point, baby."

CHAPTER THIRTEEN

ROCCO

ONE OF DOMINIC'S cronies glares at me as I stalk past, his eyes like daggers, watching my every move. I can't blame him. I'm a ring-in. One he's likely had to keep an eye on a time or two. He's right not to trust me. It doesn't mean his cocked-up stare doesn't piss me off. He's a wannabe—a tough guy. I'd kill to go a round or two in the ring with him, teach him to respect those who could hold his life in their palm, and play God.

"Rocco," Dominic greets me as I stroll into his office without knocking.

"Rein," I respond. "Don't appreciate being summoned."

He laughs, hands pausing on the papers he's shuffling around his desk. "How should I request your company in the future?" he tests. "A hand-written invitation?"

I sit without being asked.

"My understanding was that you agreed to begin working with me. Am I mistaken?"

I don't answer, only meeting his hostile glare with one of my own.

"Because if so, please feel free to leave. However, if I was correct, show me some fucking respect when you walk into my home. I may see you as an equal," he threatens, "but you are beneath me in this world, Shay."

I raise an eyebrow, shocked into silence. "Testier than usual. What's going on?"

"Why is my daughter visiting your loft?"

I school the smirk wanting to creep onto my face.

Daddy thinks I'm fucking his daughter.

Disengage the shotgun, soldier. Her virtue isn't at risk. I mean, given the opportunity, I likely wouldn't resist. But I'm smart enough to know she'd probably be doing it to get close enough to slit my throat.

"She's engaged to my brother." I shrug, enjoying playing with his temper. "They come and go as they please."

His eyes light like fire, nostrils flaring in fury.

"Chill, old man. I'm teaching Camryn how to fight. Did your minions tell you she arrives and leaves with boxing gloves?"

"York!" he bellows.

My hater walks into the room without a second's delay, hands behind his back, the picture of submission.

Little bitch.

"When you've seen Camryn arrive at Mr. Shay's loft, has she had anything with her?"

The twinkle of hope in his eyes dies, replaced by panic. "Ah." He pretends to think. "Now that you mention it, possibly boxing gloves, sir."

Dominic breathes through his nose, exhaling heavily. "Likely an important piece of information, wouldn't you surmise?"

York swallows uncomfortably. "Umm… yes, sir."

I rub my jaw, enjoying the fear in this guy's eyes a little too much. I'm sure he's shit his cheap polyester pants.

With a flick of his wrist, Dominic dismisses him.

"Does Camryn know you're having her followed?"

Hands running through his hair, the tired man in front of me sighs. "She's not silly. Of course. She graciously flips them off each morning in greeting. Sometimes she brings them coffee and accidentally drops it into their laps. Other times, she calls the cops on them. It's a lot of paperwork for me when she does that."

I don't hide my smile. "Some people are happily lost. Ever considered your daughter isn't interested in being found."

The pain in his eyes is unmistakable. Face dropping into his palms, he rubs at his forehead with a groan. "Some people are afraid to be found." He lifts his head. "They're in so much pain, they're certain it's all the world has to offer them. They want to stay lost to hide away from further hurt."

"You want to show her that the world has more to offer?"

His shoulders lift weakly. "Is that so bad? For a father to want that for his daughter?"

I shake my head. "No. But how can you be certain further harm won't find her? Maybe she's happy."

"Do you think she's happy?" he asks.

I blink, dropping my gaze to my lap. "No." I take a breath before answering. "No, I don't."

This conversation took a heavier turn than I expected it to. Fuck, this is what happens when people push themselves into your life. You get caught up in their feelings, in their perceived failings. You're compelled to want to help.

I shouldn't give two shits that Dominic Rein is struggling with a desperate need to *fix* his eldest daughter.

"I'm not fucking your daughter, Rein," I admit. "You'll be happy to know she still firmly despises my existence. She blackmailed me into doing her a favor. It'll be done in about a month."

"It's not you," he assures me, worried he offended my delicate feelings. "If I found out Parker's cock had aimed in Codi's direction before I knew they were in love, I would've threatened his life too. I think it's my paternal right, no?"

I laugh quietly. "Not well versed on parents and how they should act, but yeah, I'd guess you're well within your right."

"Good." He nods, straightening his shoulders. "Now that's out of the way... business."

"You have a lead on what I asked you to look into?" I struggle to hide the hope in my voice.

"No luck as of yet," he apologizes. "Trail isn't just cold, it's arctic, Rocco. I'll keep my guys on it, though. I've increased manpower. You should know, though, their focus is scouring death records."

I fight against the tightness in my throat. "Makes sense," I croak out, annoyed at the despair in my voice. "Keep me posted."

He nods with a sympathetic smile.

"You found your wife then?" I clear my throat, eager as fuck to change the subject.

"Not quite. But we have a lead. It seems she's closer than we originally thought. An associate of mine crossed her path in Tacoma."

I sit up straighter. "The fuck? She's only forty fucking minutes away. Why didn't your *associate* put her bullet in her fucking skull?"

My voice has moved into a frenzied yell.

"You need to calm yourself, Rocco."

"*Calm?*" I roar. "That cunt had a hand in murdering my mom. Fuck calm."

"Sarah and I agreed that both Codi and Marcus would never know Codi's true paternity," Dominic speaks quietly and calmly, irritating me further. Fury has set itself alight in my body, sparking at my toes, gushing through my veins like a potent drug. "In turn, I offered her protection. I offered her whatever the fuck she wanted."

This, right here, is Dominic Rein, the crime boss. The blue of his eyes flashes like a flame of murder. I can see his vision clearly in the quiet ferocity of his person. A slideshow of the revenge he would take on those that jeopardized the lives of his family. "She betrayed that. She put my daughter in the sight of an unhinged psychopath. She killed your mom. She threatened my daughter's life," he yells. "Whether she knew it or not," he collects himself. "One day, you'll understand that. One day you'll understand the anger you feel right now is, at best, juvenile to the rage coursing through my body. It's aimed directly at my wife."

"She deserves a fate worse than death."

Dipping his chin once, he acknowledges my words. "My associate understood his information was more valuable to me than her dead body," he cautions.

Read: Dominic Rein wants to be the one to find his wife.

Read: Dominic Rein wants to kill his wife.

"How do we know she's still there?"

He shrugs easily. "She doesn't know she's been made. She has no reason to hide. Not yet."

I don't know what to do with my hands. With my body. I'm itching for release, and yet, I feel idle.

"I have my people searching the Tacoma area for her. As soon as she's located, I'll be the first to know."

"Your people?" I spit. "You mean Dork out there?"

"York," he corrects me. "No, Rocco, not the likes of York. My company is built with a spectrum of soldiers. York is an errand boy. Would I waste someone capable of draining a body of blood, without a sign of it having been done, collect you from your home? No. That's a waste of resources. You need the meek and stupid for menial tasks."

He waits patiently as his words settle me.

"I've trusted you with this information. This means I trust you not to run off to Tacoma, waving a gun and demanding answers. You'll send her underground. We want the same thing, son. Don't fuck it up."

Arching my back, I growl toward the ceiling, cracking my knuckles.

"You're asking me to go against my nature," I warn.

"No. I'm asking you to think. Don't be your father. Don't convince yourself you're the monster the doubts in your mind attempt to tell you you are, Rocco. Don't let your hunger for revenge blind you into failure."

"Anyone ever tell you you're an asshole?"

He laughs. "Not to my face."

I groan.

"Trust can be a heavy burden when you haven't asked for it. But it's also a strong fucking shield when you need it most. Don't throw my trust away, Rocco. No matter how much you struggle to grasp it. It's not something you can pick back up after you've let go. Once it's gone, it's gone."

I hate how much sense Dominic Rein makes and how his life outlook mirrors mine. I hate that he's smarter than me. That he's honed his perspective as a weapon when I'm nothing but a self-loaded grenade waiting to fucking detonate. I hate that I know I should listen to him. I hate that he's right. But more than that, I hate that I don't trust myself to do that. I hate that my mind is so fucked up that I don't know if the moment I leave his home, I'll be strong enough not to betray him.

It's depressing that someone who should despise me has more faith in me than my family ever did, more than I've ever had in myself.

Standing, I nod once, moving toward his office door.

"Maybe Camryn is teaching you something in turn?"

I pause at the door. "Huh?"

"My men tell me you haven't been fighting. Your focus on my daughter has quelled the violence inside of you. Maybe your friendship is equally rewarding."

He looks away, dismissing me without words.

I want to tell him he's wrong. I want to give him another reason why I've kept my distance from the ring. But I don't have one. I hadn't even noticed. Fighting, pain, longing… I hadn't even recognized it'd been missing from my life.

"Stop having me followed," I bark out, slamming his office door as I leave.

CHAPTER FOURTEEN

CAMRYN

"How are the nightmares?"

He gives me the privacy I need to stomach the shock of his question. Back turned, his focus remains on the blender he's tossing ingredients into.

He forces me to drink a protein shake after every workout. Fuel, he assures me. I'd prefer a fucking Snickers.

I hadn't thought about my nightmares until the words fell from his mouth. They've been so few and far between since we started training. Especially on the days he demands a pound of flesh from my body, working me to the point of collapse. I barely have the energy to think, let alone dream.

"Better." I can hear the shock in my voice.

"Good." He nods, turning to look at me as he switches the blender on, the sound drowning out our ability to speak. He watches me carefully, the noise a barrier to our thoughts. We can stand in this moment, caught in a silent stare, watching one another without expectation. I can't hear his thoughts, and he can't hear mine.

A lot passes between us in that minute. A recognition of friendship, maybe?

We've been breaking down walls without even realizing it over the past month. We challenge one another like no one else in our lives is brave enough to do. Our families approach us like we're wounded animals. Ready to lose the final straw of our sanity if provoked. It's not only humiliating, it's exhausting. Pretending to be okay on days I feel ready to break.

Rocco refuses to let me get caught up in my head. He's comfortable with me being broken in his company. He doesn't push me to talk or to be better. He only encourages me to use what's fucking with my psyche to push through the roadblocks of my body.

"I haven't seen you with any bruising," I say when the blender stops. "Either you're untouchable, or you haven't been fighting."

"I haven't been fighting."

"Like my nightmares," I guess.

He nods. "Like your nightmares."

Giving me his back once again, he pours his awful concoction into two separate glasses. "Your dad thought we were fucking."

"He has me followed."

Sliding my glass toward me, I take it on a forced but thankful smile. Lifting the glass, I touch it to my lips, taking the smallest sip I can manage. "Mmm."

His chin dips in acceptance, pride at the fact that he succeeded in getting me to swallow this godawful drink.

"You're okay with that?"

I lift my shoulders in dismissal. "What can I do about it? It's his way of thinking he's keeping me safe. I'd be an asshole if I forced him to stop, to take that peace of mind from him."

I place the glass down.

"How are you still alive if he thinks we're fucking?"

He laughs. "I managed to convince him that we weren't." His eyes bore into mine. "I told him you still hated me." His voice has dropped, a soft scratch moving along his vocal cords.

I swallow the rock in my throat at what the rough touch of his voice does to me.

"Assuming he's still right..." he probes.

"Of course," I answer too quickly, my voice a similar volume to his.

The ring of his cell sounds, breaking the moment. Glancing at the screen, he holds it up. "Gotta take this."

He moves away without a further word. Alone in the room, I take advantage, emptying the green slush in my glass down the sink. Shifting off my seat, I rush to the sink flicking on the tap to rid the evidence from the sparkling metal. The faucet turns on too fast, and the pressure is too much. It ricochets off the base, spraying up my shirt and hitting me in the face.

"Serves you right." Rocco's voice sounds at my back.

Turning quickly, I rub at my face, wiping at the droplets racing down my skin. "Look, in my defense, it's awful."

He smiles. "It's an acquired taste."

I don't let myself read into how nice I find his smile—the soft pull of his lips showing off the white line of his teeth. The strong line of his bearded jawline pulls up in a way that hides the hatred that seems ingrained into his features.

Eyes tracking along my body, down the now see-through material of my inconveniently chosen white t-shirt, his smile drops away.

He steps closer, moving his lips to the shell of my ear. "I take it back, beauty. You're not a disgusting little hermit. A hermit, yes, but not disgusting. Not like the thoughts running through my head right now."

Teeth on nipples, biting hard enough to make me come. Forcing me to beg for it.

Ducking away from the proximity of his overwhelming body, I force a laugh.

"Get a grip, Shay. Your slushie was horrible, kind of like my sweaty self. I'm out. Catch you next week."

His smile follows my exit, my body only free from his hungry gaze when his front door closes. Even then, I feel him staring through the thick wood. His eyes are as powerful as his body.

CHAPTER FIFTEEN

ROCCO

MY BODY BUZZES WITH ADRENALINE. My heart is racing with expectation and excitement. My cock is hard, my blood pumping so steadily through my body that it throbs. My leg bounces as I drive, my fingers tapping against the steering wheel, working to rid myself of the excess energy wanting to break me apart.

But while my body is a live wire ready to put to death anything that stands in my path, I feel dead inside. My hands itch with the need to kill. This dark need only further blackens the venom of my soul. Soon it'll be all that remains; shadows of destruction that once held slivers of good. I've accepted that's not my future. Hearts and roses were never my ending. I'm at peace with the fact that I'll eventually be buried alongside misery and scorn.

Can you remain calm?

Calm? Is he fucking kidding?

I pray she fucking runs. I crave her fight. I want nothing more than for Sarah Rein to give me a reason to snap her double-crossing neck.

Who could honestly say they'd remain calm while standing face-to-face with the person responsible for their mom's death? I'd like Dominic Rein to tell me he wouldn't suck the life out of a hopeless cunt that crossed him in the same way.

The shrill ring of my cell interrupts my murderous thoughts, and I'm equally relieved and disappointed.

"Yeah?"

"Just checking you haven't skinned her alive and began feasting on her flesh."

I laugh humorlessly. "There's no way I'm putting the taint of her insides into mine. My soul is rotten enough all on its own."

I suck in a deep breath, letting it go with the temptation Dominic just offered me.

"Checking up on me? Thought you trusted me."

"I do," he implores. "I don't trust her."

I laugh again. "Your wife can do her worst, Rein. Frankly, I'm praying she does. It'll give me an excuse to hurt her."

A sigh of disappointment filters down the line. "That's what she wants, Rocco. Don't let her pick away at your self-control."

"Yeah, yeah. She'll come back to you in one piece, *boss*. Calm your fucking farm."

"I have no idea what that means, son. I hear Camryn say it to Codi regularly, but I've yet to understand how it makes sense. How does one 'calm their farm'?"

I smile unintentionally. "It means chill, Dominic. We have an agreement. Think what you will of me, but I hold some fucking integrity."

"Good. I'd hate to have to kill you."

"I'd like to see you try, old man." I hang up without another word.

Have you ever been genuinely surprised by your own weakness? Not in a mildly unexpected sense, but smack you in the face, break your nose kind of way. The type of surprise that makes you question who you are? Who you've always been?

The storm raging inside of me only moments ago had been quelled without my interference. Without blood, without pain. My ranting beast pulled back into sleep with a lullaby I didn't know was being sung.

He did that.

Dominic fucking Rein soothed the beast inside me with a few bad jokes, and what? Care and kindness?

Who the fuck am I? Am I that needy? Someone offers up the

slightest hint of effort, of prudent thought, and I roll over, begging they give me more. This family is weakening my resolve by the day. I wish I could find anger or resentment toward them for doing so. I want to hate them for coercing me into this vulnerability. Instead, I don't want to disappoint them. I want to win for them. I'm no longer a solo act— my sole purpose is protecting my brother and my slain family's legacy. I'm part of a pack. One I'd sworn my life to destroy.

I shouldn't be surprised at how quickly life can change. A blink of an eye, a thickly drawn breath, and everything you know can mutate.

When I was sixteen, my life held a semblance of normality, of happiness. Then my mother was brutally ripped from my life, and I was thrown into hell. Eighteen years later, consumed by hate and unresolved rage, I had plans to avenge my mother. I searched for peace, for vengeance. Then my brother fell in love with the very person I wanted to strip from this world. My life tipped upside down and inside out within seconds. Mira died. Marcus died. My vengeance was unwarranted and misaimed, pushing me into yet another dark path— one of self-destruction.

If my life has taught me anything, it's never to get comfortable. The moment you fall into contentment, you're weakened, and that life you're so comfortable in, it'll fuck you without your permission.

Pulling my car into a parking spot outside a derelict building, I glare at the rotting infrastructure. Why do people choose to live in a cesspit when they go into hiding? You can guarantee that if I find myself in a position that I don't want to be found, I won't be shacked up with junkies and small-time criminals. It's like a neon fucking sign. No, I'd be living it up in a fucking Four Seasons drinking top-shelf whiskey, waiting for my ending.

Tivoli, Dominic's right-hand—and my babysitter—taps at my window.

Sighing in irritation, I swing my door open, forcing him a few steps backward.

"You can stay out here."

He scowls. "Or you could."

"I don't need a fucking minder. I'll go in, grab her and be back out in less than ten minutes. She's one woman."

"One unhinged psycho in hiding. Thought you'd know better than to underestimate a cornered animal."

I smirk.

"You're hoping she does something stupid." He shakes his head. "Ah. Fuck. I wish Dominic had sent someone else. You're gonna get me fucking killed. If not by her, by my boss. You got ten minutes. Then I'm following your stubborn ass in. Don't get yourself killed. I enjoy my job."

Flipping him off, I tuck my 9mm into my jeans, my strides long as I make off toward the building's front entrance.

The inside of the building smells like how the outside looks. Putrid. The stale scent of meth, sex, and fucking death climbs up my nostrils and turns my stomach. It's eerily quiet. The sound of passed-out junkies and people not wanting to be found like a bass drum, closing in the walls with every careful step.

I move up the stairs slowly, making a mental note to burn my shoes when I get home. Fuck knows what bodily fluids I'm creeping across.

Reaching the top of the stairs, my feet pause. A group of teenage kids watch me with intent curiosity. They obviously consider themselves the keepers of this derelict castle—kings and queens of a world they've found purpose in.

I'm no stranger to kids working to prove their power. It's the only reason I don't walk past them without acknowledgment, knowing damn well that'd find me with a sharp knife lodged in my spine.

"Who ya looking for?" one of them asks. Dude, barely eighteen with a tattoo above his eyebrow and a top knot that screams douchecanoe.

"Brunette," I answer cautiously, keeping my eyes trained on their movements. "Early fifties."

"You a cop?" he pushes.

"Do I look like a cop?"

He shrugs. "Not necessarily, but can't be too cautious these days. What's your business with Sarah?"

"Old friend."

He smiles, brushing a tongue piercing along the line of his teeth. "Slim, you owe me a Benjamin Franklin. Told you she was hidin'. He guessed she was a high-class working girl."

Not feeling the need to participate in their little game, I stand silently, waiting.

"Thing is," douchecanoe speaks again. "I tell you where she is, and an avenue of my income dries up. Bitch loves her blow."

I bark out an annoyed laugh.

"She's in unit four," a blonde murmurs. Boredom coats her from head to toe. She doesn't show me the courtesy of lifting her head when she speaks, keeping her head tipped down, her concentration fixed on rolling a joint. "Straight down the hall, second door on your right."

Eyebrow raised, I wait for her to look me in the eye, to see the truth in her eyes. I don't trust these fuckers, not for a second.

She's older than the rest of them, *just*. Hair cropped at the sides, the rest artfully crafted into a smooth mohawk. Clothing purposefully worn, ripped in sections by design. She wears a safety pin through one earlobe and lipstick the color of midnight on her full lips. She's tiny, but looking at the glint in her eyes—when she finally meets my gaze— there's no mistaking the rebellious warrior that she is.

Her dark eyes scan up and down my body, her bottom lip tipping out in appreciation as she steps forward. She keeps my eyes as she slides a joint into the side of her mouth. "Bitch tried to fuck my man. She's lucky I didn't kill her. The only thing that saved her was that he isn't into crusty granny pussy." Done with the conversation, she shoves past me. "Let's go." She gestures toward the stairs, her crew falling in step behind her.

Queen fucking B, a pint-sized pixie.

"There are kids in this building." She turns back to me. "They see enough shit. You kill the bitch, make sure their eyes ain't watchin' you."

"Shouldn't you all be in school?" My eyes fall across them.

I know I sound like a fuckwit. Too young to be spouting shit about kids staying in school. Just too old to care.

The pixie laughs. "I wish people would accept that some of us aren't interested in bettering ourselves. We're happy here, thanks, dad. More so than the rest of the assholes in the big, wide world. We're not looking for something greater. We've created it ourselves. Make sure you and the bitch are gone by this afternoon."

I watch their exit. Understanding and appreciation settle into my soul. She's right. The world is hellbent on wanting and needing more. Self-actualization doesn't exist. Not in the modern world. We grab onto what we've been fighting for, onto something we've been conditioned to think we need, expecting to find endless happiness. Except, all that meets us at the end of that rainbow is disappointment. Happily ever after isn't real. We discard our accomplishments with the need for more before the present has even settled. We're never satisfied.

I move along the hallway, the carpet under my feet worn so heavily through the cement flooring can be seen. Paint peels from the walls in jagged clouds; some hanging on, others trampled into the shitty carpet.

The four on Sarah's door hangs upside down like every cliched story come to life. The door sits slightly ajar, welcoming anyone to wander in and claim their space.

I push at it with the toe of my boot, the creaking hinge loud enough to announce me. Not much bigger than a closet, she sees me the moment I enter, her soft, malicious laughter the first thing to greet me.

CHAPTER SIXTEEN

CAMRYN

"Dad!" I yell, moving through the front door and throwing my keys on the entryway table.

Brightly colored peonies fill the large vase on the table; pinks and purples, sunshine yellows and white, mahogany even. I step closer, dropping my face to inhale their scent. Intoxicating variations of citrus, spice and the delicate touch of a sweetness I can't quite put my finger on dance along my nostrils. I smile.

"Stopping to smell the flowers. That's a Camryn I haven't seen in a long time." My dad watches me from the entryway to our living room, his shoulder pressed lazily against the doorway. A fond smile greets me, as it always does, with unmistakable love and affection on his face.

I've always found it odd that people fear this man. The man who taught me how to ride a bike. The man who searched for monsters under my bed to ensure I slept peacefully. To the outside world, he's formidable, a fierce and unrelenting leader. People cower under his demand. But at home, he's *dad*. A man I could never find it in myself to fear. The one parental figure I've always known I could count on. A man who loved me without condition.

"How very Codi of me," I tease.

"On the contrary." He lets me kiss his cheek, squeezing my waist in affection. "You were always the one who needed to smell every flower we wandered past. Codi only fell into the habit of idolizing her sister, as younger siblings do."

I force a smile, refusing to let myself dwell on the sadness in my father's tone. His inadvertent reminder of how he misses the Camryn I used to be. He may love me without condition, but I've disappointed him whether he admits it to himself or not. He no longer understands me, this flawed version of the daughter he once knew.

I enter his office without invitation, dropping onto his leather sectional with a loud sigh. "Where is everyone?"

"Around," he offers loosely. "On assignment."

"On assignment," I bark out sarcastically. "Does that include our favorite psychotic Shay brother?"

"Being unkind for the purpose of being unkind is unbecoming, sweetheart," he admonishes, eyeing me with reproach. "Yes, Rocco is on assignment for me."

I pause my fidgeting, eyes slicing toward him in expectation.

Read: I've found your mother and sent the most unstable man I know to collect her.

I'm flooded by my emotions, drowned by so many I can't tell them apart.

"Does Parker know his brother is working for you?" I scold.

"Does Codi know you're spending time with Rocco?" he rebukes.

That makes me laugh. "You should really stop having me followed."

"Do you mind?"

I tip my bottom lip out in indifference. "No. Not particularly."

"I wish you would stop calling the police. It causes an unnecessary amount of paperwork for me."

He's smiling. There's no anger in the way he scolds me, only exasperation at my childish games.

"Just trying to keep them on their toes. They should learn to be more inconspicuous."

"Hm," he comments, checking the caller ID on his cell before silencing it.

"Rocco is teaching me to fight," I offer an explanation for my newfound friendship. I don't care for him to read into something that isn't there. "I was supposed to be there now, but he canceled. For you." An accusation, one he takes comfortably.

"You can reschedule."

I nod unenthusiastically. "Thought I'd see if you wanted to have lunch. Codi's working."

"Well." He laughs. "With an invitation like that, how could I say no?"

I throw a cushion his way. "Not what I meant. Are you busy? There is a new gyoza place in town, and I've been wanting to check it out."

His face lights up with an expected joy. "Never busy enough to stop me sharing a meal with my daughter. Let me make a phone call, and then we'll go."

He expects me to leave, to offer him the privacy I've always given him when he works. But I don't. I'm done hiding behind my ignorance. This involves my mother, the woman who despises me more than any other human being on this planet for the greatest imposition of being born.

Accepting my newfound rebellion, my father has his phone against his ear. "Do you have an update?"

He listens carefully.

"Follow him in."

The voice on the other end raises slightly, the muffled masculine tone drifting through the room.

"I don't care if he throws an adult-sized tantrum. I don't trust her. We've experienced enough unnecessary deaths by the hand of Marcus and Sarah, let's not add any more."

My body goes cold. My veins freezing over in dread at the thought of another death. Blood coating yet another floor, staining the world with the loss of another soul.

I should be ashamed that it isn't my flesh and blood, my mother, that I'm concerned about. But I'm not. Possibly a little shocked at the intensity behind the feeling, but my fear is for Rocco and Rocco alone. The thought of him leaving this earth hits me heavier than I would ever care to admit.

"Ready?" My father taps my knee.

"Who did you send with him? With Rocco?"

"He's fine, Ryn." He reads my concern easily, his features warming in understanding. "Tivoli is with him."

"Parker and Codi will never forgive you if... if..." I stumble over what I'm trying to say.

He watches me carefully. "Parker and Codi or you?"

I stand, feigning a look of annoyance. "Wouldn't cost me sleep at night," I say, lifting my head in a false nonchalance that he sees straight through.

I walk from the room before he can call me out on my lie. "You can drive," I tell him. "I did an overnight, status update, shattered."

⚓

THE SMALL RESTAURANT, APTLY TITLED 'GYOZA', is bustling. Small clusters of people are pushed into the space comfortably. Conversation buzzes through the room, laughter, and soft hushed tones are a melody to the loud kitchen's open layout.

Dad and I settle into a modest table toward the back, locked away in our very own cone of silence. Hidden from the bustle, I feel unfavorably exposed. Like with a simple glance, my father could look into me and discover every dirty secret I have hidden in the darkest parts of my soul.

The waiter, barely giving us time to settle, approaches, ready to take our order.

Before I can send him away, my dad nods, picking up the menu to peruse. I remain quiet while he orders, nodding along with his suggestions as he looks to me for confirmation.

"And Sake, please," I add. "Times two."

Drinks settled in front of us, I watch my dad lift his to his lips, sipping slowly.

We used to do this often when I was younger, when I was more of who he remembers and less of who he sees now. We'd escape the sunshine of Codi or the storm of my mother, hiding in plain sight at new restaurants and hole-in-the-wall cafes. Just the two of us caught up in ourselves. We'd share a meal, more often than not the food going cold as we talked for hours, too caught up in the topic at hand to remember to eat. Even at my youngest, our conversations were never surface, they never involved small talk. There was always depth. Philosophical discussions that tested our thoughts.

The meaning of life.

The injustices of the world.

Whether fate is real? And if so, does that remove our right to free will?

Will humans as a species become extinct, and if so, when?

We'd argue, agree, and happily remain indifferent if we couldn't find mutual ground. It was exciting. It was eye-opening. I felt challenged in the best possible ways, and I know he felt the same way.

Then it stopped.

I couldn't tell you if that was through a fault of mine or his. Maybe it was us both. I returned from college lost and broken, and I couldn't stomach the thought of sitting across from my dad discussing the world's problems. I was too caught up in my own. He was likely scared of who college turned me into, clutching onto his memories of who we used to be rather than making damaged new ones.

I know through it all, I hated him a little. He was my dad. Wasn't he supposed to push past those barriers? Wasn't he supposed to look into my eyes and just know? Or maybe he didn't care. Maybe his love wasn't as absolute as I believed it to be. Childish thoughts I've never been able to rid myself of.

"You found her," I announce abruptly. "You found my mother. That's where Rocco is, hunting Sarah."

He coughs, the dryness of his Sake catching on his surprise at my forwardness.

"Yes."

I appreciate his honesty, but it's not as if he could deny it. I heard his phone conversation. Lying would only create a greater divide between us, one neither of us can afford.

"Why Rocco? Why send him?"

Placing his glass back on the table, he watches me with a depth that should make me shift in my seat. Dark eyebrows pulled together, he pulls at his shirt cuffs before laying his arms along his crossed legs.

He's always so composed. I've never seen him lose his temper or break down. He's impossible to read. Not unfeeling by any stretch, but someone who is rock solid in their ability to control their emotions. I envy and hate him all at once for that.

"Why not Rocco?"

"You trust him?" I question forcefully.

"You don't?"

"Depends on the matter in which trust is required," I murmur. "I guess I'd say he's honest, based on my limited interactions with him. But do I trust that he won't kill my mother? No."

"Camryn, trust isn't yielding. It's absolute, or it's not there," he scolds. "You can't place your faith in someone only to take away without justification, giving it back only when it fits your plan. If you're balancing your trust like that, you're expecting a person to live to only your expectations."

My confusion is painted openly on my face.

"What about their expectations?" he continues. "Rocco has assured me that he won't kill Sarah. That's the expectation he's set with me, so I trust him to follow through. If he had found her without me and we hadn't discussed the situation, I wouldn't trust him not to kill her, but that's because there wouldn't have been any joint expectations set."

I frown at his words, digging deep within myself to find my own belief in his.

"What about relationships?" I ask. "You fall in love, and the expectation is that you trust one another."

He leans in closer. "Of course, but having fallen in love, you've spoken about what is important to you. If you're in a relationship with a man who tells you he wants to sleep with other women, do you trust him not to cheat?"

"No."

"Exactly, because your expectations aren't aligned. However, if you're with a man who tells you you're his everything. That he wants you and only you. Do you trust him not to cheat?"

I dip my chin in confirmation.

"My point. Your expectation is aligned with his. It's out on the table."

I consider his words as our food is delivered, leaving my dad to thank the waiter.

"Does it bother you?" he asks after the waiter has disappeared. "The potential death of your mother?"

"I guess it should." I pick up a pork dumpling and shove it in my mouth with little finesse.

"That's not what I asked."

I chew my food. "Does it make me evil to say no?" I whisper, embarrassed to admit it out loud.

"No," he answers without pause.

"How can you be sure?"

Dropping his chopsticks carefully onto his plate, he reaches for my hand. "Do you wish her dead? Or do you just have no intense feelings about her dying?"

"I feel she deserves to be punished, but if she stood before me, would I kill her? No." I shake my head. "Something inside me tells me that we should be bothered by death, which goes directly against my lack of concern about my mother's welfare."

"Camryn," he sighs. "We shouldn't be forced to think in any particular way. You'll find yourself constantly at war with yourself if that's how you live your life. Your mind is yours, just as mine is mine. We all have ill thoughts pass through us at times. Death is a given. Being bothered by it will only make you scared of it, and that's no way to live."

"I tell myself that there is enough evil in the world. I don't need to add to it with thoughts of harm and retribution."

"Drink. Eat," my father encourages, doing the same. "I look at it differently," he offers on a finished mouthful. "I've felt hate for myself, for others. I've also had it aimed my way. I lived with it for as long as your mother remained in my home. I've experienced great sadness at times, and I've felt loss. But because I've felt all that and lived through all the horrible emotions we attempt to ignore, I know what true happiness is. I know what real love feels like. The negative facets of life, both external," he gestures around us, "and internal," he points to his heart, "just let us appreciate the good in life. It's all a balance, sweetheart. The sooner we all realize that the more settled we'll all be."

"You didn't answer my question," I combat. "About us being bothered by death."

He watches me silently for a beat before shrugging. "We're all wired differently, Camryn. Things that may sit on your conscience likely won't sit on mine. So who is to say who is right?"

"But we know what actions are fundamentally wrong as human beings. Wouldn't the world be a better place if general fucking common sense prevailed? Don't kill anyone. Don't cheat, don't steal, blah fucking blah. Shouldn't we stick to that?" I argue.

"Maybe," he concedes. "But the world isn't that simple. Where is your moral compass?" he tests. "Is it aligned with mine? With Rocco's? What about Codi's?"

I don't speak, too engrossed in his thought process to even mumble a syllable.

"Codi believes in second chances, in giving someone the benefit of the doubt. Rocco, on the other hand, believes in retribution. He believes in people paying for their sins, himself included. If you wrong an innocent, you pay with blood. I imagine you'd sit somewhere in between," he shrugs, not waiting for me to confirm or deny his belief. "I don't think any of you are necessarily wrong or right. We're different, and that is where the world will always sit, Camryn, whether that makes sense to you or not."

I sit back in my seat, letting everything he said settle within me.

"I enjoy talking to you," I tell him quietly. "We don't do it enough anymore."

Sadness brushes through his eyes, dropping along his features as he blinks. "I lost you some time ago, beautiful. I don't know why, and I wish you'd talk to me about it. I gave in to your wish and left you to find yourself. But it backfired on me. In the end, you not only didn't find yourself, but you also lost who you were."

I drain my glass of Sake. "I just don't know who I am anymore." Not a lie, but also not the complete truth. "I haven't for a long time. Everything I thought I knew seems lost."

"Why do you have to decide who you are?"

I frown. "I don't understand."

"You're remembering who you were, thinking that's who you should be. Am I right?"

I shrug and nod at the same time.

"Why can't you just *be* who you are? Life changes us all, Ryn. Stop looking backward. If your focus is behind you, you'll find yourself tripping into your future, bruised and broken."

CHAPTER SEVENTEEN

ROCCO

"Always thought Dominic would be the first to find me. Connected asshole that he is."

I don't answer, letting her believe what she will. That I'm alone, working without the help of her husband's connections.

"What I don't understand." She edges away from me, feigning fear as she moves against the wall and closer to the single window in the airless dump she's now calling home. It'd be humorous if it weren't so idiotic, moving toward a window she can't escape from, pinning herself against a wall. "Is why you care if I live or die. What have I ever done to you?"

I scowl, taking two steps into the shithole she's settled into. What a fucking fall from grace. Living in the warm contentment of the Rein mansion, only to find herself in this fucking squalor, begging for fucks from a teenager and scoring drugs off kids younger than her own.

"Are you following your father's lead, relighting the Rein and Shay vendetta? Killing me ain't gonna pay you any dues."

"Stop talking."

Her feet falter at the stone in my voice. Her act of innocence wears away with every second I'm forced to stand in her company.

"You had to know," I threaten, letting my eyes drift over the ripped couch and stained carpet. "That your lies and sins would come back to fuck you in the ass. That they'd make you bleed." I kick at the trash by my feet, letting myself move closer.

Her feet stop, her fearful act dropping away altogether, the real Sarah Rein showing her face, horns and all.

"How did you find me?" she asks curiously, her head tipping to the side in contemplation. "You've been searching for that junkie ex-girlfriend of yours for years without success." Her eyes widen in mockery, the malice in her irises spiking like wildfire.

I step forward in warning, unable to hide the shock at the mention of Kendall.

"Oh, you didn't think I knew about her," she jibes, thoroughly enjoying herself. "I know a lot of things about you, Rocco Shay. Things that the remaining little family member of yours doesn't even know," she sneers, a poisonous smile tracking over her red lips. "You have a thing for the broken ones. Maybe it makes you feel like less of a fuck up. First, that street whore, and now my defective daughter."

My jaw feels ready to crack, the might in which I'm holding it shut strong enough to split stone. The ridge of my fury is ready to spill over like a volcano, violence my reign of lava. The trust Dominic forced upon me forgotten, my need to kill clouds my vision.

"Anyone ever told you to live in the moment, Shay? That focusing on the past will only drown you."

"Kendall," I ground out, my voice like sandpaper. "Where is she?"

She laughs at me. An ear-piercing chuckle that leaves me cold.

I surge forward, unable to control myself, my hand wrapping around her throat before she can register what's happened. Her skin is warmer than I imagined it. I pictured the cold touch of death coating her skin. Instead, the thick, healthy rhythm of her pulse throbs under my touch. The wildfire in her eyes dies out, replaced by tears of pain, the blue staring back at me glossed over in evidence of her lack of control.

Still, I feel five steps behind her, waiting for the penny to drop and my world to fall away.

"Shay."

Pulling my gun from the waist of my jeans, I hold it up to Tivoli, halting his movements. He contemplates me for a beat, feet balancing over the threshold of the shitty apartment.

My hand, still eagerly wrapped around Sarah Rein's throat, tightens in panic.

She smiles—the psychotic bitch—barely able to pull a full breath, grins at me in triumph. I grip harder, shooting my eyes back to Dominic's man, my chest expanding in want as I feel Sarah struggle to breathe under my palm.

Her eyes bulge in her face, looking too big to be normal. The sickly shade of her skin is marred with large, red blotches, teasing me with the promise of how she'd look dying slowly at my hand.

Hands raised in surrender, Tivoli looks unaffected by the scene before him. He expected this. Or maybe Rein did. Either way, he's not surprised or panicked by the barrel of my gun aimed at his heart.

"Get out," I command, fingers twitching to close completely around the slim line of Sarah's neck, wanting to steal the last of her breath completely.

It'd be so easy. Two to three minutes, and she'd pass out. A few more, and she'd be as good as dead. Rid from the world and, more importantly, my nightmares.

I'm out of my depth—control slipping from my resolve with every second that passes blindly by. I'm better than this. I've trained myself to be better. I'm the cunt that laughs at the motherfuckers who get caught in their heads, unwilling and unable to foresee their downfall.

"You know I can't do that," Tivoli murmurs, edging closer.

I crack my neck in unfiltered rage. I don't know what to do. I'm stuck between my savage need for vengeance and my newly formed fucking conscience.

The thought of killing Sarah Rein has been at the top of my to-do list from the moment Marcus stepped foot into my apartment, unfurling the truth like a never-ending ribbon.

I want this.

I fucking deserve this.

I was convinced I needed it.

Not anymore.

Dominic's trust aside, doesn't he fucking deserve a slice of the pie? He had to live with this piece of shit for years, knowing she was betraying him. He lived in fear that she'd steal his daughter away. She and Marcus ruined my life, but she forced Dominic to live in hell for years.

Confident Tivoli won't jump me and force my hand before I'm ready, I turn my full attention back to Sarah.

"Why'd you do it? Lila? Why did she have to die?"

She stares at me blankly before opening her mouth to speak. My hand, too tight around her neck, cuts off her ability to make a sound. It makes me smile and pisses me off all at once. I enjoy using her like a puppet, knowing her waste of a life is so feeble in my hands. I feel like a god. She's at my unbalanced mercy. But I want answers. I want to hear her traitorous mouth tell me why she thought she could play God with my mom's life.

I reluctantly loosen my grip, and she sucks in a thick breath, almost choking on it.

"I should've known you're fucking useless. Of course, Dominic found me. You're just the little bitch he sent to bring me in."

I step into her, punching a hole in the wall beside her head. "Lila!" I scream. "Tell me fucking why!"

"Why not?" she coughs out, flinching at my fist, pulling back from the broken plaster by her face. "She was nothing to me. Nothing but a fucking snitch that could get me and Marcus killed. I weighed it up for about point-one of a second and decided my life was worth more."

I step into her body, my hand lifting her up the wall to bring her eyes in line with mine. "You were fucking wrong," I seethe. "See, if you died here, no one would avenge you. Fucking no one. Not your husband, who sent me here to collect you and deliver you to death. Not your kids who begged me to make you pay. Not your dead little fuck buddy that is far better off being eaten by worms than he ever was breathing. Your life isn't worth shit, and you know it."

She rolls her eyes. "You think I care." She struggles, her legs kicking, hands pulling at mine to loosen my grip. "You think I give two shits about that asshole my parents forced me to marry," she croaks out, her words barely audible. "Or the fucking spawn I was forced to raise for him. I had hopes for Codi once upon a time, but she proved to be as useless as her sister."

My body zaps at the mention of Camryn, of how dismissive this bitch is about the life of her own flesh and blood.

"I don't fear death, asshole. This world didn't give two fucking shits about me, and I've paid it the same respect. You think you're some hero for playing vigilante for your dead mother." She laughs, and I step away from her, no longer trusting my restraint.

She massages the thick red welts marked along her skin. "You're exactly like me," she spits. "Life is worthless, both yours and that of those around you. I could put a bullet in you right now, and you wouldn't regret your life. Your stupid brother would mourn you for as long as it took for him to lodge his cock in my daughter, and you'd be forgotten. You're no one special, Rocco Shay. Never were. Marcus told me how you were your father's greatest failure. Too much heart in you to be useful in any way but not enough to make you a decent human being. He knew your brother was like his cunt of a wife, all feelings and emotion. You, on the other hand, had potential. It's a shame that you'll never reach it. You're too weak to even kill me," she whispers. "You're gonna take me back to Dominic like a good little soldier. Let him take the one thing you fought all your life for. Pathetic."

I point my gun at her face, and she steps into it, a fierceness in her eyes that reminds me so much of Camryn my arm shakes.

They're so alike. A mirror on fast forward. Their long brown hair, the soft tan of their skin, the distinct blue of their eyes.

It gives me pause—another moment of uncertainty.

"See." She moves, the blood-red of her lips a breath away from my ear. "Weak."

My fists clench with the need to pound against flesh, to break skin, and see the gush of red decorate my hands.

She might look like her daughter, but where death haunts the shade of Sarah's eyes, Camryn's shine with a scared need to hope.

Consumed by my rage, I don't see her move.

A taser being fired sounds like a thousand cicadas swarming around my ears or like that irritating static of a radio or TV that hasn't been tuned. Small and needling, but fuck does it hurt.

My entire body tenses involuntarily, locking me in place. Pain slices through my body like a bolt of lightning striking through me from the top of my head to the tips of my toes. Within seconds my body drops to the ground without warning.

Tivoli moves in my peripheral, having stayed quiet up until this point. But she's faster, picking up the gun I'd dropped when I hit the ground, aiming it in Tivoli's direction in silent warning.

His feet stop.

"I'll fucking kill you," he warns.

"Not if I get you first," she taunts, one hand held tightly to my gun, the other on the taser she dropped me with.

Lowering the aim of my gun, she doesn't hesitate, and I watch the bullet pierce Tivoli's leg, sending him to his knees with an agonized grunt.

I move to sit up, but she points my gun at my face. "Next time I see your face, I'll kill you and that useless daughter you seem caught up on, just for shits and giggles. It'll be nice watching you bleed that pain again. It'll be like Lila and Kendall on repeat." She grins.

She steps over me.

"Where is she?" I bite out, the ache stopping my body from attempting to move.

"She ain't anywhere, handsome. Like your mommy, the bitch is dead."

CHAPTER EIGHTEEN

CAMRYN

THEY LOST HER.

Not in the way someone will tell you they'd lost their wife or husband, with sadness in their soul and tears in their eyes.

She's gone, but not dead. They lost her. As in, she escaped.

My pathetic excuse for a mother overcame two grown fucking men to flee.

One with a score to settle.

The other trained to kill.

I take my hat off to her, she's one sneaky bitch. But no one ever claimed otherwise.

Dad got the call as we were finishing up our lunch. Tivoli, who had been shot in the leg, was on his way to the hospital to be stitched up. Surface wound, he assured my father, his pride having been dealt a more significant blow than his leg. Sly as she is, apparently Sarah has horrible aim.

Rocco is now MIA. Tivoli said he took off after her as soon as he could stand. She'd tasered him. Shot him straight in the chest with five thousand volts. Apparently, her aim isn't as bad with a taser as it is with a gun. I'd laugh if I didn't hate her enough to wish they'd succeeded in forcing karma down her throat. What I'd give to taser that son-of-a-bitch and watch him fall to the ground.

I can't tell if I'm more pissed off at the fact that Sarah got away or relieved that Tivoli and Rocco aren't severely hurt. Maybe a mixture of both. I'm comfortable with my concern for Tivoli. He's family. He started with dad as a teenager, only a few years older than me, he's more of a brother than a soldier. And he's earned his place as a trusted right-hand to my father.

Rocco, well, apparently, I'm still in denial about the fucked up friendship we seem to be feeding into.

The elevator door slides open on a soft chime, and I step into the hallway, irritated that I'm even here. I'm just checking he's not dead, I tell myself for the twelve thousandth time. Or, more likely, checking he's not on his way to kill someone else.

That's all.

Nothing more.

Nothing less.

I'm doing my duty as a good citizen to the world and checking their well-being with an angry Shay on the loose.

I tell myself there's a good chance he's not even home. He's probably run off to one of his illegal fights, letting someone beat his skull to dull the pain.

Jackass.

The scars on my leg throb in a silent reminder that I have no right to judge his way of coping. I feel attacked and ashamed of my body all at once, grinding my teeth in irritation at my weakness.

I knock softly, rolling my eyes at how pitiful the sound of my knuckles is. I knock harder.

The door opens with force, a bristling Rocco standing on the threshold, sans shirt.

He can't hide his shock at my presence, eyebrows pulling down in thick slashes over his crazed eyes. "Fuck are you doing here?"

I hide the hurt that his cutting accusation causes.

He doesn't want you here, Einstein.

This isn't the first time I've seen him this way. He looks just like he did the day Mira died. Pacing his loft like a panther, ready to claim your jugular with his bare hands. Only this time, he remains still, the veins on his arm protruding in fury.

"Nice wounds." I gesture to the superficial injury on his chest, ignoring the nasty voice in my head.

He grunts in annoyance, eyes skating over me like I'm a stranger—an unknown unwelcome in his space.

"I just thought I'd—"

"Rocco." A blonde steps into my line of sight, cutting the sentence off in my throat, a bottle of whiskey in her hand. "Oh, hey," she greets with a surprised smile.

I lift a hand lamely in silent acknowledgment.

She's exactly who I'd imagine would be Rocco's type. Large fake tits, superficially tanned skin, and her figure enviably curvaceous. A skin-tight leopard-print dress covers her body, a tank-style top that follows the line of her body down to her bare feet.

"I'm Maggie," she introduces herself eagerly.

Before I can reciprocate, Rocco steps closer to me, the door moving with him enough to cut her out of view.

There's chaos in his eyes. Uncertainty and a hint of *regret* as he scans my face intently.

I want to reach out and reassure him. Ease the skittishness in his person. He resembles a caged animal, wild in the way he wants to rip out your throat, savage in the silent burn to be loved.

"I should go." I speak before he does, turning on my heel and making for the elevator in an awkward rush.

The world, obviously working to do me a solid for delivering the ultimate embarrassment, lets the doors open immediately. I don't hesitate to jump inside, tapping the close button faster than a new judge on The Voice.

Maggie.

She's even got a nice wholesome name. What the heck is she doing with the likes of Rocco Shay? More importantly, why the fuck do I care?

I rush onto the ground floor, making a beeline for the exit doors. But I can't walk through them. My feet pause, the automatic mechanism forcing the doors open, only to close them again when I make no attempt to move.

I won't fucking tell anyone you don't hate me as much as you pretend you do.

The truth is I don't hate Rocco Shay. Not even a little, and that's a bitch of a reality check to swallow. He's the closest thing to a friend I have in this world. Someone who sees the broken pieces of my mind, the fractured shards of my soul, and accepts them without question. Moreover, he seems to appreciate them.

Since the tumultuous end of my last relationship, I have thrown myself into work. Work couldn't harm me, not in the way trusting another person could. My work couldn't raise havoc in my life. It never made me question who I am or who I used to be in the way another person could.

My career took me in like a guardian angel, keeping me busy enough in an attempt to forget every horrible facet of my life.

Only recently has the brutal reality of loneliness crept in. Years spent alone in the darkness have finally caught up to me. Codi and my father aside, I have no one. Dad has his work, and Codi now has Parker to steal away her free time. That leaves me with the company of me, myself, and I. Not to be a bitch, but me, myself and I can be a total cunt to chill with at times. She's jaded beyond belief and can be downright hostile. Not to mention she is boring as fuck.

Enter Rocco Shay. The absolute brute that fell into my life, bleeding and as broken as I was.

The man I'd sworn to hate for the rest of my days.

The man who could have stolen my sister's life away from me.

My best friend.

Jesus Christ. I deserve to be stoned to death.

Closing my eyes, I take a deep breath.

I came here to check on a friend. One that, from a simple look into his slate grey eyes, is not okay.

"Fuck," I exclaim, apologizing to the middle-aged woman walking into the building with a graceless smile.

He's occupied, I concede. Happily so. Maggie is beautiful—I don't let myself read into the pain that slices into me at that—she'll gift him some peace. Even if it is for the limited time it takes to get his rocks off.

I should leave, I tell myself as I move toward the lone couch in the lobby, dropping myself down.

I'm a fucking idiot, I think, settling into the soft leather and making myself comfortable while I wait.

Stalker much, Camryn? I curse myself as the elevator sounds.

Maggie steps out, waving over her shoulder as she steps from the giant metal box, a smile on her pretty face. She notices me immediately, offering me a quick wink before stepping through the exit doors and disappearing down the street.

When I can no longer see her, I glance back at the elevator, a silent and somber Rocco braced against the frame, keeping the doors from closing as he watches me.

I stand without invitation, keeping his eyes as I approach. I step past him without speaking, standing at the back of the small space, my lower back pressed against the glass as I wait for him to move.

He presses the button to his floor silently. Standing with his back to me the entire way up, his eyes remain pinned to mine in the door's reflection. Indecipherable in the metallic blur but poignant enough to make me swallow.

He doesn't wait for me as the doors slide open, stepping onto his floor, expecting me to follow.

Which I do.

I feel like the ultimate third wheel as I step into his loft, Maggie's presence screaming at me for being the loser I am.

Rocco watches me cautiously, moving into his kitchen to place the counter between us. A shield of sorts. From what? I'm not sure. But I appreciate it as much as he seems to need it.

"Why are you here?"

I lift my shoulders, only to let them fall heavily in indecision. "To check on you."

"Why?"

I lick my lips. "Because Dad said you were hurt."

"Lie," he accuses. "You're a nurse. You know what a taser does. You know I'm fine."

I exhale purposely. "I was more concerned about this." I tap my temple, looking away, afraid to see what's in his eyes.

"Careful," he warns. "Someone might think we're friends."

"We are friends, asshole," I bite out. "Likely the only ones either of us have got. I hate myself for it, but here we are." I throw my hands up in the air, growling in frustration. "Taser aside—which I would've paid money to see hit you—you lost her. It has to be playing heavily on your mind. I thought I'd make sure you're not murdering helpless animals to cope."

He looks as shocked by my admission as I feel.

Rocco Shay and I *are* friends, and I just admitted it to him.

What the fuck world do I live in?

"You were worried about me."

"I shouldn't have been," I scoff. "You were clearly fine with your friend *Maggie*."

"Jealous?" He rounds the counter.

"No," I groan. "Put your ego back in place. More worried about your friend and whether she knows you're not capable of deeper feeling."

His loud laugh booms out, even his genuine amusement cut down by the rage begging to escape.

"Ah, fuck. I can't wait to tell Mags that." He sighs in exasperation. "Maggie uses me more than I do her."

I look affronted and don't care to hide it. "I doubt it."

He shakes his head at me, retrieving a bottle of whiskey and holding it in his lap like a shield.

"Maggie is married to some seventy-year-old foreign investment manager. The guy is fucking loaded, but he prefers dipping his cock in twenty-year-old men. Maggie is for show. She's down for it. She came from nothing. She pretends to be his devoted wife until he carks it, and she's an instant multi-millionaire. Win-win for them both."

The judgment within me eases, understanding tipping my bottom lip out in appreciation.

"I'm not the only cock she likes to ride. Not that we talk about it, but I go months without seeing her, and then she pops up for a quick fuck. She's got plenty of money, a cushy companionship with a nice guy, and a selection of cocks she can service herself with. She's not complaining."

"Oh."

"Yeah." He grins. "Oh."

Unsure of what to say, I choose my silence, watching him carefully.

He does much of the same.

"So are you?" I finally ask. "Okay?"

He drops his head, letting his feeble act of composure drop away.

Lifting his head, his eyes look black in savagery. A storm of violence overtakes, making his large frame quake with barely held onto restraint.

Head tipped back, he releases a yell so broken down with anguish, I step back in fear. The bottle of whiskey he had in his hand is thrown across the room, smashing against the wall with a loud and haunting shatter.

I didn't see him stand, too focused on the glass exploding against the plasterboard. But I watch him pace. Up and down.

He throws anything that stands in his way.

A table.

Chairs.

A vase.

His phone.

He only stops when he reaches the mantel. His mom stares back at him from the worn photograph.

"Do I look okay?" he roars. "Does this fucking look okay?" He gestures around his apartment.

"No."

Most people would leave him. Let him descend into madness, afraid he'd cause them harm. But it shocks me to realize I'm not scared. Not for myself. For him, absolutely.

His hate and rage are aimed inward. Being left alone is the very last thing Rocco needs right now.

"Anything I can do?"

"Wanna suck my cock to help me forget?" he asks sarcastically.

"No."

"Then leave."

"No."

He smiles viciously. "No?" He steps toward me, a warning painted across his face.

"You don't scare me," I tell him confidently.

"I should."

I shake my head. "Why? Because you're losing your shit right now? We've all been here, Shay. Your temper isn't anything I haven't felt before."

He looks saddened by my declaration. "You're nothing like me,

126

beauty. Trust me when I tell you it's a good fucking thing. Everything I touch... everything I love... *it dies.*"

A statement. One he wholeheartedly believes.

"Mom. Mira. All my doing. Parker was smart," he urges me to understand. "He found someone to love more than he does me. He saved himself by finding purity to erase his sins."

"Surely you don't believe that?"

"Give me another reason why anyone that gets close to me seems to be stripped of their last breath."

He looks so broken down by his unreasonable belief.

"Anyone who got close to Marcus died, Rocco. Lila, Mira, even Kane... they're on Marcus. Not you."

Eyes boring into mine, he looks disgusted by my argument. How could I think anyone *but* him is the reason for life's downfall? Every shitty thing that this world has on offer is a weight on his shoulders he's burdened with holding.

"You know," he ponders, refusing to discuss his responsibility for his mother's death any further. He drops his ass onto a kitchen stool, thick arms crossed over his chest. "Control is the one thing in my life I crave. I pride myself on it. I can stand in a ring and have some jerk lay blow after blow to my body, but I control that. I let them hit me," he confesses candidly. "I want them to think that they're in control because there is nothing that fucks with your psyche more than realizing you have no fucking control. The awareness that you're helpless. I wait until they're most confident, and then I claim it back."

"Sarah played you at your own game," I guess.

His head shakes side-to-side, a look of distaste twisting his features. "She didn't need to. I was outta my depth the moment I stepped into that room. She knew it. I knew it."

His large palm rubs down his face.

"You have it back now," I push. "Your control. You could've gone out and lost your mind, but you didn't."

Shame stares out at me from the agony in his eyes. "That's not true. I couldn't fight, Cami. I would've fucking killed someone. I locked myself in this cage, all but begging Maggie to come over to stop me from leaving."

"She could stop you from leaving?"

"She can be pretty persuasive."

"Ew."

He stands. "Doesn't matter, you interrupted before I could tell her to fuck off and go on the search for a concussion."

He's telling me he didn't fuck her. That he didn't want to. Not in the end.

"Who you fuck is none of my business."

"Was just letting you know," he murmurs distractedly.

"What about Parker?" I change the subject. "Why not call Parker?"

He eyes me with contempt. "I haven't shared that your father and I are working together. Add that to the fact that I have no intention of sharing that I'm on the search for your mother. He'll go all sensitive Parker on me. He'll tell me he needs me, that I matter to him. He gets in my fucking head," he complains.

"Oh, no," I gripe sarcastically. "Not someone who loves you. How inconvenient and insensitive of him."

"Fuck off, Rein," he grumbles, opening and closing cupboard doors in search of something. "You came to see if I'm okay. I'm not, but I've had my meltdown. Your conscience can rest easy."

Grabbing a bottle of tequila from the last cabinet, he holds it up triumphantly. "I'm about thirty shots away from being comatose. I can't fucking kill anyone then, can I? You can go now."

I move into the kitchen. "You're unhinged, Shay. You're about two-point-five-seconds away from severing someone's head from their body. Congratulations, you have a babysitter once again. Where are your fucking limes?"

He glares at me for a beat before tipping his head to the fridge.

CHAPTER NINETEEN

ROCCO

MY NIGHTMARE WON'T END.

The screaming. High-pitched and panicked. Over and over again. Their pain is so real, it beats inside of me in time with my heart—a thick and steady strum of surrender.

I can't place the voice, my head throbbing with recognition, but my mind is a step behind.

My stomach turns, ten tequila shots too many twisting in my gut, even in sleep.

Please, the voice begs.

No, it cries.

A woman. One begging for her life.

"Mira?" I groan, pushing through the clouds in my head. It's not just a fucking storm. It's a tornado of its own making. The horrors of my past rotate so rapidly that I can't tell the collateral of one fucked-up decision from another.

"HELP!"

Startled into consciousness, I sit up in my bed. My breathing wracks through my body sluggishly. My shoulders lift as my chest expands, dropping back wearily as it deflates. I suck in the deepest breath I can, filling my lungs.

Thumb and finger to my eye sockets, I press down, working to relieve the throbbing in my temples.

Crying.

It's soft—a haunting echo in my eardrums.

It also wasn't part of my nightmare. It was, *is*, real, infiltrating my unconscious and forcing me awake.

It hasn't stopped—gentle whimpers of pain filtering from my living room.

Stumbling down the hall in a sleep-induced stagger, I take in the scene before me.

Camryn sits alone on my couch, body quaking with stuttered sobs. Dark hair, loose from its usual confines, hangs in a knotted mess, shielding her face from view.

Unsure if she's still asleep or awake, I approach slowly.

"Camryn," I test, afraid to startle her.

Shaking shoulders aside, she doesn't move.

Kneeling in front of her, my chest tightens. Beautiful enough to be a painting, memorialized for eternity, she's the saddest muse I've ever laid eyes on. Misery shades any light shining from within her. Caught in the dark corners of her mind, she's hollow, and her soul is looking for an escape.

I recognize the despair she's trapped within. Her thoughts and memories are her straight jacket, keeping her as an unwilling prisoner. I recognize it because I've sat in that very spot, I've seen it all from her view, and it's an ugly place to be.

Caught between the limbo of slumber and consciousness, she stares at nothing. Heavy, wet tears drop from her eyes and slide down her sleep-creased face.

"Beauty," I call, my hands framing her face, trying to get her eyes to look at mine.

Blinking slowly, she brings me into focus. "Rocco?" she stutters quietly.

"I'm here," I assure her.

Hands lifting to touch mine, she looks at me like you would a ghost. Both afraid and intrigued.

"Are you real?" she whispers.

My heart thunders in my chest, my ribs piercing it in pain. "Yeah, baby, I'm real."

She can't tell the difference between her nightmares and reality. To her, they're the same.

After a stuttered breath, her head nods in relief. Eyes closed, she leans forward, pushing the damp touch of her forehead against mine, needing to feel me to believe me.

"You're here."

"You're safe," I murmur, the salty smell of her tears tickling my nostrils.

"Safe," she repeats, touching her lips against mine.

"Safe," I hum against her mouth, too afraid to move.

She kisses me tentatively. A soft press of her tear-stained lips tasting mine. I don't kiss her back, not confident enough to know that's what she wants. This is her coping, managing whatever is fucking with her head enough to make her *need* to kiss me.

She explores my lips slowly, gentle brushes of her mouth caressing mine.

It's a foreign feeling to be kissed without frantic need. Without the carnal need to fuck. I'm more exposed than I care to be. Stripped bare for her to read with her heart on her lips.

I should pull back, push her away, stop her before I'm tangled up enough to let her keep going. But she stops herself. Her mouth pulls back, teeth grazing along her bottom lip to savor my taste.

What we shared wasn't a spike of need. It wasn't a push of desire surging through—a thirst needing to be quenched. No lustful urges were fusing our mouths or forcing my hand to grip her hair not to lose her taste. We weren't fighting to tear off one another's clothes, to feel each other, skin to skin. I didn't need to fuck away her fears in the same way she couldn't fuck away mine.

It was more. So much fucking more.

What Camryn just shared with me was a broken moment full of gratitude. A not-so-simple thank you. An intimate recognition of bearing your soul completely. Letting another see it in all its ugly glory and recognizing they didn't decide to turn their back.

Her eyes open, looking directly into mine. "I'm sorry," she whispers.

"We're good," I refute. "Nothing to apologize for." A gruffness catches along my throat, making me cough.

Comfortable that she's settled, I pull my hands from her face, dropping them onto the couch.

"You taste like tequila."

I smile. "You brought the salt." I glance at her lips, annoyed at my craving to touch them again with my mouth.

She pushes my chest, her cheeks darkening in embarrassment. "Twice now you've rescued me when I've been battling monsters in my sleep."

"Hey." I grab her chin, forcing her to look at me. "Don't you dare be embarrassed about that. I told you, I'm no stranger to nightmares, Camryn. Do I look weak?"

She shakes her head as best she can with my hand still gripped against her jaw.

"The shit that haunts you in your sleep doesn't make you weak. Fuck, even the shit that haunts you when you're awake doesn't make you weak. Those monsters up there..." I lift my chin, gesturing to her head. "They're weak, having to wait until we're most vulnerable to gain traction. Fuck them for being too pansy-ass to go up against us at our strongest."

Her eyelids drop in acceptance, and a small smirk pulls along her lips.

"Do your nightmares cause you physical pain?"

Desperate to know she's not alone, her eyes widen in anguish, begging me to tell her that they do. She wants to hear that I wake up with a rope tied around my heart, the frayed edges squeezing tight enough to stop it from beating. She wants to know that my body aches, recalling every blow I've taken against my skin, my bones feeling brittle enough that they'll break if I breathe. She needs me to acknowledge that the simple act of breathing feels like the world's greatest burden.

Fear grips my vocal cords. It strangles my voice box, stopping me from speaking. I look like the world's biggest cunt, but I can't tell her there are days I wake up in so much pain, I wish for death to claim me. To rescue me from this existence I've twisted myself up in.

I can't confess that my nightmares are enough to make me bleed.

That I wake up with tears tracking down my cheeks, making me feel like the fragile little boy who lost his mom and not a grown-ass man who shouldn't be crying over something that happened almost twenty years ago.

"Pick a movie," I sniff, standing abruptly, ignoring her plea in favor of my self-preservation. "I'll make you a herbal tea."

She looks torn down, humiliated that she showed me the inner workings of her mind, and I all but shit on them. I, like her bad dreams, have taken her power. I pushed her down. Happy enough to let her feel fragile to save myself.

"I'm just gonna use your bathroom," she mumbles.

Standing in the kitchen, I launch my knuckles against the marble of the counter, infuriated at myself, at her, at whatever fucked her so badly in the past.

I should've just told her. I should've just admitted that I live in a constant state of pain. That she should be stronger than me. I've let my past mistakes define who I am now, and I pay for it in blood.

"Fuck."

Without second-guessing myself, I follow her to the bathroom, ready to confess my sins. Wanting, needing her to know that if she's alone in this world, she doesn't have to be. My mind is as chaotic as hers. We share a devotion to pain neither of us can evade.

"Cami," I call out, pushing at the bathroom door, still currently ajar.

She doesn't speak, choosing to keep her silence. Her breathing is thick. Long, measured breaths forcing the hairs along my arms to stand on end.

"Look, I'm sorry." I step into the bathroom, refusing to let her ignore me.

Sitting on the closed toilet lid, her eyes are mesmerized by the river of blood sliding down her thigh, tracking along the back of her knee and calf in a red ribbon.

"What the fuck?" I bellow. "What are you doing?"

My voice startles her enough that the small grey razor blade in her hand falls to the ground, bouncing in a chime that resembles the elevator down to hell.

I grab a towel and push it against the cut along her tanned skin.

"It feels better," she tells me. "To hurt from something I've done. I'm in charge."

It's then that I see them—too many to count. Scars littered along her upper thighs, letting me know that this isn't the first time she's harmed herself while searching for power.

"Cami," I whisper.

"You wouldn't understand," she accuses quietly. "My nightmares hurt, Rocco. They—"

"Why the fuck do you think I fight?" I yell. "I lied. Of course, my nightmares fucking hurt. They carve away everything I am, slicing me open and letting me bleed out."

Her hand grabs onto mine, still grasped tightly to the towel at her skin. She's shaking, or maybe that's me. I can't tell.

"I fight to find power. I let others make me bleed in search of freedom. The agony their fists cause distracts me from every fucked up thought drowning me." I sigh, dropping my head. "I'm always fucking drowning, beauty."

"But you're strong," she argues meekly.

"Physically, yes. Mentally, I'm as feeble as they come."

That's it. Me. No question. No doubt. A show of muscle on the outside, but cracked on the inside, ready to shatter.

And now Camryn Rein knows it.

"Will you keep my secret?" she asks, the plea in her voice as desperate as I've ever seen her.

"This isn't healthy." I gesture to her leg.

"It's been getting better. Since..."

She goes quiet, her eyes anchoring to mine in indecision.

"Since me," I answer for her.

"I'm lame."

I cough to clear my throat. "I haven't fought since you."

She searches for the lie in my confession. One she won't find.

Camryn Rein has become my greatest defense against myself. A distraction I hadn't believed was a possibility.

She wraps her arms around my neck, pulling me into her body. Like her kiss, her embrace is a silent recognition of what my fucked-up version of friendship has brought into her life.

I don't think about it too hard, hugging her back and showing her my gratitude.

"Aren't we just a fucked up pair?" She barks out a laugh.

I pull back, a lazy smile on my face. "It's not as if we could share these broken parts of ourselves with Parker and Codi."

She nods. "It's nice to be accepted. To not have someone try and *fix* you."

"Let's get this leg cleaned up. You're staining my tiles."

"It's not deep," she says softly. "Do you have any of those steri strips from your eye left over?"

I place her hand on the towel, making sure she has hold of it before I stand.

"I think so." I open my bathroom cabinet in search of something to stop the bleeding. "When did it start? The cutting?"

I watch her reflection in the mirror, the dismissive shrug of her shoulders. "Few years. These were all from just after I left college. I wasn't lying. I don't do it often. Only when I'm really struggling."

"Shouldn't you speak to someone about a healthier way to cope?" I turn around, handing over the strips she had asked for.

"Have you?" she bites back.

"My mind is a maze no one is making it out of."

I answered my own question.

"Why?" I test, more than confident she'll tell me to go fuck myself.

"I told you why," she argues defensively.

"You know what I mean." I lean against the vanity, arms crossed against my chest. "What was the catalyst? What was so painful that you find peace in harming yourself?"

The line of her throat bobs thickly as she swallows.

"What was yours?" She throws back at me, eyes focused on the cut, no longer than an inch, carved into her thigh.

"My mom," I answer without delay. "The way she died. I was weighed down by a pain I could never lift off my shoulders. Then Marcus hit me, Kane, too, and for a split second, the physical pain brought down by their fists was enough to erase the pain in my heart."

She looks up, looking into me deeper than I'm comfortable with. "But that's not everything."

It's my turn to swallow my hesitation.

"Someone else left me."

She watches me carefully. "A girl?"

I shrug, not willing to divulge any more. "Your turn."

Placing the small white strips across the cut, she dabs at the spot, cleaning away the dried blood. "I can't," she chokes on the words.

"Can't or won't?"

She shakes her head, refusing to answer.

"Why?"

Glancing up, she lets me see the pool of tears collected in her eyes, readying themselves to fall. "It hurts too much. I've never spoken to anyone about it, not completely," she begs me to understand.

"You're scared."

She blinks, her tears racing down her face silently.

"You find something that scares you, beauty, you stand the fuck up and confront it head-on. You stare it right down the fucking eye, and if it forces you down... you push it back. Harder. You stand tall— squared shoulders. And push. It. The fuck. Back. You own it. You let that fear know it won't fucking control you. That's how you destroy it. With strength. With the force of you."

She rejects my words, that head of hers shaking vehemently. "I'm not strong enough."

I frown, irritated by the lack of belief she holds in herself. "That's not true," I condemn, forcing myself to stand tall. "Because even if, for some reason, you falter, you're forgetting your reinforcements."

That offers her pause, the constant shaking of her head stopping, confusion settling in its place. "Huh?"

"Me," I declare. "At your back. Holding you up and helping you push those fucked up fears down. I'm an impenetrable wall, baby, and I've got your back."

Her face softens. "Why don't you let people know that you're good? Why do you force us to only see the villain?"

Scratching at the hair along my chin, I shake my head. "We're not talking about me, Camryn."

I watch her inhale deeply. "I fell in love when I was eighteen," she starts. "My first year of college. That stupid teenage love that you're convinced will last forever. I thought he was my everything."

"How long did it last?"

"The relationship?" she tests, and I nod.

"Four years. Eighteen months of young, happy love. Two and a half years of pure vitiated hell." There's no emotion in her voice. No feeling of love or despair, or hostility or heartache. Just… *nothing*.

"I was isolated from my family. The few friends I'd made in class abandoned me because he was such a dick. I was just too blind to see it. At first, anyway."

My anger starts off small, tiny stab wounds of fury poking at my shoulders. Typical predator, he needed her weak to feel powerful.

"By the time I realized how poisonous he was, I was pretty much as alone as anyone could be. I was ashamed of the position I'd put myself in. I was so fucking stupid." Her head shakes in disgust. "I pushed Codi away. I pushed my dad away. They stopped calling, thinking I was too busy with my new life to care about them."

She swipes at the tears falling down her cheeks without permission, not wanting to give him the ability to make her cry anymore.

"He controlled everything about my life, and in the end, I let him." Too ashamed to look at me as she speaks, her eyes focus on the floor, the soft mumble of her voice almost too low to hear. "When I ate, what classes I'd attend, what I did socially, and when we'd fuck." Her voice splits open, cracking along the word like a lashing across her back.

He starved her when he felt the need.

He isolated her because he could.

He dictated her life because he tore her down for her to think his wants were hers.

He raped her because he could overpower her.

I'll kill him if I ever have the chance.

"I'd fight." She finally looks at me, her tone begging me to believe her. "Sometimes. I'd fight sometimes. He'd hit me. I think he enjoyed it more when I fought. When he could subdue me."

It catches her, then. The pain she'd been avoiding by slicing her leg open. Face falling into her open palms, her sobs overwhelm her. The agony she'd caused herself by holding it in, letting go like a dam wall breaking, a tidal wave of truth surging forward, destroying everything in its wake.

"I was nothing. He knew it, and he made sure I did too."

I don't move. My body itches to comfort her, but her shame is strong enough to keep me at bay. She doesn't want my pity. She doesn't want my comfort. She needs this. She needs to cleanse herself of the toxicity he injected into her life. To share the ugly parts of her soul and know that it doesn't make her less of a person. To release her burden, and know someone else will hold it for her. *That I'll hold it for her.*

She cries for a long time. Her tears are brimming like the crest of a waterfall, unrelenting and freefalling. I like that she's comfortable enough to cry in my presence. She hasn't attempted to stop, flee or apologize. It's the most authentic version of Camryn I've seen, that anyone has seen.

She's breaking and healing in front of me, and it's the most courageous thing I've ever seen another person do.

"How'd you get out?"

The back of her hand rubbing along her nose, she sniffs ungraciously. "Codi came to visit. One of his friends took a liking to her."

Her head shakes, the fear of her thoughts spiking.

"I couldn't... I couldn't let her fall into the abyss as I did."

"You saved yourself because you were strong enough to save her."

Standing, she moves to the basin, wetting the towel to drop to the tiles, cleaning away her smeared blood. "Why do you think we do that?"

"Do what?"

"Put more value in the lives of those we love than our own?"

Tiles clean, I lean forward to retrieve the towel from her, dumping it into the trash can under the sink. "Because we don't know all their flaws like we do our own. We look at Parker and Codi and see how they're better than us. We don't consider their weaknesses or how they've failed in life because, to us, that's insignificant. We're harder on ourselves. We judge ourselves more than we judge others. It's depressing as fuck, but it's easier to find forgiveness for others than it is for yourself."

CHAPTER TWENTY

CAMRYN

I GAVE birth to my feelings.

Every sordid one of them.

They spewed forth like an untamed rapid, turbulent, and catastrophic.

I vomited my damaged heart onto the floor, laying it at his feet, asking him not to judge me for how scarred it was.

My shame exploded in our faces, decimating the wall I'd spent years building up. Only the rubble of my past remained, laid between us like a sacrifice.

I had divulged my most hallowed secret.

To Rocco Shay.

Questionable decision twelve thousand and eighty-five.

Or maybe not.

In that bathroom, standing before me with warmth shining from his icy eyes, he looked like a broken angel.

My imperfect savior.

He wasn't repulsed. He was captivated.

He wasn't uncomfortable. He was engaged.

He didn't pity me. On the contrary, he felt my hatred and met it with his own malevolence.

My fight became his. He vocalized nothing, but I could read the promise in his eyes, storming forward in thick grey clouds of assurance. He'd kill my monster if he could. He'd slay my demons without mercy. Moreover, he'd do it with a smile on his face.

From that fractured moment, something shifted. *We* changed. A titanium connection was built—an attachment forged in the one thing neither of us ever expected to feel, *acceptance.*

I wasn't worried that he'd betray me. Just as he wasn't concerned that I'd forsake him. Trust flourished, and we knew without discussing it that it was solid.

The expiration of our previously agreed-upon arrangement has come and gone. Forgotten like our animosity.

Two months have passed by in a blur. Our dependency only grows with each day. We've managed to replace our nightmares with one another. Freed from our everyday masks in one another's company, we're too afraid to sever our connection for fear of the incidental harm it would cause.

My body is stronger than I've ever seen it. Muscle sits on my limbs like foreign additions. Agile and lithe. Rocco has succeeded in crafting my body into a weapon. I feel energized. I feel capable. I feel strong.

"Are you listening?" Codi snaps her fingers in front of my face.

Smacking her hand away, I nod. "I can't believe you're getting married today."

"I know." She drops beside me on her childhood bed, the silk of her white robe brushing my leg.

"Are you nervous?"

Her shoulders lift dismissively. "Not about marrying Parker. I love him. The day seems over the top."

Dropping my head to her shoulder, I inhale the sweet scent of her skin. "I'm still surprised he was insistent that you marry in a church."

Her head moves to rest atop mine. "It's what Lila would've wanted."

"I'm sad that his mom won't be with him today."

She sniffs. "Me too."

"You don't find it odd that he didn't want to invite anyone to his wedding?"

She stands, moving to the box of donuts on her dresser. "No," she answers, picking up a glazed one and taking a bite. "He's never told me outright, but I don't think he or Rocco have any close friends. I guess they've kept everyone at a distance their whole lives."

I frown. "That's sad."

"No sad faces." She points at me. "It's my wedding day. We aren't allowed to be sad. Here, eat a donut." She throws one toward me. "Sugar fixes everything."

Attempting to catch it in my mouth, I fail, the sticky dessert hitting my chin before falling to my lap. Dipping my tongue out, I lick at the icing on my skin.

"Has anyone ever told you that you eat like a rabid dog?" Codi laughs.

Shoving the entire donut in my mouth, I shake my head. "No." The word is entirely unintelligible, my jaw struggling to let me chew around the dough.

Opening her mouth to tell me I'm disgusting, a knock at her door interrupts us.

"Hi." A middle-aged woman pops her head in. "I'm Linda."

"Hair and makeup," Codi tells me. "Hi. I'm Codi. This disgusting little human is my sister, Camryn. She's going to shower to remove the excess food from her face."

Linda smiles at us. "I'll set up over here." She points to the window. "We'll start with you, Codi."

Brushing the crumbs off my chin, I stand awkwardly. "Nice to meet you, Linda. I'll clean up and be right out."

ST. Paul's Episcopal Church was Lila Shay's sacred place. She would sit in this very church, her two boys by her side, participating in evening prayer or morning mass. She asked for guidance when her future path was not clear. She'd seek comfort in this place of worship. This space was where Mira would visit following her sister's untimely death, mourning a loss she couldn't understand.

Heaviness leans on my heart the moment we step inside the church. I can sense Lila Shay watching us all from the wooden beams framing the building. Her spirit filters across the ocean-colored windows in a welcome none of us had expected. She infiltrates every corner of the space, and I'm humbled and honored by her presence.

I can't see Rocco or Parker, but I can feel them. Their grief wraps around me, finding their peace in this bittersweet moment.

It makes sense that Parker would feel close to her here. That being married in this place of prayer would let him feel as though she was sitting on the very front pew, watching him marry the love of his life with a smile on her face. A smile not different from his or Rocco's. Wide and infectious. Her gray eyes glistening with unshed tears. She'd celebrate louder and with more delight than any other. Her boy was happy. He was loved. The goodness she'd nurtured within him had flourished, letting him fall irrevocably in love.

"Do you think she's here?" Codi whispers, her purple eyes, wide in awe, skating over the church in hope.

"She's definitely here," I assure her, blinking back the emotions threatening to wet my eyes.

I turn to my sister, my emotions getting the better of me.

"You're so beautiful."

It's been said at every wedding since the dawn of time. Likely believed with everything within the preacher's heart. But going forward, it'll never be true. Because standing in front of me, lace contoured to her body in perfection... Codi is timeless. She's the definition of elegance.

Long sleeves, a scalloped neckline, a daringly-low back, and a bottom-hugging gathering; she's the dream of every bride on their wedding day.

Beyond exquisite, her curves are tastefully accentuated. Her blonde hair is pinned up intricately, showing off the slim line of her neck.

"I feel so out of place not wearing my Chucks and jeans," she whispers.

"Oh, Codi," Dad interrupts before I can tell her she looks like a modern-day princess. His chin wobbles and I look away before I hold a similar look on my made-up face. "You're a vision."

"You're gonna make me cry," she reprimands, encouraging him to come closer with a wave of her hand. "Hug me."

"They're ready for us. Parker looks ready to storm down and steal you away from us all."

"Is he nervous?" she worries.

"Not about making you his wife," he soothes her. "I can't believe you're going to be a Shay from today. My littlest Rein is leaving me."

"Let's not start the waterworks. I don't want this day to be memorialized with mascara running down my face like a clown in every photo."

Dad and Codi laugh. "Where are your flowers?" he asks her.

"Here." I pass them to her.

"White roses."

"For Lila," Codi whispers, linking her arm through our father's.

The soft strums of the violin and piano twist through the church like an ode to love. Delicate and graceful, a beautiful ribbon to tie Parker and Codi together for eternity. Schubert's Ave Maria settles the quiet hushes of the people into nothing as I step forward, my feet sliding down the aisle to a silent and severe Parker.

Dressed in an impeccably tailored tux, he looks ready to burst with anticipation. I wink at him as I approach, bringing a small smirk to his lips.

The guests stand as Codi and my father step forward, a collective inhale echoing the room's acoustics in awe. Not that I doubted that would occur, like I said, she's the most beautiful bride ever to exist.

My sister's beauty is all-encompassing. It's not just the prettiness of her face, it's what she holds inside. She's golden, from her heart and soul to the picture-perfect face people pay money in search of.

I choose to watch Parker as Codi approaches. Their happily ever after within their grasp. I lose myself in the affection softening the severity of his features.

His gray eyes shine like silver, a possessive devotion watching Codi without blinking.

The stiffness in his posture relaxes into relief. She's here. She's standing in front of him, ready to promise her forever to him and only him.

I've never seen love this up close and personal. The way a man and a woman lose themselves in one another. The potency of their affection is intense. Their lives forever entwined as they carve out large chunks of their hearts to hand over to one another—a sacrifice to a legacy they will build together.

I was starved of its realness as a child. My mother and father didn't care for one another in this way. Their feelings were staked in obligation and regret. Sure, my father loved Codi and me. But romantic love is different when it's true. The friendship nurtured, an eternal flame of devotion sparked with a simple look between two people destined for forever.

Unable to stare at its vividity any longer, I glance away as Parker recites his vows. My eyes fall on the man standing behind him.

His best man.

His brother.

Rocco is watching me unabashedly. I know, without an exchange of words, that he's too afraid to look directly at the adoration in front of us. Scared of what it will do to him.

I watch him as candidly as he does me. My eyes drift over his appearance in a greedy need to drink him in.

My armor, weakened by the love in the room, wanes enough for me to recognize the beauty in the beast standing before me. A warrior, his body built for combat. His height and muscle are intimidating to regular mortals. Rocco Shay is his own shield. His blonde hair is styled away from his face, sides shorn close to his head, bringing my focus to his well-groomed beard. His cheekbones are carved out like a contour you couldn't fake, bracketing the line of his beard. Icy gray eyes look at me so deeply, I'm certain he's sliced open any guard I've managed to build, seeing everything I've kept sacred. I know his teeth to be a perfect shade of white, his incisors a little sharper than the rest. His smile is rare, a sight on the verge of extinction. But when I catch a glimpse—goodbye heart, farewell ovaries—I've lived a good life and died by the prettiest of knives.

Dressed in a suit identical to Parker's, he looks dangerous. To my life. To my heart. The currency the same, knowing he could claim them both and destroy them without hesitation.

My tongue peeks out, wetting the dryness in my lips. The discomfort at my feelings is both alarming and exciting. His focus drops to my mouth, eyes recognizing the way I tasted.

I kissed him. A fact neither of us has brought up. My lips have pushed against his in a desperate need to feel grounded, and he didn't pull away. I don't regret it. On the contrary, my eyes eating him up, I wouldn't mind doing it again.

As though he can read my thoughts, his teeth bite at his tongue, grazing against it in need. Something I'd never imagine I'd see. Rocco Shay is holding an arrow of desire and aiming it my way.

The clandestine line between love and hate was now blurred by lust.

I hated him until I didn't.

I was indifferent until I wasn't.

I was content until it all shifted.

Now I'm *wanting* and afraid of how that morphs moving forward.

Hate was our beginning, but that surreptitious line has been erased. Leaving me in a trap I never imagined I'd find myself in.

Love.

CHAPTER TWENTY-ONE

ROCCO

Random fact, my brother is whipped.

Beyond saving.

Tied around the pinky of his new wife like a tattooed thread. Lost to the promise of eternal love.

Companionship. Support. Affection. An endless supply of your preferred pussy.

I don't blame him. Shit, I'm pleased as fuck for him. He's happy. An emotion I didn't see him wear until we barged into Codi's life, swords of revenge at the ready. Now it rarely shifts. It oozes from his skin, a charged current coursing through his veins, highlighting my bitterness.

Their ceremony was nice enough. From the snippets I could bring myself to listen to when I wasn't being suffocated by my mother and aunt. My throat constricted with panic as Codi walked down the aisle. Their presence was screaming at me, demanding I acknowledge them. I couldn't, though. It was too hard. Parker made it difficult enough. Two white roses were placed on the front pew in their place. I knew if I looked in that direction, I'd see them. Their smiling faces watching Parker marry his woman. Love in their eyes and joy in their smiles. A moment in his life they should've been front and center of.

The church was a path down memory lane I wasn't ready for.

Parker's heart was in the right place, searching for a way to include Lila in the most important day of his life. I've learned the hard way, though. The road to hell is paved with good intentions. Maybe my intentions weren't exactly good, but they were significant to me. They were important. Still, I all but dug a path into the depths of nothing. Today was just another reminder of that.

I couldn't stomach staring directly at Parker and Codi. They were too bright. A glow of happiness surrounded them. A light I couldn't meet head-on for fear of the damage it could cause.

Then I found Camryn.

A safe harbor I never fucking wanted.

A woman I have no right to.

The Rein family has twisted me up and turned me inside out. I don't know who the fuck I am anymore.

When mine and Camryn's eyes connected, peace hit me. I wasn't fighting against myself. I felt Lila's smile aimed *at me.* I felt Mira's joy shining down *on me.*

Camryn Rein shifts my perspective. She looks at me like I'm worthy. No one has looked at me with such reverence since my mom. Sure, Mira loved me unconditionally, as does Parker. But their concern for my mental well-being was always clouding their acceptance.

"Why are you hiding around here?"

Speaking of the devil, the soft click of her heels taps against the cement of her father's driveway.

I knew she was beautiful. Even in grimy work clothes and messy hair, she sends blood straight to my cock. But standing in front of me, body encased in a thick red fabric, her long chocolate hair in waves down her back; she's that dangerous temptress come to life. Ready to slay me.

"You look good, Rein," I burr.

"You scrub up alright yourself, Shay." She sits beside me, the addictive scent of her perfume wrapping around me.

"Where is the happy couple?"

"Mind if I smoke?" she asks, holding up a small pack of cigarettes.

I can't hide my shock.

"It's a dirty little habit I partake in very rarely." She rolls her eyes.

"It's bad for you."

"So is coffee and sugar… and *you*…" She drifts off, placing a smoke between her lips.

Inhaling the nicotine like a potent drug, she smiles, her eyes closing in pleasure. "Parker and Codi are mingling with their guests. Touching one another inappropriately in public and making out in a way that should be illegal in front of others."

I grimace.

"Tell me about it." She flicks her cigarette, the loose gray ash vanishing in the drag of wind before it hits the ground.

We attempt to speak simultaneously but stop, the awkwardness lulling us back into silence.

"Wanna have breakfast tomorrow?" she invites, rubbing the butt of her smoke on the ground to put it out.

"Yeah, beauty."

She looks pleased by my answer, her shoulder nudging mine in tenderness.

"Beauty," she repeats. "Does that make you my beast?"

I laugh. "No, Cami." I lean back, resting my arms behind us, my eyes trailing over her thick hair. I refrain from reaching out and touching it. "The beast is merely misunderstood. He's a kind heart trapped in ugly wrapping. He's lonely and looking for purpose."

She glances at me over her shoulder. My body itches to sit up, to lean forward and claim her mouth. "I'm the opposite. An ugly fucking heart housed in a body that makes you wet," I whisper. "I'm Gaston, baby, and that ain't ever gonna change."

"Gaston was a giant douchebag who wanted to be put on a pedestal," she argues. "He would've fucked himself if he could have. He didn't want Belle's love. He wanted the triumph of winning her. She was an object to him. You're not Gaston. But you're right. You're not the beast either."

Stretching her legs out, she moves her feet side-to-side, watching her brightly colored toenails glitter in the night sky. "You're lonely, though," she ponders, more to herself than to me. "And you're always searching for purpose."

She's not wrong. Camryn isn't dumb. She knows I'm searching, she doesn't know what for, but she knows it's important enough that I won't ever stop.

"And your heart isn't ugly," she implores. "Different than most, but different is good."

Her lips purse, a silent contemplation hitting her. "Not Gaston, but not the beast."

She shakes her head. "You're Rocco. You have too many layers for a villain in a Disney movie. They're always fighting for power. You don't care for power. You fight for what your heart deems is right."

I pinch her side. "Poetic."

She laughs. "That one was all my own too. No Dominic influence. He's rubbing off on me."

"Or maybe you're trying too hard to see me as more than I am."

"Maybe," she muses. "Can I ask you something?"

I don't answer, knowing she'll ask me anyway.

"Do you wish you kissed me back?"

The whispered words freeze between us, caught across the cold night air in expectation.

"No," I answer honestly.

Bottom lip tipped out, she doesn't look hurt by my response.

"You didn't want me to kiss you back," I explain.

Turning, she faces me, throwing her leg over the bench we're sitting on, straddling the concrete structure.

I follow her lead.

"You didn't kiss me out of craving. It wasn't attraction that triggered you."

She looks at the bench between us, her cheeks changing in color before my eyes. "Would you now? Kiss me back? If I did it again."

I clear my throat, waiting for her to look at me. I wait a full minute, using a finger to lift her chin. "I don't know. All I know is, I won't kiss you until you're ready."

Shifting closer, she touches her forehead to mine, our noses touching.

"Are you ready?" I murmur.

"I don't know," she whispers.

"That's a no, beauty. You'll know when you're ready." I pull back, searching for disappointment in her eyes.

I stand reluctantly. Her big blue eyes watch me, an appreciation twinkling up at me.

Leaning down, I touch my lips to her forehead. "Come." I hold my hand out for hers. "Let's go watch our siblings all but procreate in front of their guests."

The warmth of her skin slips into my palm as I pull her up. I wait while she readjusts her dress one-handed, unwilling to let her hand go.

"Please don't joke about that. They're too much. And they live with me."

A loud boom of laughter jolts out of me unexpectedly. "If I didn't find so much joy in your misery, I'd feel bad for you."

"Rude!" She balks. "Don't talk too soon, Shay. If they become too unbearable, I'll be moving into your place, messing with your bachelor vibes."

I squeeze her hand. "Wouldn't work. My loft has an all-around sugar ban. You wouldn't survive."

"You suck the joy out of life."

I push her away gently, our hands holding on until we can no longer reach. "It's part of my world domination plan."

Flipping me off, she moves toward her sister, leaving me to stand on the edge of the Rein patio, watching her retreat.

"Rocco." Dominic approaches, a whiskey in his hand.

"Nice setup." I gesture to his backyard. The grandiose decorations transform the space into a wonderland of tulle, white roses, and lanterns.

"Sarah's been spotted in the city." He ignores my praise, drawing my attention immediately.

"What? When?"

"Earlier today," he worries. "I don't like it, Rocco. She should've gone deeper into hiding. But, instead, she's out in the open. Something's happening. I don't know what, but I can feel it. She's planning something."

"You sure she's not just cooked on meth and making stupid decisions?"

"No." He throws the contents of his glass down his throat, snapping his fingers toward the closest waiter, demanding a refill.

The waiter brings me one, too, and I mumble a thank you, eyes set on Dominic.

"But we can't rely on that. Prepare for the worst and hope for the fucking best."

I sip the amber liquid, letting the earthy flavors soak into my lips. "Do we have any leads of where she's staying?"

His head shakes, a fake smile on his lips, waving to Codi as she drifts past.

"No. Which means she has connections here I don't know about. Fuck," he spits, rubbing a hand roughly down his face.

"Boss," the asshole, henceforth known as Dork, interrupts.

"What?" Dominic snaps, inhaling heavily to calm himself before turning around. "Apologies. What do you need?"

York shifts uncomfortably on his feet. "Tivoli has asked for you inside. Says it's urgent."

I walk with Dominic, but he stops me with a hand on my chest. "Enjoy your brother's wedding. We'll reassess tomorrow."

I scowl in indecision.

"Go." He taps his jacket pocket, opening it to pull out two Cuban cigars. "Find your brother, celebrate."

CHAPTER TWENTY-TWO

CAMRYN

THE HOUSE IS QUIET, uncharacteristically so. *Unnervingly* so. A hush of disharmony has been cast over the vast space. It should be bustling with people. Staff should be marching through with purpose; food and drinks leaving the kitchen continuously to satisfy the guests outside. Instead, it's empty. Mayhem is spilled through the open plan like it was placed on pause. Servers and cooks seemingly dismissed without warning, whatever they had been doing at that particular moment, left in limbo.

I stop, listening for voices, but I hear none.

Turning on high-heeled feet, I move toward my father's office with purpose.

"York," I call out as I approach.

He turns to me, appreciation in his beady little eyes.

Total. Creep.

"Where's Dad? It's time to cut the cake."

He clears his throat, straightening his shoulders in a show of importance.

Douche.

"He's busy."

My face screws up. "Yeah, no. It's Codi's wedding."

"He's with someone." He steps in front of me, cutting off my path as I move toward the door.

"Do yourself a favor, jackass, and move your ass out of my way."

He swallows in uncertainty. "It looked important, Camryn. He has two teenagers with him. I think they were snooping around the property."

I lift my hands in a who-fucking-cares gesture. "Cool story, bruh. *Move*."

He hesitates for a split-second before shifting out of my way, muttering, "I better not get fired."

I slip through my dad's office door without acknowledging York further. I honestly have no idea why my dad hired him. He is insufferable—some rich kid with a point to prove to his daddy.

"Everything okay?" I ask my dad, closing the door behind me.

My eyes slide over the two kids sitting on Dad's office couch. Their spines straighten with uncertainty, and I turn, giving them my full attention. The familiarity in their gray eyes forces my feet closer to them. "Holy shit," I speak before thinking. "You look so much like—"

"Camryn," my dad cuts me off. "We're in the middle of something."

"Codi wants to cut the cake," I offer distractedly, my eyes glued to the boy in confusion.

"That'll have to wait. I'm sorry. Can you please grab Rocco for me?"

"No need," Rocco's voice echoes behind me as he moves through the door. "You forgot to give me a guillotine and lighter." He closes the door behind him, Parker a step in front.

"Fuck me," Parker speaks first.

Why do movies pretend integral events unfold in slow motion? I wish that were true so I could take it *all* in. But it happens in fast forward. I'm caught between the look of utter bewilderment in Rocco's eyes and the rough accusation in Parker's tone. "You look exactly like me."

I don't know where to look.

He's right. This kid, who can't be much older than fifteen, is a picture of Parker with a reverse aging filter. Same dirty blonde hair and virulent jawline. Eyes so similar, they look plucked from Parker's face and placed into this random child's.

"And you're the spitting image of Lila." Rocco finally finds his voice, eyes trained on the young girl looking a little too entertained by the influx of people.

Parker inhales fiercely. "*Fuck.*"

"Who is Lila?" The girl's voice is like honey.

"Our mom," the boys answer in unison.

On recollection, they're right. She could be the woman in the photo that sits proudly on Rocco's mantel. Long blonde hair, wolf-like eyes not unlike her son's, and a smile of mischief and joy pulling at the side of her mouth.

"We shouldn't have come," the boy speaks, the potent regret in his voice too panicked to be comfortable. "Let's go." He turns to the girl, stretching out his hand.

She takes it without issue, holding on like a lifeline.

They're connected. A set. Inseparable. It's evident in the way they lean on one another, both physically and emotionally.

"How do you fit?" Parker steps forward, wholly lost to himself.

"That would be none of your concern, Shay," the boy spits, hate dripping from his tongue like a poison he doesn't want to touch.

"Jesse and Blake came to me out of appreciation," my father speaks, moving toward the kids cautiously.

Our heads all turn his way.

"They were raised by Marcus Dempsey. They told me they saw news footage of his demise and my subsequent arrest."

Rocco looks ready to explode, his fists clenching and releasing in time with his breaths, quick and sharp.

"You look like us," Parker says, working to understand. "How?"

"Don't know, don't care. We want nothing to do with any Shay."

Rocco steps forward, and the boy does the same, placing himself in front of the girl, warning in his stormy gray eyes.

"Are you siblings?" I finally speak, drawing the girl's attention.

The boy refuses to look away from Rocco.

"Yep. I'm Blake. This bristling hero is my twin brother, Jesse. He's a little intense." She rolls her eyes.

I smile. "Seems it runs in the family," I joke, hoping to put her at ease. "I'm Camryn Rein, Dominic's daughter. Parker here" —I point— "is my new brother-in-law, and Rocco is his brother."

"We know who they are," Jesse grits out, unimpressed by my introductions. "Monsters. Just like their fucking uncle."

"We're nothing like that piece of shit," Parker snaps. "Don't ever compare us to that scum."

Jesse narrows his eyes. "We'll be leaving now. Let's go, Blake."

"He told us you were dangerous," she ignores him. "He told us you would want us dead if you knew we existed. That he was our safest option."

"Marcus killed our mother and our aunt, who also happened to be his *wife*," Parker repels her argument with a fervor that sets the room on edge. "The only person ever dripping in blood was that asshole. He was evil."

"Well aware, Einstein." Jesse pulls at his sister's arm, working hard to get her to move.

"How'd you find yourself with Marcus?" Parker continues. "You can't be Lila's. Mira? Did Mira have kids we didn't know about?"

"No," Rocco answers stoically. "Their mother is Kendall Montgomery." His voice is vacant. An empty pool of misery he looks ready to drown in. His body visibly shakes.

Parker turns, questions in his eyes. "You knew?"

Rocco doesn't speak.

"Rocco knew Kendall was pregnant," Dominic answers for him.

"You never said anything," Parker accuses, hurt scoring across his face openly.

"Who is Kendall?" I ask.

No one answers.

"I—" Rocco's voice cracks. "She left a note saying she didn't want me. She told me she would rather die than give birth to something that was part of me, part of my family."

My heart cracks in my chest.

Rocco.

"You're our *dad*?" Blake asks, pushing past her twin brother to move closer to the blonde giant in the room.

Jesse grabs at her, but she shakes him off.

"How old are you?" I ask.

"Sixteen," they answer in unison.

"Where's your mother?"

Blake looks at Rocco like he's an artifact in a museum. Untouchable but beyond intriguing. "Dead."

"How?" Rocco looks in physical pain.

Someone else left me.

The idle statement he let go in his bathroom weeks earlier.

He meant Kendall. His ex-girlfriend. One he'd knocked up and has spent half of his life searching for.

He'd been searching for his family when I'd been dissecting our every interaction, certain feelings I'd never hoped to experience again were holding me hostage.

"Overdose," Jesse answers, the word almost too painful for him to speak.

My eyes blink closed in condolence.

These two kids have lived a life no person should—one of loss and betrayal, pain and mistruths. You can see it in their guarded, gray eyes. Older than their sixteen years, worn down and cynical about the world around them. Not that I blame them; while other kids their age were playing team sports and arguing with their parents about the injustice of their worlds, Jesse and Blake were fighting to survive.

Rocco shakes his head, rejecting their words. "Kendall was no junkie. It doesn't make sense."

"That's the only Kendall we knew," Blake rebukes. "You didn't know her anymore. Not after you blew a load and demanded she abort your illegitimate child."

"You asked her to do that?" Parker recoils.

"Of course I fucking did," Rocco yells unexpectedly. "I was nineteen and in no frame of mind to raise a fucking kid. It was an initial reaction when she told me. We fought. Then before we could talk it out, she disappeared."

"How convenient for you," Jesse barks out a humorless laugh.

"I *searched* for her. For *you*."

"To what? Make sure she followed through with your demands?"

"What? No. To make sure you were safe," Rocco argues, begging them to believe him. He's fraying at the edges. His composure is bursting with panic, ready to rip him apart.

"Well, we weren't," Blake vilifies, her soft sweet voice delivering the words like a dagger, making sure they maim. "We lived with the devil, and when we finally escaped that hell, we were forced to survive on the streets. I didn't know anything about you. About who you were or what you were like. I'd convinced myself you were dead."

I can't bring myself to look at Rocco, knowing the heaviness that he'd be loading himself with.

"Because if my dad were alive," she continues. "He would've found me. He would've found *us*. He would've rescued us from the wretchedness we were caught in."

"I tried," Rocco whispers. "Every fucking day. Kendall was a ghost. You... you were ghosts."

"That's where you disappeared to all those times?" Parker asks, the pain in his voice not dissimilar to his brother's.

"You didn't try hard enough." Jesse ignores his uncle, eyes scanning his sister's profile in concern.

That declaration hangs in the room like a grenade ready to explode. Destruction at the ready, mere milliseconds of panic as it flies through the air, ready to blow the final pieces of Rocco's heart to smithereens.

"He'd leave." Parker steps forward, gesturing for the siblings to sit, following suit after their asses reluctantly meet the couch once again. "For days on end. Sometimes weeks. He'd never tell me why, but I knew it was important. Important enough that he never stopped trying. It started seventeen years ago, I'm assuming while your mom was still pregnant, and it hasn't stopped."

He lets that sink in—a cold, hard truth neither of them was expecting. "You can drag our name through the mud," he offers vehemently. "It's not like it doesn't deserve it. The Shay name is fucking poison. We know that better than anyone. You can claim we didn't understand, but you're wrong. *We* lived with Dempsey too. He killed our fucking mom, took a gun to her head, and shot her. We were left with him and our piss weak excuse for a father, who wasn't much better. The only light we had left was our aunt, and he took her from us as well. You had it worse. There's no doubt. We had our mom until our teenage years. You didn't, not the way you should've. Not in the way I remember Kendall. But you can't say my brother didn't look for you."

Jesse and Blake look at one another, uncertainty dancing between them.

"Whenever he came up empty-handed, which was every fucking time, he'd throw himself into a ring. He'd let some fucker beat him for failing you. I didn't understand it. Now I do. Your dad looked for you; he searched high and fucking low. He *bled* for you. He lived for you all these years. Whatever Marcus Dempsey told you, it was a fucking lie."

"He's right." Codi's voice echoes the soft click of the office door. "Marcus Dempsey was a monster."

The twins stand as she steps into view.

"Your eyes," Blake breathes.

"Are his," Codi answers freely. "He and my mother had an affair, and I was the result—a child born of hate and disloyalty. I was lucky that this man" —she steps toward our dad, grabbing his arm, hugging him— "took on the role of my dad and never looked back. I found out Marcus was my father the day he died."

Jesse looks torn by the information being unloaded, his eyes looking at each of us, working to see deeper. Fighting to read lies in amongst the truths. "This is all too much to take in," he murmurs, the initial bite in his words lost to bewilderment. "Blake and I need time to think all this through. We came to thank Dominic for slaying a demon we couldn't and have found a family we were convinced we didn't want."

Quiet descends on the room, and no one is sure what to say or do.

"We have a *dad*." Jesse looks at Rocco in an ambivalent rapture. Not quite sure the man before him is real. More a figment of his imagination, one he'd dreamed of as a child but never let himself hope for as he matured by circumstance.

"It's too much all at once," he confesses, looking to his sister for support.

"Jesse looks like a cloned version of his uncle. I'm apparently the spitting image of my murdered grandmother. Our father looks as unhinged as Marcus promised he was, but also kind of sweet in the way he'd kill anyone that would hurt us, which is *so* confusing. Our uncle is also married to the daughter of the guy who forced us to grow up in purgatory all because he was all kinds of deranged. *Too much* is the understatement of the freaking century. We need to decompress."

"You can stay here," Dominic offers.

"That'll be a hard no." Blake smirks. "We've survived this long without handouts or help. We're good. But a bit of that food you had circling for Uncle Tattoo and his model wife here would be awesome."

"Please," Rocco begs of them, the desperation in his voice slicing across the room in heartache. "I don't expect you to accept an invitation to stay with me, and that's cool. But you came here with trust for Dominic. You were right. You can trust him. I promise you that. I'll leave if that's what you want," he grits out, hating himself for saying it. "But let Dominic give you a roof and food while you're sorting through this mind fuck."

Looking at one another, they share a silent conversation none of us are welcome in on. "We'd feel comfortable if you weren't here."

Ouch.

He hides the hurt their words cause him, dipping his chin once in understanding. "I'll be back tomorrow." Turning to my father, he nods. "You'll make sure they're comfortable?"

"Of course," Dominic assures him.

"It seems all hopeless right now." Rocco stuffs his hands in his pockets, unsure what to do with them. "But we'll work it out. I don't wanna frighten you, but I've searched my whole adult life for you. I'm not gonna let you go without a fight. You deserve that, someone to fight for you. That's me..." He trails off, swallowing against the lump in his throat. "You might not believe it, but... you're mine, which means my life is yours."

He walks out without another word, the power in his declaration left in the room like the aftermath of a wedding reception; messy and chaotic and overflowing with evidence that love is real. And it's confusing as fuck.

"I'll go with him," Parker offers, but I stop him with a hand on his arm.

"I will. He needs a friend right now. He'll feel like you need an explanation. One he's not ready to give you." I look at the twins. "My dad, Parker, and Codi have got you. Please don't leave before you give him a chance. He wouldn't recover... *please* give him a chance."

"Ryn," Codi calls after me as I step through the front door. "You sure you're up for this?"

I shrug. "I'm the only friend he's got, so as hard as it might be, it's my job to show up."

Looking back to the house, Codi nods in apprehension.

"You've got this, Codi." I read her reluctance. "They're just kids."

"They won't even look me in the eye," she laments.

I step closer, grabbing her shoulders. "They're scared, Codi. Looking into your eyes is like looking into the eyes of a monster that breathed fear into them all their lives. Tell them your story. Show them who you are."

Exhaling heavily, her eyes close with a nod.

"I'm sorry all this happened on your wedding day," I apologize. "You should be locked away with your husband celebrating."

"Are you kidding?" She looks at me like I'm crazy. "Rocco and Parker have a family we didn't know about. This is the greatest gift I could've asked for."

CHAPTER TWENTY-THREE

ROCCO

"MOVE."

She doesn't. Her feet remain stationary in front of my door, halting my exit.

"Where are you going?"

"Out," I grit, my nostrils flaring in a fit of anger I can scarcely contain. "*Move.*"

"Can't do that, Shay." She tips her head to the side, drinking me in. I know she's trying to read my inner thoughts. It's futile. It's a fucking tornado in there. Swirling around so fast I can't decide if I'm elated, petrified, insane, heartbroken, or just fucking incensed.

"You think you can stop me?"

Crossing her arms over her chest, she shrugs. "I can't imagine you'd put your hands on me, so, yeah, I do."

I growl, wanting to put my fist through a wall. "Fucking move," I bellow, the veins on my neck straining enough I can feel them protruding from my skin, bulging thick and blue, ready to burst.

She doesn't react. Not a flinch, barely a blink. "Where are you going?" she repeats, and I grab my hair, ripping at it roughly. My control is slipping with every second she stands in the way of what I need.

Pain.

"Where the fuck do you think I'm going?" I seethe, pacing in front of her like a wild animal, caged against my will. "I'm going to fight. I need to fight."

"No, you don't. You want to. There's a difference."

I inhale, my muscles aching with the need to be used. To be pushed. To be punished. My entire body is shaking. My emotions are bubbling under the surface with the energy I need to disperse.

"You should understand this," I snarl, pointing a finger at her in accusation. "More than anyone. You should get my need to do this."

"Okay." She steps away from the door. "But if you walk out, think about how you'd feel if this situation was reversed. Think about how you'd feel knowing I felt like slicing my thigh open with your razor blade. I will. I'll cope with my past with pain instead of talking to you about it. Instead of punching a bag or two to find my power."

I step forward, my hand on the door handle twitching in indecision. I open it, and the corridor mocks me in a way that makes me hate myself. Because I'm considering it. I'm considering walking out and not giving two fucking shits about the fact that she carves open her skin for relief.

"What do you want?" I slam the door, stalking toward her. "What the fuck do you want?" I roar. "You want to know that I need someone to beat the fucking shit out of me because it's what I deserve."

She flinches at the agony my words are laced in.

"I searched my whole life for her. And not because I fucking cared about her, but because she just fucking up and disappeared. I had no idea if she had my kid. I had no idea if a piece of me was out in this world without me. And now I find out I failed not just one but two of them. Twins. I have fucking twins, Camryn, and I'm such a giant fuck up, I couldn't save them." I want to vomit. Empty my insides in the hope that it'll offer me even a sliver of relief. "Me. Their dad. The one person who should always be around to protect them… failed them."

"You didn't know where they were."

I laugh. A sarcastic bubble of hate slicing between us. "It's not good enough, Camryn. They're sixteen. They've gone their whole life without feeling safe, and that's on me. They've been living on the fucking street." I don't even bother wiping away the tears that fall from my eyes.

She frowns, meeting my step backward with a forward one of her own. "Rocco, you need to stop blaming yourself for everything that goes wrong around you. The burden of the world isn't on your shoulders. Stop taking responsibility for its failures."

My back hits the wall, and I slide down it, my legs refusing to hold me up any longer. Knees bent, I drop my head between them—a complete and utter image of despondence.

"Talk to me, Rocco. Fucking lean on someone for once in your life."

She kneels in front of me, the palms of her hands pressed on my knees.

"They're why I fight," I confess.

"I know," she soothes.

"Kendall and I weren't in love. We were two messed up kids fucking around to make ourselves feel alive. I met her after my mom died. She was everything I was; broken and angry and full of hate. When we were together, it's one of only a few times in my life that I didn't feel so alone."

She squeezes my knee.

"I remember her clearly. More than I do my mother. Maybe my need to find her never let me forget her face. The ghostly white skin, the brown eyes that sat bitterly in her face. She was pretty, sure, but she was sad. Happily so. She didn't want to better her life. She was content in being miserable, in blaming the world for her shortcomings. She turned up at my place a few months after we started fucking. She was so messed up." I remember it with such clarity. The way her tears reddened her skin, making it blotchy with grief. The panic in her eyes. "She was crying and ranting about me being another stupid fucking mistake."

"She was pregnant."

I nod, my head dropping back against the wall.

"You asked her to abort your baby?"

I shake my head. "Not like that. I asked her what she wanted to do. Fuck, Cami. I'm not gonna lie, I wasn't ready to be a dad. I'd lost my mom. I was lost and hateful, and vengeful. Kendall sure as shit wasn't ready to be a mom either. I put the ball in her court, and she took that as me telling her I didn't want the baby."

"What happened?"

"Kane came outside to see what was going on. She got scared and ran. I told him what had happened, and he beat the shit outta me for being so stupid. He broke three of my ribs and split open my eye socket. I spent the night in the hospital and never saw Kendall again."

I've always hated sympathy and despised pity. It's always made me feel weak. But not with Camryn. There's a tenderness to the way she calls me out. An affinity in the way she listens.

"Do you think…" She trails off, too scared to vocalize what I now already know.

"That my father called his sick-son-of-a-bitch right hand and demanded he deal with my off-the-rails booty call? Yeah, I think that's exactly what happened. I just don't know why he didn't kill her straight away. Why keep her alive to have to raise her kid?"

"Knowledge is power, Rocco. He had something over you, whether you knew it or not. It made him feel like a king."

"I'd kill him," I vow, knowing it's all in vain. "If I could bring him back to life, I'd kill him. I'd make him pay, make sure he felt everything."

"The kids were the something that left you," she surmises. "Not Kendall."

She's thinking about our conversation in the bathroom. The one that stripped us bare and solidified a connection we're now sewn together by.

"I didn't realize they were a plural. But yeah, I've been searching for Kendall with the sole purpose of finding my kid."

I clear my throat, happy that Camryn still hasn't removed her hands from my knees. The warmth of her touch is grounding me. In a time when I thought all I needed was pain and violence, she became my beacon.

"I'm sad for Kendall," I tell her honestly. "But I hate her too, Cami. I fucking despise her. I'm so fucking furious that she let them live that life…"

Unwanted thoughts flood my mind as they've done for years. Only now, I know they're not fears. They're real. My kids weren't thriving. They weren't loved and cared for. They weren't protected. Like Parker and me, they've had to learn how to *survive*. When life should've been easy and carefree, they were fighting. They've struggled. They've had no one to lean on, save one another.

"I could've... I would've given them something better."

"Maybe," she counters.

"Maybe?" I feel wounded by her statement. Unsure of how to let go of the hurt, I drop my knees, no longer wanting her touch.

"You were angry for a long while, Rocco. You were ready to kill. You were what Kane and Marcus wanted you to be. You may not have been the right place for them either."

Fuck. Straight for the jugular. "Anyone ever tell you honesty isn't always the best option?"

Crossing her legs, she sits in front of me. "Is that what you want? Lies to make you feel even worse. Maybe their mom failed them, but that doesn't mean she didn't love them the best she could. Who knows what happened to have her become tangled in Marcus' web? All we know is that in the end, it was bad enough that she sought to escape the best way she knew how."

I swallow the bitter pill she all but shoved down my throat.

"They're forever scarred for whatever that asshole put them through, for what they saw with Kendall. I can't take that away. I don't have the power to fix it, to *fix* them."

I'm empty. The fight only minutes ago coursing through me has dissipated into nothing. Into numbness. I'm broken and tired.

"You don't fix them," she declares indignantly. "You make sure this next phase of their lives is a new world. One of love and acceptance. You show them there is no longer anything to fear."

My eyes sting. My heart aches.

"You're one hundred percent right; you can't take away their past. But the scars of yesterday aren't ugly scrapes on our souls that will forever mar us as imperfect. They're survival wounds, Rocco, for which we've fought tooth and nail. Scars are perfect, no matter how unsightly they look. Your kids are strong. They're survivors. Exactly like you and Parker."

"How do you do it?" I ask.

"Do what?"

"Pull my guard down before I've realized. Make me show you my insides without my permission. I give you everything. I give you all of me... all before I've realized it's happened."

She moves to speak, but I cut her off.

"Tell me it's not just me. Tell me I give it to you too. Tell me I'm not the only one leaning here, begging for something I didn't even know I wanted."

"You give it to me, too," she admits almost shyly. "Likely more. I share the deepest parts of myself, daring you to look away. But you don't. You move closer."

I realize at that moment, there's something sacred about bearing yourself completely to another. Something jarring. You're jumping off a cliff, hoping, praying someone will catch you before you hit the ground.

This is it. Me. In the flesh. Ready to run yet?

CHAPTER TWENTY-FOUR

CAMRYN

I WAKE, mentally spent, my head still reeling from yesterday.

Rocco is a dad.

Rocco Shay.

Has *twins*.

My temples pound, and I stand before I'm tempted to pull a cushion over my face and suffocate myself.

His apartment is quiet. The sterile silence is welcome after the deep conversation we dug ourselves into last night. We took a hammer to Rocco's emotions. We cracked open a box he'd kept sealed away with the power of a million padlocks.

Searching through his kitchen, I open the cupboards, disappointed to find zero chocolate. I make a note to bring a stash to hide away next time to save myself this disappointment again.

Moving to the fridge, I glance through the greenery on the shelves, grimacing over the thought of eating whatever the fuck it all is. Settling on a carton of juice in the door, I pop the opening, glancing over my shoulder to make sure I'm alone before drinking straight from the cardboard.

"That's fucking disgusting."

I freeze, orange juice still on my lips, carton balancing in the same spot.

Sleepy Rocco has an incredibly rough voice. One that creeps across your skin like whispered promises of things I shouldn't want.

"In my defense, I was doing you a favor." I turn, closing the juice carton. "Firstly, your kitchen is so clean I felt wrong dirtying a glass. Second, surely this has too much sugar for you. I was ridding its poison from your life."

Sleepy Rocco also has super hooded eyes that trail along my body in a way that also makes me think of things I shouldn't crave.

"Sleep well?" I change the subject, hoping like hell my thoughts aren't dusted across my cheekbones in a blush I can't hide.

"Not a wink."

"Want coffee?"

He nods, moving into the kitchen in long, lazy strides. "You sit. I'll make it. Coffee is too important to me to have you fuck it up."

I roll my eyes, trying my hardest not to sniff him as I walk past him to see how sleepy Rocco smells.

"You?" he grunts out.

Moving into the living room, I sit, legs out along the cushions, my front pushed to the back to ensure I can still see him.

"Meh," I answer non-committedly. "Your couch, as comfy as it is to sit on, sucks as a bed."

"Could'a used Parker's."

"Eww." I scrunch up my nose. "He and Codi have done unmentionable things in that bed."

"Could'a just crashed in my bed with me."

I bite my tongue, unsure of how to respond.

Sleeping in a bed with Rocco Shay. It doesn't repulse me as much as it should. In fact, the thought alone is enough to kickstart something deep in my stomach that excites and scares me.

"As long as you don't snore," he jokes, saving me from my awkwardness.

"I absolutely do not snore. I don't think," I add as an afterthought. "Not that it matters," I rush out. "I am not sleeping in your bed with you."

His shoulders lift in dismissal. "Your loss. I'm cuddly as shit."

"Cuddly as shit isn't exactly appealing."

A soft smirk pulls along his face, and his long strides bring him closer to me, coffee in hand. And look, I'm woman enough to admit that Rocco Shay, shirtless and sleepy, bringing me coffee isn't the worst way to spend my morning.

"Did you put sugar in this?" I eye him suspiciously.

Sitting on the coffee table across from me, he nods. "Sure."

"Lies." I inhale the rich aroma, eyes closing in pleasure.

"Just fucking drink it."

Watching him over the rim of my mug, I drink him in as I sip the smooth liquid. The perfect mixture of bitterness and sweetness explodes along my tastebuds in the promise of a good fucking day.

A small moan falls from my lips. That first taste of morning coffee like taking my first breath.

Rocco's eyes zero in on my lips, watching as I lick them, savoring that first drop.

I watch him, watch my mouth, the silver of his irises deepening with every second that passes. Coffee, forgotten in my hand, plays second fiddle to the violent need staring at me from the imposing man in front of me.

Desire is a funny thing. The amplified yearning for another person that settles within your body. An overwhelming feeling that is built solely around attraction and anticipation. The belief in your mind crackles like a bonfire, burning through you with the promise of pleasure only *that* person can bring you.

Not just any person. Him. *Rocco*.

Before I've realized he's moved, he extracts my coffee from my grasp, placing it on the coffee table he sat atop seconds ago.

Settling in front of me, he offers me the power of position. I'm above him, looking down on him in expectation.

"I see how you look at me, Cami," he tells me quietly. "The lazy want in your pretty blue eyes. The color that hits the top of your cheekbones when you're thinking about all the things you want me to do to you. You want me to fuck you," he states, arms stretching out behind him, palms pressing into the soft carpet of his living room.

I don't dispute his words. Even though I should. I will myself to laugh in his face, to tell him he's delusional. But he's right. Denying his statement would only make me look like a fool. I know I should feel shame. That I should be disgraced and disgusted at myself for letting myself want him. But I can't. Because rejecting what I genuinely feel seems hopeless at this point.

I seek him out more than any other person in my life. I'm a stronger person when I'm around him. Rocco Shay has sparked something inside of me, something I long thought dead. Attempting to deny that would be like extinguishing my own flame. And I'm selfish enough to admit I don't want to do that.

"The thing is, Cami," he sighs. "I'm not interested."

Embarrassment fists itself around my heart. I attempt to swallow it down but find myself choking on it instead. I clear my throat, unsure of what to say or how to act. I shift in my seat, wanting nothing more than to flee his space. Would he let me leave with my dignity? Would he let me walk from his home and pretend he didn't just cut me with a heavily serrated knife of disregard?

He watches my humiliation in unaffected silence.

"I need more," he finally adds. The words are barely audible, so quietly spoken I can scarcely hear them over the heavy drum of my heart.

"More?" I ask stupidly.

"More," he concurs.

I blink, and the fist around my heart eases its grip, letting it run away with the thundering rhythm of uncertainty.

"I never imagined I'd want someone to call my own," he confesses. "Have someone that fed my obsession and was borderline psychotic in their need to possess my heart in the same way. Truth be told, I questioned the existence of an actual heart inside my body. Shocks me to admit it's there, and it's just as crazy as the rest of me."

Silence settles between us.

"For you," he murmurs. "It's fucking head over ass crazy *for you*."

"Me?" I ask, dumbfounded.

That makes him smirk. "Yeah, beauty." He shifts closer. "Do I want to fuck you? More than anything. I want to possess every inch of your beautiful body. I want to bury my cock so deep inside of you that there isn't a single part of your body I haven't claimed. I want to own you the way you unknowingly own me."

I stare. He shifts closer once again until he's kneeling between my legs.

"Question is, what do *you* want? Because if it's just a quick hard fuck when you feel in the mood, my answer is no."

He reaches up, swiping his thumb against the collection of freckles that decorate the bridge of my nose and cheeks.

"I can't seem to read you, Rein. Do me a solid and tell me what you feel?" he asks, the palm of his hand wrapped tightly around my forearm, keeping me close.

"About what?"

His eyes bore into mine, pools of gray that never seem to end. Eyes that I forever want to become lost in.

"About me," he murmurs.

My throat tightens, the intensity of his gaze cutting off my ability to breathe.

"My heart and my brain are at war," I whisper. "I'm broken."

"You're perfect," he combats quietly.

"And you're broken," I continue.

"We're both broken, but together all our fractured pieces, they make a beautiful fucking whole, Cami."

I bite my lip to stop the wobble in my chin, my eyes squeezing shut as I nod quickly.

"My heart is screaming for you," I confess. "But my mind won't let me forget everything you've done. The damage you tried to inflict. Every time I think I've silenced the power in its voice, it rears its ugly head, making me believe I should still hate you."

He watches me in understanding.

"Tell me you regret it. Tell me it was all a mistake, Rocco. Make me believe you," I beg, pulling my arm free of his grasp to cup his face.

His nostrils flare, panic painted openly across his features. "I can't," he insists. "I can't do that."

The wet line of my lashes brush along my sockets. My tears fall in heartache.

"I can tell you I'm sorry that I had so much hate inside me. I welcomed it spreading like cancer. I can tell you I'm sorry that my stupidity hurt so many people. I can tell you that losing Mira sliced away a piece of my heart that I'm never getting back. I can tell you I'm sorry," he declares. "But regret it... no. I can't do that."

My eyebrows, pulled together in confusion, ease with the touch of his thumb brushing down my forehead.

My hands fall away from his face, and I see the hurt that causes him.

"I don't regret Marcus dying," he argues, more to himself than to me. "I don't regret Codi and Parker finding love in the hopeless situation I created."

He watches me quietly for a beat, shifting closer so that when he breathes in, his chest touches mine. "I don't regret finding the best friend I've ever had," he admits, his words a quiet promise. "I don't regret loving her harder than I've ever loved anything or anyone in my whole life."

He pauses, choosing his words carefully. "Which is saying a lot, considering I was ready to kill for my mom. There's no limit to what I'd do to protect you, beauty. No fucking limit. It scares the shit outta me."

My nose stings, and my eyes ache as I attempt to hold back my tears.

"How can I regret the reasoning behind finding myself in someone else? Something I never thought would happen to me. Tell me, beauty, how the fuck do I regret that?"

I lean forward, wanting to feel his lips against mine. Wanting my lips to decide if I've forgiven him because I no longer trust the war inside me.

He grabs my jaw, stopping me before our lips connect. "Are we doing this? Because I'm not interested in just a taste."

I hesitate. "You love me?" I test, shocked and confused that someone with a heart as dark as Rocco's could find itself able to beat for another. More, that my cold, splintered heart could do the same.

He laughs. "Baby, love isn't a strong enough word for what I feel for you. I love Parker. I fucking *bleed* for you. My heart only started beating again when you saved it from giving out."

Warm, fresh tears fall from my eyes, dropping along my cheeks.

Barely a breath from my eager lips, he whispers, "And I think you feel the same for me, too. I need to know if your love for me is loud enough to drown out those doubts that are keeping you just outta my reach."

I answer him with a kiss. A push of my salty lips against his. He kisses me back without hesitation. His large palm fisted into my hair to deepen our touch.

There's a desperation in the way his mouth moves over mine. In the way his tongue swipes into my mouth, dragging against mine in thick, wet caresses.

It's not a pretty kiss. No soft moans of pleasure or teasing flicks of a tongue. It's messy and chaotic and altogether frantic. Longing exploding in our faces in our need to be as close as possible.

Ass sliding to the edge of the couch, my thighs press against his obliques. I swallow his rough groan, drinking it down like it's only ever been mine. Like no one else has ever heard the ragged sound of need breaking from his eager lips.

Palm pressed into my spine, he lifts me from the couch, sliding backward. His ass to the carpet, my legs remain stuck to his sides, letting us feel his potent want thickening against my core.

His kiss, unbreaking, only intensifies as the seconds tick by. There's an agony in the way he kisses me. An endeavor on his lips. A silent prayer sealed in the fusion of our mouths.

Love me, he asks. He begs. He pleads.

Harder, he urges.

Completely, he burns.

Who am I to deny him?

Tearing my lips from his, I let the promise in my eyes bore into his.

"Are you sure?" I ask, pressing my forehead to his. "About this. About us. You've just discovered you're a dad. You have teenage twins, Rocco. Do you need this complication?"

Inhaling heavily, he shakes his head, our skin still touching. "You're the one thing in my life I *am* sure about. The best part of each day is you, beauty. You settle me," he concedes. "You've become the best part of me."

"*Rocco*," I whisper.

"With you, I no longer have to hide the hideous parts of who I am," he admits, almost hesitantly. "You make me believe you love those parts too... all the ugly."

I want to cry. I want to grab his hand and force it into my chest so he can feel what he does to me. "I don't love your ugly parts," I whisper.

His eyes flash in understanding, in a defeat that weakens his valor.

"I don't love your ugly parts because they don't exist, Rocco. Every wretched thing you've done has been done through love. That's not ugly, baby. It's beautiful. You're beautiful. You're everything to me, and I love every part of you. There's no ugly, not to me."

It's taken me almost too long to recognize that. I pinned him as an unhinged psychopath, refusing to see his purpose. Rocco Shay, unbeknownst to everyone, might very well be the most devoted human being I've ever known. Lawless, sure. A chaotic devotion drives him. He's possessed by a love so fierce it's read as hate.

Talk about poetic. This striking man has been reared by the most hateful of souls, judged by the rest of us, and for what, loving too hard?

My hands frame his face, and I look into his eyes. "I'd bleed for you too. I poured so much effort into hating you that you bulldozed your way into my heart without me noticing. Without either of us noticing." We smile. "Rocco, you showed me how to love myself. You gave me something I thought was lost. You let me be free."

CHAPTER TWENTY-FIVE

ROCCO

I HOLD HANDS.

Who would've thought?

But driving to her father's house, ready to face the scorn of the two people I've dedicated my life to finding, Camryn's hand resting comfortably in mine, I feel centered.

So, yeah… I hold fucking hands.

As if reading my thoughts, she squeezes my palm. "How are you feeling?"

Taking my eyes off the road for a second, I glance in her direction. "I don't know," I tell her honestly. "I don't know how to navigate this shitty situation. I want them to accept that I'm their dad, but they have every right not to."

"You're scared," she deducts.

Scared. "Fuck, beauty. I'm petrified."

"That's good," she tells me. "Love is scary. You love them. You want it to work out."

Lifting her hand to my mouth, I press my lips to her knuckles.

Love isn't just scary. It's a catastrophe waiting to happen. It's a constant test the universe enjoys throwing at you, measuring your commitment to the feeling, waiting for you to fuck up. If my life has taught me anything, it's that. My mother. My kids. Mira. Shit, even Kane. The most important people in my life and my love for them have been pushed to their limit. Time and time again. The problem is, more often than not, I fail.

We walk into Rein's home hand-in-hand. My feet a step ahead of hers, daring someone to comment. Maybe I should've checked whether she was ready to divulge our new status to her family, but I didn't want to give her the option to back away from me.

I told her that.

All. In.

I've given her everything. I'm not interested in taking steps backward.

Blake sits at the breakfast bar, Dominic cooking bacon and eggs as she chats away eagerly. Her face lights up as she speaks, her hands moving in quick, excited movements to emphasize her story.

She reminds me of Lila. The soft chuckle that trails off as she laughs. The wide, infectious smile that stretches over the entirety of her face, crinkling her eyes, carving small dimples into her cheeks, showing her slightly crooked teeth.

It gives me pause.

I have a daughter.

One my mother will never meet.

A miniature version of her that she would've adored on sight.

The smell of their breakfast drifts through the house, making my stomach rumble. It's loud enough to hear, alerting them to our presence.

Blake's voice cuts off immediately, eyes darting to me in uncertainty, her smile disappearing almost immediately, replaced with a thin line of caution.

I hate that she was comfortable alone in Dominic's company. A stranger. One that owes her nothing. But I stand a few feet away, her father, and she shuts down.

"Hi," she tests after an awkward beat of silence.

"Morning," I respond. "Sleep okay?"

"Dad," Camryn interrupts. "Let's, uh, check on that thing you wanted to show me."

My eyes close with a sigh. "Smooth, Cami."

"Yes." Dominic places his spatula down stiffly. "That thing, good idea."

Blake and I watch them disappear, their quick-moving feet only slightly more awkward than their made-up escape.

"They're, uh, graceful."

I smile. "Wanna walk out back?"

Jumping from the stool, she nods. "Sure."

"Where's your brother?"

"Sleeping." Her face softens at his mention, the love shared between the two of them enough to chip away at a small cluster of my guilt for leaving them without family for too long. In reality, they weren't alone, and from experience, it makes a world of fucking difference.

"He has nightmares," she tells me openly. "They can be pretty bad. He crashes out pretty heavily after really awful nights."

"Nightmares are something I have a lot of experience with."

Neck twisted to scan my profile, she nods in understanding. "I see that."

We sigh at the same time.

"I'm not really sure how to navigate this whole situation," I say.

"The situation being Jesse and me?" she tests hotly.

"The situation being I'm a dad with two teenagers who have been conditioned to hate me."

"We don't hate you," she whispers, her hand brushing across the foliage of a plant as we move past it. "We've just spent sixteen years only having one another to lean on. You may be our biological father, Rocco, but you're a stranger."

That reality burns my throat.

"Can you tell me about you?" I ask.

There's a dismissal in the way she shrugs. "There's not much to tell. I'm a happy loner. My brother is my best friend. I like to think of myself as a good human being. In saying that, I've stolen, lied, and cheated to survive."

Her feet stop at the base of a large tree in the backyard, her neck tipping back to take it in. "I have this obsession with sitcoms. The canned laughter and idiotic jokes. They make me laugh." She smiles at me when she says that. A beautiful grin that reminds me so much of my mother. It lightens my heart in the same way it causes it pain. "It used to make me feel as though the world can't be that bad of a place if people like me could see the humor in a joke like someone riding in their private plane did."

She circles the base of the tree, and I follow. "I fell out of a tree like this once. I was hiding from Marcus. I broke my arm, and Mom was too out of it to take me to the hospital. Jesse and I had to find our own way there," she muses.

"How old were you?"

Looking at me over her shoulder, she pauses, considering not telling me. "Eight."

"Jesus." I scratch at my beard.

She laughs. "It was an adventure. They *obviously* called child services, but not before they'd put my arm in a cast. We hightailed it out of there when they weren't looking before they could take us away from one another."

She recites the memory with a fondness that stabs at my conscience.

"Don't look so murderous," she sighs, her big eyes rolling to exaggerate her distaste at my self-pity. "I survived. I'm alive. I'm happy-ish."

"Blake—" I start, but she cuts me off.

"I'm not going to lie to you, Rocco. I want to know you. But my brother is more important than my need for a family that may or may not work out."

I stare at her, unblinking, unsure of what she's trying to say.

"If he wants to leave and never see you again..." she offers apologetically.

"You'll never see me again."

Refusing to look at me, she nods her head. "I like knowing you exist, though."

"Tell me how to make it work," I beg quietly. "Tell me how I get him to want to know me too."

"This house is ridiculous. Do you live in a house this big?"

Hands stuffed in my pocket, I shake my head. "I can take the two of you to show you? I have a picture of Lila. My mother." I sound pathetic, a street dog waiting for scraps. But if scraps are all they want to give me right now, I'll fucking take them.

The eagerness in her eyes flashes openly, firing my hope. "The one I look like?"

"Blake!"

Spinning on her heel, she waves at her brother enthusiastically. "Morning, sunshine."

Stalking toward us, he frowns against the sun.

"You show him you give a shit," she whispers. "Jesse is the best person I know, but he trusts no one. Not even me. We've been screwed over our entire lives. That's where his expectation now sits. You change that, and he'll stay."

Fuck. No pressure.

"Morning," I murmur, and he echoes the sentiment with a quick jerk of his chin.

Playing with his hair, Blake turns her back to me. "Rocco invited us to check out his home," she tells him quietly. "Show us some photos of our family."

Jesse's eyes never waver from mine, the intensity unwelcome on a teenage boy.

"Sure," he finally agrees.

I expected an argument—a decisive and unmovable no.

"You're the best," Blake sings.

THEY WALK into my loft with hesitant steps. Feeling as unwelcome as I am uncomfortable.

"It's so, uh... homely," Blake jokes impassively.

"Parker moved out a few months back."

"Took all the character with him, I see," she retorts.

"Blake," Jesse reprimands miserably.

"What?" she quips. "It's like a show home. I feel my mere presence is unsanitary."

A first good impression. Failure, a million. Rocco, zero.

"I like order. Cleanliness. It makes me feel..."

"In control," Jesse offers distractedly, eyeing my gym setup earnestly.

I should've let Camryn come with me. She offered, and I told her it was something I needed to do alone. Now I'm regretting it. I have zero idea what to talk to them about or how to put them at ease.

"You look fit." I look Jesse up and down.

He's tall. Even at sixteen, he doesn't stand much shorter than Parker and me. The kid's got broad shoulders, but he's too skinny; bones sticking out where there should be muscle.

"Nice try." He barks out a laugh. Not exactly humored, but not entirely sarcastic either. "I'm a weed."

"So was Park at your age," I assure him. "Some good food, a few sessions training your muscles, and you'll see some positive growth."

"Are you a personal trainer?" he asks. "For work?"

Walking from the gym, he assumes I'll follow, which I do. "Nah. Parker and I own a club."

"And you work with Dominic?" he tests.

My shoulders lift non-committedly.

They're not stupid. They know Dominic's line of work, which means they know I'm not exactly a stand-up citizen.

"Is this her?" Blake interrupts. "Lila."

Glancing up, the photo of Parker, mom, and I held in her hands, she looks to me for confirmation. "That's Lila," I cough out. "My mom... your grandmother."

"She's beautiful," she sighs.

"She looks like you."

Her smile touches my face, but my eyes are on the photo.

Fuck, what I'd give for my mother to have met them. For her to look at them and know I created something worthwhile.

"What was she like?"

Scratching at my beard, I look away, unable to look them in the eye and talk about Lila at the same time. "She was the best person I've ever known. She was kind and funny and giving."

"Why'd he kill her?" Jesse interrupts. "Marcus? Why did he kill her?"

This was the last thing I wanted to talk to them about. I didn't want to spend the first, and possibly, my last bit of time with my kids talking about death and the implosion of my family.

But they deserved the truth.

"Marcus was having an affair with Sarah Rein."

They shift uneasily.

"You've met her," I surmise.

"Unfortunately," Jesse mutters.

I look to Blake for confirmation, but she looks away, unfazed by my curious gaze.

"He knocked her up, and my mother found out," I continue when she gives me nothing. "Sarah was feeding dodgy intel to Marcus about Rein's business. Marcus freaked about Kane—my dad—finding out, so he and Sarah killed her."

Confusion settles across their faces.

"Why didn't Kane retaliate?" Blake places the frame neatly back on my mantel.

I gesture for them to sit down, only doing the same after they've settled. "He didn't know. He thought Dominic was responsible. He spent the three years before he died plotting his revenge."

"And Parker just married Codi?"

I nod. "I took on Dad's revenge. I wanted to hurt Dominic. My plan to do so involved hurting Codi." I feel sick. "Parker fell in love with her instead. Everything went sideways, and we found out the real story. My aunt Mira died in the fallout, Dominic killed Marcus, and the world kept turning."

They watch me with wide eyes.

"I'm telling you this because I want you to know that I've done some seriously shitty things in my life—unforgivable things. I'm not the greatest role model. I'm not sure I ever will be. But I promise you I'll try. I want you both in my life. I want to be a father figure. I want us to build the relationship we should've always had. But, if that's too much to ask of you, I'll take a relationship in whatever capacity you will consider. You've never had anyone in your corner fighting for you. I understand that." I implore them to believe me. "You have me right beside you now. And Parker, Cami, Codi, and Dominic. You have a family, whether you're interested in it or not."

Standing abruptly, Jesse rolls his shoulders. "Can I use your bathroom?"

I scared him. Or he thinks I'm full of hot air, spilling shit that I think he wants to hear.

"My ensuite is down the hall, on the right."

He leaves the room without another word.

"Nice speech."

I move my gaze to my daughter. Her body is settled comfortably into my couch, her arms crossed against her chest, one leg crossed across the other, kicking back and forth.

"Wasn't a speech."

"Mmm," she dismisses me. "Do you have any food? I'm starving."

"Thought we could go out for lunch?"

"Sounds good to me." She stands, strolling into my kitchen lazily to open my cupboards.

Shaking my head, I move down the small hall toward my bedroom.

Jesse, head bent down, hand rifling through my side table, doesn't hear me approach.

"Anyone ever tell you it's rude to snoop?"

Standing quickly, he turns, slamming the drawer shut. "Just trying to get a better read on who you are."

He's not in the slightest bit apologetic, and I respect the hell outta him for it. I'd lose my head if anyone else was going through my shit. I'd be fucking furious about my privacy being violated in that way. But the truth is, if the situation were reversed, I'd be doing the same thing.

"Sit." I gesture to my bed.

He drops his gaze to the comforter, then back up. "I'd rather stand."

"Please," I exhale.

Shifting forward, he sits along the edge, his reluctance making his movement jerky.

"Kid," I start. "I don't want us to fuck this up before we've even had a chance. I know you owe me nothing."

Palm pressing against a closed fist, he cracks his knuckles, refusing to look at me.

"But I owe you patience and understanding and a whole lot fucking more. I won't stand for you coming into my home and sneaking around. If you want to know something, Jesse, ask me. If you need something, it's yours. You don't need to steal from me."

Teeth grabbing his bottom lip, he rolls it back and forth.

"Blake wants to start staying here," he says. "Instead of Dominic's," he clarifies unnecessarily. "I want you to say no."

"I can't do that," I deny him. "I could, but I won't. If you belong anywhere, it's with me. You're a Shay, Jesse, not a fucking Rein."

CHAPTER TWENTY-SIX

CAMRYN

"You need to sit down before you wear a hole in the floor."

He stops the constant pacing of his bedroom, glancing at me and then back to the door.

"I offered to buy him a bed, but he refused," he tells me for the millionth time. "He's sleeping on the floor at the foot of *her* new bed."

"It's very sweet, Rocco," I assure him. "He's being protective. They're in a new place. Let them settle the best way they know how."

Throwing himself back onto his bed, I bounce at the way his large frame shakes the mattress.

"I'm gonna suck so fucking bad at this," he groans, palms pressed into his eye sockets. "At least when you fuck up when they're babies, they don't know. Two sketchy-as-shit-on-me teenagers will hang me out to dry the first opportunity they get."

"First of all," I combat. "Give them some credit. They're not expecting the world. Secondly, who says you're going to fuck up?"

Pulling his hands away, he tips his head backward, looking at me upside down. "Me."

"You know who sucks at parenting?"

He remains silent.

"People who *don't want* to be parents. I have no doubt you'll make mistakes along the way, but that doesn't take away your parent card,

Shay. You panicking about it makes you a better parent than you already realize. Take it as it comes."

Pushing his body upright, his elbows rest on his knees. "I caught Jesse going through my shit today."

I frown, removing it from my face before he looks at me. "He's sixteen. He's used to hustling to survive. You didn't go all Rocco on him, did you?"

That makes him laugh. "What the fuck is that supposed to mean?"

"Did your head start spinning around on your neck? Did you rip your shirt open and bang on your chest like an animal ready to attack?"

"No," he bites out defensively. "We had a fucking conversation."

Arms crossing over my chest in awe, I smile wide. "Look at you being a dad."

Moving to his feet, he grabs my ankle, pulling me down the bed. I squeal, the sound echoing through the room.

"Shh." He laughs lightly, hand cupping my mouth to cut off the sound.

I lick his hand.

"Didn't realize the whole daddy thing would make you hot." He releases my mouth, grinning down at me.

Palm to his face, I push him away. "Gross."

"Distract me for a bit?" His mouth moves to my neck, his teeth skating across the delicate skin tenderly.

Tenderly. Never a word I'd associate with Rocco Shay, but here we are.

Hands to his cheeks, I pull his face to mine, letting my mouth find his.

He's overwhelmed and elated but so far down a tunnel of self-doubt that he can't see straight. He's geared himself up for failure. Anyone can see that. He's afraid to get too close but petrified of keeping his distance.

Patience isn't a virtue Rocco holds in spades. But it's a quality he knows he'll have to embrace if he wants to build a lasting relationship with his children.

He spent the day with them, working to connect in any small way. They're a closed fucking book, though. Their feelings, thoughts, and, dare I say, motives are indecipherable. All I managed to pull out of him was that for every step forward, it felt like a falling elevator back down when he'd stumble.

It's now eleven pm, and after a cumbersome dinner that we clawed through, the twins finally crashed out. This is the first time we've been alone since this morning. Since the moment we promised *all in*, sealing it with a kiss I won't soon forget.

I have my doubts that he's ready to commit to something so significant with everything he has going on, but he seems resolute in his declaration.

He told me he loved me, and maybe I'll be left brokenhearted in the end, but I believe him.

I've avoided relationships since Jonathan for obvious reasons. Trust wasn't high on my gift list to others. I was afraid and rightfully cautious. I've *slept* with men since Jonathan. I forced myself to claim back my body in the way that *I* wanted, but I could never lose myself enough in the moment to get out of my head. I let men fuck me for the sake of doing so. I pushed myself to open my legs to prove I could. I didn't necessarily enjoy it. But I did it. I used faceless men to erase his hold over me.

Then my feelings for Rocco sparked. Burst to life with butterflies in my stomach and a *want* to touch him. I longed for him to look at me with desire in his eyes. No matter how much I initially rejected the thought. I wanted his hands on me, caressing my skin, breaking down my walls. I no longer needed to *force* my legs open; they craved to wrap around him, to feel the strength of his waist between them.

I'm giddy over Rocco Shay. *Jesus.* I was never this person. Before Jonathan and after. I was never gaga about sex. I enjoyed it, sure, but it was never powerful enough to scatter my brain.

Rocco shot through me like a surprise I wasn't ready for. The person I've learned he is, is healing my heart and mind in a way I didn't know was possible. Now my body wants him to do the same. I need the passion he holds for me to heal my wounds. I was done with being lonely. I hadn't realized it until Rocco stumbled into my life, showing me the beauty of a broken soul.

The rough brush of his beard tickles my mouth as he kisses me.

Lips softer than I imagined. Our tongues push together in tender strokes.

A lump in my throat forms, my emotions wreaking havoc within me. He tastes like freedom, lips closing over mine in the promise of safety.

I'm ashamed to admit that I made assumptions about Rocco. I judged his appearance and decided he'd be a pushy lover. One that would be consumed by his own pleasure.

I was wrong.

Hands, large enough to swallow my throat, remain planted against the mattress by my head. The weight of his body, heavy enough to pin me down, remains suspended above me. I'm pleasantly possessed with only his lips and tongue drifting across mine. Brazenly adored.

As lost to the moment as I am, he groans into my mouth. The rough burr shoots desire through my body, the feeling exploding wickedly at the apex of my thighs.

This is how it should feel.

I moan, hands twisting into the soft cotton of his shirt, pulling him closer. He fights me, pushing himself up higher, almost out of reach. My mouth chases his, neck arched uncomfortably to ensure he can't disconnect.

Yanking at his shirt again, he laughs into my mouth.

"Stop it."

Breaking our kiss, I look at him in confusion.

Eyes focused on the swell of my well-kissed lips, he growls. "I'm not gonna touch you, Cami," he tells me, his voice rougher than I've ever heard. Thick with the hunger he's refusing to give into. "Not until you're ready."

Pushing my elbows up beneath me, I kiss his jaw. "Who says I'm not ready?"

"I do."

Teeth gnawing at my lip in indecision, I pressure my voice to speak. "How will you know I'm ready?"

Dropping his mouth to my ear, his tongue caresses my lobe, pulling it between his teeth. "You'll beg me."

I laugh, the sound wholly lost to the moan I let out as his lips drift across my neck. "Beg you?" I whimper.

"Yeah, beauty. You'll *beg* for my cock." He sucks on the delicate line of my neck hard enough that I know it'll leave a mark. "You'll plead with me to put you out of your misery and make you come. You'll walk around with damp panties for *days, weeks* before I'll give it to you. You'll move past the juvenile feeling of want and into a desperation only I'll be able to cure."

Lifting his head, a salacious smirk tips his lips upward. "That's when I know you'll be ready."

"But..." I argue meekly.

"But what?"

How do I tell him I need him now? My body is buzzing in a way I haven't felt in *years*. I don't want to lose that. I want to grab hold and let it be mine.

"You want to be touched?" he murmurs. "You're wet for me now?" He presses, his tone begging me to say yes.

I nod, my voice unable to find its power.

"So touch yourself."

He shifts backward, taking my hand to cup it over my pussy through my pants.

I cry out in pleasure, the simple thrill of my hand gripping me sending tremors through my body.

"In front of you?" I swallow, unable to remove my hand. The feeling too addictive, too gratifying to stop.

"Yes," he answers coarsely.

"You wanna watch?" I ask hesitantly.

"I'd kill a man to watch, beauty. You want me to watch?"

I don't need to think about it. "Yes."

Head tipped back, he growls at the ceiling.

Palm rubbing across his jaw, he rights his head, watching me. There's something about lust that changes someone's eyes. The way their eyelids drop, heavy and hypnotic. The change in color, the darkening that promises a carnality you're not entirely used to.

"I'm gonna stand against the wall," he husks out. "Control my hands reaching for you."

"No," I rush out. "No," I repeat more calmly. "Stay close. I want you to do it too. Touch yourself for me, Rocco."

His hand falls to his crotch, his large hand gripping it tightly—the generous bulge of his Adam's apple slides up and down the line of his throat.

"Please," I beg.

He says nothing, watching me in silence.

Unable to stand the quiet any longer, my hands grip the waist of my lounge pants, and I tip my hips upward, sliding them over my ass and down my legs before I can second-guess myself.

His hands move on their own accord, yanking at his belt in haste.

All the while, his eyes refuse to leave mine.

Naked from the waist down, I bend my knees, sliding my feet outward, opening myself up to him. A sacrificial lamb presented for the slaughter. My predator too beautiful to be good for me.

Cool air hits the warmth of my center. Anticipation buzzes through my veins, expending itself in a pleasant trickle of wetness dripping from my pussy down the crack of my ass.

Sucking two fingers in my mouth, I trail them down my body slowly, pussy throbbing in foretaste as they move toward the tight knot of my clit. I rub myself in soft circles, moaning loudly.

"Look what you do to me," Rocco bites out, the words breaking off on a pained groan as he squeezes his hand around his length, pulling it from the confines of his pants.

My hand moves faster, my body shaking in titillation. I'm numb and oversensitive, and rapacious all at once. I want to come. I want to hold out. I want to *scream*.

"Inside," Rocco commands, and I follow his instruction, surprised at the ease with which I forgot he was here. Too caught up in my pleasure to care.

Forcing my eyes on him, I watch his hand fist his thick cock, pumping it in hard, lazy pulls. My fingers slide inside my eager body, hips lifting without direction. The sleek line of my fingers push deeper, seeking the one spot that will have me seeing fireworks.

"*Rocco,*" I whimper, my fingers moving in and out, the sound of my excitement, the melody of my fingers loud enough to make him grunt.

I'm mesmerized by the sight of him. The brutal aura of a man lost to lust. Spellbound by a carnal need to dominate his prey yet submit to his pleasure.

The silk luster of his skin tells me he'd feel like velvet in my hand. Hard and smooth. The thought alone enough to make me salivate.

I want him in my mouth.

"Soon," he rumbles.

So lost in the moment, I hadn't realized I'd spoken aloud.

My tongue peeks out, licking my bottom lip in dreamlike anticipation and wishing, hoping, praying for his thick head to rest heavily against my lips.

The impressive length of his cock points at me, the crown of his head dripping with the translucent white of pre-cum. The veins of his hand pulsate with every slide of his wrist, giving away *just* how hard he's gripping himself.

My body is on fire, a sheen of sweat kissed across my skin. Every muscle in my body tightens. I can hear myself panting, the thick need to come jumping from my throat in quick, short spurts.

"Keep going," Rocco orders, his arm moving faster, his breathing climbing higher.

I do as I'm told.

Feet planted on his mattress, my hips fly upward, my fingers delving deeper still, needing... *"More."*

"Your pussy's so wet," he mumbles, the veins in his neck like ropes, heavy and corded. "Fuck. I can't fucking wait to taste you, to touch you."

I cry out at his words, my entire body convulsing, readying itself to explode into a million pieces.

"Cami, baby, I can't hold on for much longer," he growls.

"Come," I whimper.

Stepping closer, he pumps his cock harder, the velvet head darkening just before he groans. Ribbons of cum shoot against my hand, the warmth of his climax mixing with mine.

It's my undoing. Back arched, breath caught, I unravel. Rocco's name breaks from my lips, my body dropping to his bed in an orgasm so intense, my heart leaps from my chest.

I hear nothing. A quiet buzz surrounds me as my breathing evens out. My eardrums feel blocked, shut out with the thundering beat of my heart.

His calloused fingers wrapping around my wrist feels like a

security blanket I never knew I needed. Slowly pulling my hand from my body, he lifts it. Tongue outstretched, he licks up my fingers, pausing as he approaches the tips to bite his lips, savoring the taste.

"Taste like heaven right now," he muses. "Know what you'll taste like after you've begged?"

I raise an eyebrow in question, too tired to speak.

"You'll taste like hell, beauty. Like every sin pushed together, set alight to entice every motherfucker to this sweet cunt."

CHAPTER TWENTY-SEVEN

SARAH

UNKNOWN

Five-hundred thousand and not a cent less.

JONATHAN LOOKS OVER MY SHOULDER. "Ready to tell me who your contact is yet?"

I don't bother answering. I might be a junkie, but I'm not stupid. My cards aren't just held close to my chest. They're tattooed there. Inked faced down, refusing anyone access. I might need muscle to execute this plan, but I'm the brains.

"Whoever they are, their price jumped fifty grand overnight."

I refrain from telling him to fuck off. It is, after all, his money we're using to pay the asshole on the other end of the line.

Jonathan Waith might be pretty, but he's as stupid as they fucking come. A wannabe boss with too big balls and not enough drive.

I have no clue how my daughter spent four years with him. I'd likely carve my eyeballs out if I had to spend too much longer in his presence. He's a means to an end. One with a hefty trust fund that consists of too many zeros and a vendetta to take ownership of my daughter. Five hundred grand is a drop in the ocean to him.

"Do you want Camryn or not?"

He stares at me. "You better not be playing me. I'll fucking kill you if you are."

I roll my eyes. "Swallow your little threats, boy. Drop the cash, and we'll both get what we want."

His dark eyebrows pull inward. "Why are you so hungry for revenge? Who is Rocco Shay to you?"

"He *was* no one," I answer. "Until the asshole put hands on me. Now he'll fucking die."

"And Dominic?"

"He'll be in a world of hurt when one of his precious daughters goes missing. He dotes over them like nobody's business. It's sickening."

He smirks.

"That family wants revenge on me. They chose the wrong fucking person. I was happy living in hiding. My cunt of a husband put a dollar sign on my head, and my daughters cheered him on."

"They all need to pay."

"They're all *going* to pay," I correct him.

Sliding a cigarette into his mouth, he watches me over the stick, the flame of his lighter dancing in his eyes. "How confident are you in your contact?"

"Dominic forgets what I know, *who* I know. He's not the only person who can claim control in this situation. Trust me."

Jonathan laughs. "You've got to be kidding. You're not a threat, Sarah. You're a junkie whore with a score to settle."

"I sought *you* out," I bite back. "I can just as easily find someone else. Don't tempt me. We have the same end goal here. Maximum damage. Fucking relax."

"I'll relax when I have my Kitty Kat back in my bed. Until then..." He holds up a bag in front of my face, the small white shards of rock inside quickening my heart rate. "Pure. Only just hit the market," he teases.

"Give it." I stand, skittish as fuck like the junkie I am, dying for a taste.

"Oh. I'm already giving you five hundred grand, sweetheart. You're going to have to pay for this."

I step forward. "That's right, on your knees, whore. Don't speak or look at me while my cock is in your mouth. I'll be imagining your daughter."

CHAPTER TWENTY-EIGHT

ROCCO

"Nice right hook, dude," Parker praises.

Jesse's shoulders lift in pride, the feigned glower on his face not enough to erase the pleasure he feels at his uncle's approval.

Seeing them side-by-side like this is surreal as all hell. Jesse is a replica of Parker fifteen-odd years ago, albeit a little thinner.

The dirty blonde hair, currently cut too short, emphasizes the severity of the angular line of his face. Eyes, not unlike our mother's—filled with the anguish I see in my own—shine with a hope that is all too common in his uncle. Their skin tone is a carbon copy. The only difference is the ink tattooed onto Parker.

At Jesse's request, we've been boxing for a good few hours. I'm not complaining, I'm spending quality time with my boy.

Fighting strips away your walls. It doesn't just open you up to physical harm, it cracks you wide emotionally, everything rushing out through the fire of your fists.

I've learned more about my son in the last few hours than I ever would have sitting down for a deep and meaningful conversation. I've discovered that as much as he looks like Parker on the outside, he's as torn up about life as I am on the inside.

It wasn't hard to discover his reason. To work out where his want to fight stems from. Where I fight for freedom, his aim is centered around love. He wants to learn how to protect himself and, more importantly, his sister. According to Jesse, the blame for their shitty start to life rests solely on his shoulders. It doesn't take a genius to work out he wished he'd done more to protect her. He didn't have to say the words. It was bleeding out of his eyes as he powered through punches that almost broke his body.

"Bathroom," Jesse grunts out through labored breaths.

Hand tapping his back, I grab his shoulder in affection, squeezing it once before letting go.

"You two look like you're connecting," Parker reflects, watching his nephew retreat.

I wish he were right. Today is an exception. The kid is unwavering in his withdrawal. He's afraid to get too close, predicting this attempt at a happy family will blow up in our faces.

"I don't know," I answer honestly. "He's cagey. It's like trying to connect with a me that looks like you."

A peel of laughter rolls from my brother's mouth.

"So what you're tryna say is that he's superiorly handsome?"

I jab him in the ribs bare-fisted.

He grunts. "Fuck, dude." Rushing forward, he twists an arm around my neck, attempting to pull me down.

"I've gotta head out," Jesse interrupts our play fight, and we stand up straight, watching him curiously.

"Where are you going?"

He smirks. "Bit late to start the dad thing, yeah?"

I don't know what to say.

"Maybe," Parker answers for me. "But when you're only sixteen and staying as a guest in someone's house, you pay 'em some common courtesy."

Jesse's eyes flit between the two of us. "Well, which is it? Houseguest or family?"

Touché, kid. Tou-fucking-ché.

"Just trying to look out for you."

He refrains from rolling his eyes. "Done okay thus far on my lonesome."

I'm caught between my want to tell him that things have changed.

He needs to understand he now has a parent—one who gives a shit. But I'm petrified of pushing him away by coming on too strong.

"You need any cash?"

He shakes his head.

"I'll get you a spare key," I sigh. "Just in case I'm out when you get back."

"Appreciate it."

I move to walk past him, stopping. "I'm working on giving you guys space to settle in, but any chance you could make sure you're home at a decent hour to save me thinking you've run off?"

A soft bark of laughter is my answer. "Sure thing, Rocco."

SITTING ON THE COUCH, whiskey in hand, I frown at Parker. He's staring at me, thinking too hard to make me comfortable.

"I think you should give the twins tighter boundaries. They can't just disappear without telling you where they're going."

I shoot my drink, spinning the empty glass in my hand.

"You would know," I answer. "With all the parenting practice you've had."

"Don't be a dick," he bites. "They're fucking kids, Roc. They need to know there are rules."

I sigh. "Park. They've been in my house for a week. To them, I'm still a stranger. I'm treading carefully."

His head shakes. "There's treading carefully and being neglectful."

"The fuck?"

Hands lifting in surrender, he apologizes. "That came out wrong. I'm saying they don't want to go back to the street any more than you want them to. Don't let them walk all over you for fear you'll lose them. Being a parent also means laying ground rules, Roc. Don't let them dictate how shit is gonna be in an attempt to connect with them. Show them you give a shit."

I stand, moving back toward the bottle of whiskey, dropping my glass down, thinking better of having another drink.

"How are you so much better than me at this?"

Tipping the remainder of his drink down his throat, he stands, placing his empty glass next to mine.

"I learned from the best."

If I look confused, it's because I am.

"You, Roc. You were hard as fuck on me growing up. It showed you cared. As much as I bitched and whined, I secretly fucking loved having someone looking out for me."

I don't know what to say, so I say nothing. But I grab him, pulling him into an embrace I didn't know I needed.

"Aww. Cute. Can I join in?" Blake's arms wrap around us without warning, her cheeks pressed against my shoulder.

Pulling back, her eyes fall across the loft. "Where's Jesse?"

"Said he had something to do."

Bottom lip tipped out, she hmphs. "Nice of him to tell me he was leaving."

"What've you been doing?" Parker asks her.

"Dude. I've been street bound for *months*. I've been giving Rocco's Netflix, and Amazon Prime accounts a total workout, catching up on all my shows."

He frowns at me. "Since when do you have Netflix and Amazon Prime?"

My shoulders lift in dismissal. "Since Blake told me she had shows to catch up on."

She blinks at me widely. "You didn't have it before?"

"Had no need."

"So you got it for me?"

"It's just some TV subscriptions."

She laughs it off uncomfortably. Embarrassed that I would reject something that she deems important as nothing.

Fuck.

"I was happy to do it. It's important you get to be a kid, that you can binge-watch trashy TV and talk my ear off about it, even though I have no idea what you're talking about."

Her smile starts small. The sides of her mouth tipped upward before moving into a fully formed grin, lips stretched wide, teeth on show, and dimples present. "Ha. I knew it." She laughs. "You secretly love my recaps."

"I don't," I assure her.

"You do, don't worry, Uncle Park, and I won't hold it against you."

Uncle Park, but I'm still Rocco. Like that doesn't hurt like a serrated knife to the throat.

"Just like hearing you talk."

Every delicate feature on her face softens, the chip on her shoulder disappearing like a puff of smoke.

"Any idea where your brother has gone?"

Moving into the kitchen, she opens the fridge, grabbing a carrot out to bite it. We watch her chew, her focus never leaving the orange vegetable.

"I know where he is." She finishes her mouthful. "I followed him one day. You'll find he does this a few times a week."

"So?" Parker prompts.

"Oh." She giggles. "I'm not going to tell you. I'd have to kill you. Twin code and all."

She winks as she walks past us, that chip having found her again.

"Dinner is at six tonight," I yell to her retreating back.

She gives me a thumbs up.

"Why is it so annoying that your kids are so much like us?"

Talk about nature over nurture. Jesse and Blake have had nothing to do with us growing up. They were shaped well before they'd heard our names, but here they are, so much like Parker and I, you'd think someone had cloned us into smaller versions.

"How are you doing with all this?" I ask my brother. "It's the first time we've had a chance to chat since the bombshell of the twins was dropped."

Grabbing his shirt from his duffle, he slides it over his head. "I'm confused as to why you never told me Kendall was pregnant, that you thought you had a kid."

I should apologize, but I know my brother, he doesn't expect it.

"I could've helped you."

"Kendall told me she was getting rid of the kid. It could have been a wild goose chase, doll face. Why get your hopes up that we had family if it weren't true? You'd lost enough. I didn't want that hope in your eyes to cut me open whenever we came up empty-handed."

"What about you, though?" he argues. "What about your hope?

Rocco, you've lost just as much, if not more than I have. I'm sick and tired of you balancing the burden of our lives by yourself. I'm not a kid. Let me fucking *help* you. Show me you fucking trust me."

"I do trust you," I combat defensively.

"Do you? Really? Look me in the eye and tell me you aren't keeping anything else from me."

Lips pursed, I can't bring myself to look at him.

"I fucking knew it. Tell me."

Hand reaching up, I scratch at the back of my neck in discomfort.

"You're a real prick." He slings his duffle over his shoulder. "You know that, right? God forbid anyone does anything without your permission, but you're a law unto your own, isn't that right, *brother?*"

Showing me his back, he moves toward my door. His shoulders are clenched in disappointment, the stench of bad blood widening the gap between us.

"I'm working with Dominic," I call out. "To find Sarah."

Feet paused, he doesn't turn.

"I found her," I confess to his back. "Well, Rein found her. He sent me to bring her home."

He turns slowly. "And?"

"Bitch tasered me and shot Tivoli in the leg."

"Who else knows?"

"Camryn."

"Are you fucking her?" he accuses.

"It's not like that."

Quiet hangs between us. "Where is she now?"

I swallow. "Contacts of Rein have spotted her in town."

"What the fuck is she doing?"

"We don't know," I answer truthfully. "But it's set Dominic on edge. He thinks she's planning something."

"Jesus fucking Christ," he spits. "You don't think Codi and I should've been made aware? Fuck, Rocco. My *wife* could be in danger, and you're keeping secrets."

"She has people watching her," I vow.

He has to know that Dominic would never leave Codi unprotected. That *I* would never leave him unprotected.

Arms outstretched, he looks at me with disgust. "I don't give a fucking shit about *people*. *I* keep her safe. *Me*. Her fucking *husband*. Her security isn't your responsibility."

With that, he slams the door, exiting the loft with the fight of a man whose family is at risk.

Fuck.

It's not lost on me that we're back here again. Me forcing my brother into a situation he wants no part in. One that threatens the lives of those he holds most dear.

"That was awkward."

I startle at Blake's voice, watching her closely to determine how much she heard.

She's good, though. Not just a closed book. She's one that's padlocked shut and twisted up in chains, not letting a single thought escape from her eyes.

"You know, Jesse and I lived with one unhinged psycho for too long. One hellbent on making everyone pay for his stupid mistakes repeatedly."

I take the insult in her words without judgment.

"We won't do it again," she declares.

"I'm tryna fix it all," I tell her. "I'm trying to make sure Marcus' stain or Sarah's vendetta can't hurt the people I love. They took my mom, which lost me my dad. Then they stole my aunt."

The padlock pops open on her consent, sympathy clouding her eyes.

"I won't let them touch you or Jesse. I won't let her close to Camryn, Codi, or Parker. I'm fucking petrified of the damage she can inflict. I'm trying to stop it before it blows up in our faces."

"Why can't you just leave it?" she questions, trying to understand.

"You told me you knew Sarah. You knew Marcus. Do you think she'll stop? Do you think she'll rest until the threat of her family is extinct from her life?"

She doesn't even pause to consider my question. "No."

CHAPTER TWENTY-NINE

CAMRYN

"You're restless," I tell him, watching his leg bounce up and down in agitation.

He stops the constant movement, pausing to look at me. "I haven't fought in months."

I can't decide if he's relieved or pained by the thought.

"Do you miss it?"

"Yes," he answers immediately. "No," he corrects. "*Fuck*. I don't know."

I sit beside him on the bed, my hand reaching for his.

"I miss the outlet." His thumb traces my hand. "When I'm stuck. When I'm fucking confused. When I'm lost," he finishes quietly.

"Could you find somewhere to do it safely?"

Twisting his neck, he looks at me, a smile growing on his face. "Fuck, you're cute." His arm hooks over my shoulder, bringing me into his body.

"I'll take that as a no."

Lips to my temple, he talks against my skin, the burr of his voice kissing me. "You know I don't do it for the fight, Cami. I do it searching for pain. Tempting fate, gambling on my life."

"*Oh.*" My heart cracks.

"I can't do that anymore. I *don't* want to do that." He eases my hurt. "But..." He trails off, unsure of what more to say.

"Sometimes life gets hard."

He shakes his head. "Sometimes I don't know what the fuck to do, and I don't know how to take control. Everything is so fucking uncertain."

Neck tipped back, he growls at the ceiling.

"I haven't told my mom about the twins, about you."

I try hard to hide my shock, failing miserably. "You talk to your mom?"

"Mm," he confirms distractedly. "I visit her grave. Talk to her about how much of a fucking failure I am. She listens, and I think I still have her love. No matter how much I disappoint her."

"*Rocco.*"

He shakes his head, standing to distance himself from me. "Talk about a buzzkill."

"Baby." I stand, walking toward him. He attempts to move away, but I halt him, hand on his arm, pulling him back. "Let's go now. To Lila. Tell her about Blake and Jesse. Tell her about me. Tell her about the things that make you happy."

Rocco's eyes are consuming on a good day. Days like today—tumultuous days—they're like caverns, dark and deep voids you could quickly become lost in.

He doesn't speak for long, drawn-out seconds. Enough to make me second guess myself.

"I... I shouldn't have suggested it. I—"

"You'd do that with me?"

His vulnerability slices away at my heart.

"Of course," I implore.

"It's your dad's birthday, the party—"

"Is hours away," I cut him off. "We'll go and be back with plenty of time."

His arms wrap around me tightly. The obvious strength in them squeezing me in appreciation. "I love you."

"I love you, too."

I SHIVER as I step onto the well-kept grass of the cemetery, my arms wrapping around my body to shield myself from the cold. I offered to stay in the car, and while he didn't respond verbally, he did so in true Rocco form, through action. He opened my door, reaching for my hand.

The place is deserted. Not a single soul in sight. The smell of fresh-cut grass and warring floral aromas an upbeat and pleasant scent to attribute to death. To those who left us behind.

Rocco is comfortable with me following at a distance. He didn't want me to wait in the car, but I'm betting he doesn't want me listening to his conversation either.

It might be strange, but I feel like I've met Lila Shay. Her presence was so heavy at Parker and Codi's wedding, she was a little hard to ignore. Add that to the love she poured into her two boys. She's someone I admire.

In the beginning, I refused to try and understand Rocco. I pinned him as a poisonous human. Everything in his vicinity was decaying. But as time passed, I saw through that smokescreen. Lila Shay loved her boys so hard that her loss was catastrophic. Rocco and Parker were never fueled by hate. They were inflamed by love. A devotion so chaotic, few people would ever understand it.

Her name, carved into her headstone, reads the same on Rocco's heart. Forever ingrained, a marking that will live long after we all die.

Loving wife. Adored sister. Devoted mother.

The words on her gravestone. *Devoted. Mother.* If Rocco were to die today, his would read something similar.

Loving brother. Devoted son.

He's more like his mother than he's ever realized. I wish he could see that the good that lived in her is also very much alive in him.

"I wish it was raining," he says.

"Rain and tears aren't the same, Rocco," I tell him. "You can't camouflage emotion with mother nature. Trust me, I've tried."

"Says who?"

I shrug, eyes skating across the cemetery, taking in the flowers offered to those we've lost. It surprises me how you never come across another person in a cemetery, yet headstones are always adorned with fresh flowers. Are we so overcome with our grief we refuse to see anyone else? Or does fate let us select our timing, ensuring our suffering is our own?

"Emotional tears have a different makeup than other secretions of your eyes," I tell him distractedly. "It's all science, but they move through different tissue, which makes your eyes puffy. Basically, your body is a traitorous bitch when it comes to emotion. It wants everyone to know you're breaking."

Glancing between his mother's headstone and myself, I take his hint.

"I'm going to sit over there." I point to a large Dogwood tree, the white flowers in full bloom.

It's hard not to watch him. To let my eyes wander to where he sits in an attempt to work out what he's saying.

Did he jump straight into the twins?

Has he mentioned me?

Is it selfish to consider he would with everything else he has going on?

He's with her for over an hour. Sixty minutes I'm sure he's in no way filling with mindless conversation. Which means she's either talking back or he's enjoying their shared silence as he decompresses.

Standing abruptly, his hand moves across his cheeks, swiping at the tears he doesn't want me to see.

My broken soul—so afraid to let anyone see the cracks in his armor for fear they'll turn their back.

Hands stuffed into the pockets of his jeans, he keeps his face downward. "I just have one more person to see."

"Of course. Take as much time as you need."

He waits, a sharp inhale as he moves to speak, but he stops, thinking better of it.

I watch his retreat, waiting until he's out of sight before moving toward the ghost of Lila Shay. I don't know why I wait for him to leave. Whether it was a conscious decision or one my mind made for me. Would he be mad? Am I overstepping?

Sliding my hand along the grey stone, I feel the damp chill under my palm.

"You don't know me," I tell her. "Or maybe you do. I'm not sure how all this works."

Dropping to my haunches, I pick at the dead grass around her headstone, tossing it aside to leave only the green. To leave only *life*.

"My name is Camryn Rein, and I'm so sorry that you were taken from this world too quickly. You're missed, I'm sure you know that. But just in case you had your doubts, please know that you're thought of every day."

I stand again, comfortable that her headstone is perfect.

"I just wanted to let you know that I love your son. I think it's a hope for all parents that their children find someone who loves them as much as you do. I don't know if you were ever concerned that Rocco may not find that..."

I sigh.

"Actually, from what I've been told about you, I think you knew he'd own someone's heart one day. That he'd guard that heart with everything he holds inside of him, scarred or whole. I want you to rest easy knowing that I love him that way too. I own his heart as much as he does mine. I promise to protect, cherish, and love it through its darkest moments."

I see him approach, eyes searching for me at the Dogwood where he left me.

"Thank you," I tell Lila's gravestone, hoping she hears me. "Thank you for filling him with a love so deep most people can't understand it. It's a beautiful kind of love, Lila."

The touch of his hand brushes my shoulder, and I turn. Eyes filled with tears, he stares at me in complete diffidence. I pull him into a hug.

"Mira?" I ask, my face pressed forcefully against the hard plane of his chest.

"Yeah," he stutters. "Hardest conversation I've ever had, and the other person couldn't respond."

"That's almost worse," I tell him. "Because you never really know whether you have the forgiveness you've asked for. It's all unknown, and nothing is more debilitating than the unknown."

My chin resting over his shoulder, his face buries into my neck, finding comfort in the steady rhythm of my pulse.

It's only then that I see her.

Blake Shay is watching us.

Our eyes catching, she brushes at the tears she's shedding before turning on her heel and disappearing as fast as she appeared.

I have no idea how she got here. How she managed to follow us, or why. But I keep her presence to myself. This was a private moment for Rocco. One of reluctant grief and a step forward he wasn't sure he was ready to take. A show of vulnerability I'm not sure he'd be willing to share with his kids. Not yet, anyway. Not while the blame still has his heart tied in knots.

Walking back to the car, he's quiet, contemplative even.

"Do you think they'll stay?" he questions. "Blake and Jesse."

"I don't know," I answer honestly.

"If they could tell me what they wanted... I want them to tell me who they want me to be, and I'll strive my fucking best to be that person for them."

I pull at his arm, stopping him from opening his car door. My hands brush along his chest. "Roc, baby, what makes you think they want you to be anyone other than who you are?"

"I'm not exactly the pick of the bunch, am I, beauty?"

I take a step back, angered by his self-loathing. "Stop it."

"Stop what?"

"This." I wave my hand in front of his face. "All the fucking contempt you wrap yourself in. You're a good fucking person, Rocco Shay. A little psychotic at times, sure, but love is all about the extreme. In my opinion, anyway. No one wants to be loved half-assed. They want to be fucking *consumed*. My dad has me followed, for fuck's sake," I gripe. "But I know it's because it's his neurotic way of making sure I'm safe."

I move a step forward. I press my hands against the sides of his neck. "Rocco. Stop holding yourself to this warped idea of your imperfections. No one is fucking perfect. No one."

"You are," he whispers.

"Well, yeah, obviously." I smirk. "I'm serious," I say. "I love who you are. Parker loves who you are. They will too. I wish you'd find it in yourself to love the real version of yourself. He's kind of amazing."

"Just kind of?" A finger dips into the line of my shirt, pulling me closer.

"Maybe a little bit more," I murmur, thumb and forefinger held between us, showing an inch of space.

Head dropping, he smashes his lips against mine. A simple closed-mouth kiss that is full of appreciation and fierce love.

IT'S NOT every day that your dad turns fifty-two. Or so Codi says.

My dad hates celebrating his birthday. In fact, I'm pretty confident he despises it. What he doesn't hate, though, is having everyone he cares about in one place, enjoying one another's company. So for that reason, each year, Dominic agrees to a birthday get-together at Codi's suggestion.

This one seems bigger than the last few years. I mean, York is here. Fucking *York*. Did Codi actually invite him? Don't get me wrong, Rocco called him Dork when we entered the house, and I'm not going to lie, my life was made.

I've also had at least five margaritas and am on my way to grab my sixth.

"You don't find it weird that the older Shay brother has just been brought into the fold?"

Tipsy enough, I didn't hear his approach.

"No, Dork. I don't."

He scowls. I smile.

"You do realize you're talking about my guy. Like, Rocco and I are involved, and you've just told your boss that you aren't a fan of one of his family members?"

I hiccup.

"You're not my boss."

"I kind of am."

He stomps away.

"Fucking loser," I mumble, searching the room for Rocco.

He's talking to Tivoli, lounging back on our sectional with an untouched beer in his hand.

Stone-cold sober to my wobbly and more-amusing-than-attractive intoxication.

Stalking over with a sway to my hips that likely makes me look like a newborn giraffe, he smiles. A smile that promises a million and one things. Not all appropriate, some downright filthy, but some overflowing with infatuation and love.

"Oh hey," I slur, that last margarita twisting my tongue.

Having seen my approach, Tivoli makes himself scarce, with a look of judgment in his eyes as he passes me.

I look back, surprised at his scrutiny. Like they haven't done shitty things in their lives. Yet they're sitting on their throne of importance, thinking they're better than Rocco?

Rocco's hand brushes against mine, a thick blonde brow raised as he pats his knee.

I glance at it, tracking up to his face. "You have a nice face," I compliment, sitting on his lap. "I'd like to sit on it."

"You're drunk," he observes.

I scrunch my nose up in affection, pinching his cheek. "Pretty *and* smart."

"And irritated by drunk people."

I stick my bottom lip out. "And a total party pooper."

"Where's your dad?"

"Bed. He went too hard too early."

Rocco frowns.

"Okay, fine. He's old and hates celebrating his birthday. He hates the extra attention."

"Smart guy."

"You can marry him in another life," I tease. "Right now, *I'd* like to kiss you."

Instead of kissing me as I'd hoped, he lets his eyes run along my face.

"What?"

"Nothing," he murmurs, lifting his thumb to drag it down my bottom lip, resting it along my chin. "Just thinking I like you looking like this."

"And what do I look like?"

"Mine," he speaks quietly. "You look like nothing but fucking *mine*, beauty."

I let my lips slowly chase his. My soft pout bracketing his with a whisper of a kiss. One that tells him I love him. That being *his* makes my heart sing in a way it never has.

He offers me the same touch back. The rough whiskers of his beard a stark contrast to the tenderness in his lips when they caress mine.

"Well, aren't you two just the cutest."

We break away from one another reluctantly.

Arms around Rocco's neck, I smile up at his daughter. "We're in love."

Her smile falters, only slightly, but enough for me to notice.

"Gross."

I shrug. "It's true, so best get used to us kissing in front of you *all* the time."

She looks almost sad at my terrible joke, and I want to kick myself. She's sixteen, likely still mourning her mother and possibly dreaming of a life where the four of them lived happily ever after.

Kendall may be dead, but her memory will forever remain. A ghost that, in Jesse and Blake's eyes, I'm a poor replacement for.

An awkward beat of silence ensues, one hundred and fifty percent driven by me, but I can't help it.

"I should let you two catch up," I stutter, struggling as I move off Rocco's lap.

Fingers circling my wrist, he stops me, a look of confusion twisting along his menacingly beautiful face.

"I'll catch you in a bit," I promise.

He lets me go reluctantly, but only after his lips skate across my knuckles.

I move through our living room, unsure of what to make of myself. I was a mess just then—a bumbling fool. If I want to be in Rocco's life, I need to handle this shit better.

"Hey, Camryn." Blake's footfalls sound behind me, and pausing, I take a deep breath to steady myself. "Wait up."

"I was only joking about that kissing remark," I stumble over my words awkwardly. I've had too many margaritas to have a proper conversation with Rocco's daughter.

"Oh." She waves me off. "You're funny. Gross. But it was funny."

I nod in fear of slurring my words if I attempt to speak.

"I heard Parker talking the other night," she confesses. "Maybe I was eavesdropping, but..." She shrugs. "Semantics. He said you used to hate my dad."

My mouth opens in shock, closing again when I can't think of anything to say.

"Now you love him?" she tests.

"Yes," I croak out, clearing my throat in discomfort.

"What changed?" she asks earnestly. "You're a good person. How did you go from hating him to loving him?"

This poor girl. I want to hug her. Pull her into my body and assure her everything will work out.

I exhale heavily. "I'm a little too drunk for this conversation," I tell her honestly. "But I'm a big believer in talking shit out, so if I slur or repeat myself too many times, please don't judge me."

Glancing around the room, too many listening ears present, I tip my head toward the kitchen, and she follows without issue.

"Sit." I point to a stool, depositing myself with an eye to the entryway so I can see anyone approach.

"I don't think I ever hated him," I tell her. "I didn't care to understand him, and I refused to *see* him."

My mind travels back to those moments. To those bleak snaps of time when my grief and uncertainty consumed me, and I refused to see anyone else's pain.

"It's funny," I muse. "I used to only ever see hate when I looked at your dad. To the outside eye, I guess it's a perception he doesn't care to refute. He was molded that way, Blake. By Marcus. By Kane. Through *loss*."

She nods, swallowing my words eagerly. She's searching for something. I'm not sure what, but it's important to her. Enough to coat her eyes in tears she's not willing to shed.

"But through all that, through all that hate, through all that venom and cruelty, you know what shined through?"

Her head shakes side-to-side.

"He wanted to avenge his mother because he *loved* her."

She swallows.

"He took fists meant for Parker time and time again. Because he wanted to *protect* him."

Her lip trembles.

211

"He poured every cent he had into finding you and Jesse because *nothing,* and I mean nothing, was more important to him than knowing whether you existed."

Her teeth bite into her lip.

"He refused, up until today, to visit Mira's grave for fear she would never forgive him for her death. A death that Marcus was responsible for."

Her eyes flash in shame.

"We were so far from friends that I don't even think you could call us enemies. It didn't matter. He helped me in a way *no one* else has."

"He's a protector," she whispers.

"He told me I no longer needed to fear my demons because he'd always be right there with me, fighting, and who the *fuck* would go up against him."

"That'd be nice," she hums. "Knowing you had that."

I sit up straight. "*You do,* Blake. You have Rocco loving you harder than he's ever loved anything else."

"You think so?"

Leaning forward, I grab her hand. "I know so. How can you not see that? He's petrified of you leaving him. He'd lay his life on the line for you and Jesse. Whatever you're so afraid of, it's got nothing on your dad."

CHAPTER THIRTY

DOMINIC

I STARE at the photo in front of me, unsure of what to make of it.

"Do we know who he's meeting?"

Tivoli shakes his head. "I haven't been able to ID him as of yet. But I'll keep on it. It just seemed off. I wanted to check it out."

Nodding, my eyes remain fixed on the photo. Jesse Shay meeting with an unknown man in a suit worth the same amount of money that could pay someone's mortgage.

"You did the right thing. How'd you know to follow him?"

Tivoli, shifting forward on his chair, glances over his shoulder, making sure the door to my office is closed. Confident we're alone, he still drops his voice. "I heard the kid talking to York. Threw a message under his nose and asked for directions."

Makes sense.

"Weird thing," he continues. "Is that York didn't give him directions. As soon as York recited the address, the kid was gone."

My lips turn down. "Odd."

"Mm-hm. I'll keep digging."

Moving to stand, he pauses as Camryn taps a fist against my door. "Knock, knock."

"Hey, sweetheart."

"Oh, good. You're here too. I wanted to talk to you both."

Tivoli looks at me uncertainly. Shrugging, I gesture back to the seat he was only moments ago sitting in.

He waits for Camryn to sit down before taking his seat again, and I clock the way he looks at her. A soft longing disguised by his impassive mask.

Frank Tivoli has been infatuated with my eldest daughter for years. I don't blame him, she's beautiful.

He's never told me, which means he values his job more than he does his feelings for Camryn. In my eyes, that means he doesn't care for her enough.

"York and Tivoli are making me uncomfortable."

"What?" he blusters out, his usual calm caught off-guard by the directness in her declaration.

"York made an unsavory comment about Rocco to me at your birthday party. He questioned why we'd welcomed him as family. I refrained by firing him on the spot, thinking you'd prefer the satisfaction."

I manage to hide my smirk.

"And Tivoli?"

"He glared at me all judgy the other night when I was sitting with Rocco," she adds haughtily.

"Sitting with him," he spits. "You were sprawled over him like a cat on heat."

"Frank," I burr, clear warning in my tone.

"What I do with *my* boyfriend is *none* of your concern."

"Shall you have me fire Tivoli too?" I ask, not in the slightest bit serious.

He moves to argue, but I hold a hand up, silently requesting he let my daughter speak.

She straightens her shoulders. "Well, no. He's family. He just needs to closet his judgment."

"I'm sitting right here, Camryn."

Turning to him, she looks him dead in the eye. "Fine. Closet your fucking judgment. Rocco makes me happy. That's all that should matter to this family, *you* included."

I'm pleased by the look of remorse that crosses his face. "That's all I want for you," he tells her. "If he's the one that can give it to you." He pauses, maybe praying she'll interrupt, which she doesn't. "Then I'm happy for you. But just for future reference, I'd get judgy eyes looking at Codi and Parker sucking face too."

A lie. One she happily accepts.

"Perfect." She stands. "I'll leave York in yo—"

Her words cut off like the edge of a cliff. Brutal and final. Moving closer to my desk, she looks at the photo I had blown up of our mystery man's face.

"Why do you have a photo of Jonathan Waith?"

Fear is something I'm used to seeing in people. It doesn't bother me. I can stare it straight in the eye and take joy in the emotion.

Not in my daughter's, though.

"You know him?"

She swallows, stepping back so she can no longer see his face. "Jonathan Waith was my college boyfriend."

"Waith as in *Waith Industries*."

"Yes," she answers Tivoli's question. "I don't even know why he was at college. His trust fund alone could feed the world's starving population many times over. I assume his father needed him to occupy himself for a few years."

She goes silent.

"I'm gonna go," she announces abruptly, visibly shaken. "Don't forget to fire Dork."

"It's *York*," I call after her.

"I'm gonna kill that motherfucker." Tivoli grinds his teeth, gesturing to the photo.

No explanation is needed. My daughter feared this asshole, which means he has to die. I'm not one for getting my hands dirty. Our line of work can stain your hands for longer than you'll likely live. But if this cunt thinks he can build fear in my daughter, he's going to learn first hand I'll happily live with that stain on my conscience for the rest of my days.

"You'll have to wait in line. Firstly, let's find out why the *fuck* he was meeting with Jesse."

I NEVER QUESTIONED my offer to allow Jesse and Blake to stay in my home. They were the family of Rocco and Parker, which meant they were family to Codi and, in turn, me. You never turn your back on family. Not the ones that haven't given you a good reason.

I also don't question myself often. I'm a leader. A doer. A man with a focus on protecting his family and building his business. One hundred percent in that order.

Now I'm questioning my hospitality. I'm questioning whether I can trust Rocco's sixteen-year-old son, which doesn't sit well with me.

The guy I have sitting at Rocco's apartment tells me the kid leaves the loft alone twice a week. For a teenager that refuses to stand more than two feet away from his twin sister at any given time, this lights a bulb of uncertainty in my brain. At first, I didn't think anything of it. I told my guy to leave it.

Now I'm not so sure.

"Thanks for the dinner invite, Dad." Codi smiles at me, picking at the tomatoes in the salad I had our kitchen staff prepare earlier.

"Always, sweetheart. I'm just glad we could all be here," I offer her distractedly, not that she notices, her focus on the food in front of her.

My eyes remain on Jesse Shay. If he clocks me and my overly zealous observance, he doesn't act differently. Staring broodily off to the side, he avoids everyone and everything. So much like his father, it's almost uncomfortable to be around.

Blake shoots daggers at him from across the room. Staring at him intently, I'd be certain she'd skin him alive if she had the mind control to manage it.

The twins, usually as close as any two people can be, are distinctly separated. A purposeful distance pushed into existence through hostility and opposition.

Annoyed by her constant bristling, Jesse walks from the dining room, Blake quick on his heels.

"Camryn," I call. "Can you get everyone a drink? I'm just going to make a call, and then we'll eat."

Their voices are easily recognizable from the other side of my front door—their hushed tones heightening as they argue.

Positioning myself by the door, I place an ear against it, listening intently.

"What did you do?" The panic in her voice rises, her whispered tone more of a spit than anything else.

"I took care of us," her brother replies just as hotly.

"You did no such thing. *You've* put us in danger. What were you thinking?"

"The only thing I'm only ever concerned with doing, Blake," he accuses. "Keeping you safe."

She growls, the sound more feral than feminine. "When are you going to get it? I'm not your fucking responsibility."

"Everything okay?" Rocco walks up beside me, as stealthy as a tiger.

"Jesus," I speak loud enough for the kids to hear. "You scared me. I was just about to grab the kids."

Opening the door, they stare at us with wild eyes.

"What's wrong?" Rocco steps in front of me, moving closer to them.

"Nothing," Blake lies like she's breathing, entirely at ease in the action. "Jesse is just being a little bitch about Dominic putting feta in the salad. He's not a fan of cheese."

Her phone rings, dragging our attention away from her oddly believable lie.

"You gonna get that?" Rocco asks her.

"No," she answers easily. "Probably just one of my many admirers." She winks, pushing past us into the house. "Let's eat."

Rocco, following his daughter, leaves Jesse and me alone.

"Deceit can hurt a lot of people, Jesse."

His eyes flash in worry.

"Mostly those you love. You'd do well to remember that."

CHAPTER THIRTY-ONE

SARAH

UNKNOWN

Deal's off.

I STARE AT THE TEXT, anger bubbling through my veins. I'm going to rain *hell* on fucking earth.

CHAPTER THIRTY-TWO

BLAKE

I FUCKED UP.

CHAPTER THIRTY-THREE

TIVOLI

THE KID IS A SNEAKY FUCKER.

"Dominic," I speak into the line. "I lost him."

CHAPTER THIRTY-FOUR

CAMRYN

"W ʜ ᴇ ʀ ᴇ's J ᴇ ss ᴇ?" Blake walks from her room, arms reaching upward in a long stretch.

They've made themselves a comfortable space in Parker's old room. Jesse's living on a swag fit for a king at the end of the queen-sized bed Blake claimed as her throne. The room is covered in books and clothes, messy in the way teenagers are. Much to Rocco's discomfort. He offered to renovate the loft to add an extra bedroom, but they shut it down. They're most comfortable in close proximity, even when they're on the outs.

Look that up under the definition of *siblings*.

"I haven't seen him all day."

"Where's Rocco?"

"At the club," I tell her. "He and Parker had some work to do."

"He realizes I don't need a babysitter, right?"

I shrug, placing my coffee mug down. "He wants to make sure there's always someone here if you need it."

Appreciation pulls a smile from her blank face before worry turns her eyes in, her frown line coming on heavier than I've seen it. "Jesse should've been back by now. He only ever goes for an hour, maybe two."

"Goes where?"

She ignores me, pulling her cell phone from her pocket. Fingers moving like fire, she rings him, the call going straight to a generic voicemail. A quick inhale, and she calls again, the outcome the same.

Rocco bought them both phones the day after they arrived. Blake, like every teenage girl in the world, is attached to hers. She doesn't even pee without it. Jesse, on the other hand, is impartial. But he keeps it with him at all times, a security blanket he's never had before.

"What time did you say he left?"

"Blake, you need to calm down. Jesse's fine, I'm sure."

"I asked you what time he left?" She bites out unkindly. "Not for your opinion on how I should be feeling."

I refuse to answer.

"Please, Camryn," she pleads.

"I don't know," I answer honestly. "Maybe ten*ish*."

Her hand comes up to massage her stomach. "It's now two. He's been gone for four hours. That's not right."

Her big gray eyes have moved past her initial worry and into a hysteria that makes me move toward her.

"Hey," I soothe. "You need to relax. Shoot him a text, and I'm sure he'll call you as soon as he gets it."

She shakes her head. "I can't."

"Can't what?"

"Text," she stresses, calling him for the third time.

"Blake—"

"He can't read," she yells at me. "I can't text him because he can't fucking read, okay?"

I take a step back. "I didn't know."

"No one knows," she cries. "He thinks he's stupid. He goes to the library twice a week. Some old lady there has taken pity on him and teaches him how to read."

My heart breaks. "Why didn't he say anything?"

She laughs, the sound the exact melody of a broken heart. A sonnet to the betrayal she feels she's now painting her brother with by telling me this.

"We're street kids, Camryn. Kids who get by through hustling. We lie, we cheat, and we steal to live day-to-day. Who would want us?"

"*Rocco*," I state categorically. "Rocco wants you."

"Well, we didn't know that." Tears have now sprung to her eyes. The gray of her irises, so wet with emotion, they're almost transparent.

"Jesse was convinced that if Rocco found out he couldn't read or write that he'd be embarrassed his son was such a fuck up. He begged me not to say anything."

I grab at my chest, working to calm the pain in my chest.

"But, you—"

"Know how to read?" she guesses.

I nod.

"Jesse forced me to go to school while he stayed home caring for our mom. Whether it was to make sure she didn't choke on her vomit or to protect her if Marcus decided to visit. He never got an education but made sure I did."

I can feel my tears now, sitting uncomfortably against my eyes, waiting for permission to fall.

She begins pacing the room, thumbnail caught between her teeth.

"Blake," I start.

"You don't understand," she accentuates, stepping toward me only to step back again.

"You guys are attached, I get it," I soothe, working my hardest to talk her down from the ledge she's hellbent on balancing upon. "You're worried, but he'll be fine."

An unamused cry falls from her lips. "Jesus. We're not fucking useless without one another."

Her cell sounds, and she jumps at the sound, hand diving into her pocket to retrieve it.

I've seen a lot of people through grief. Both strangers and family. Interestingly enough, I've never met two people who react the same way. Tears are tears, but crying, that's strikingly individual.

Watching a teenage girl break is high on my list of things I'd happily never experience again. Witnessing the moment her world falls into pieces around her has never made me feel more useless.

Her knees give out before either of us has noticed, my reflexes far too slow to catch her. Her cry strips her vocal cords so violently that no sound comes out. Her mouth opens in a silent scream that would disturb peace on earth.

But it's the way her body shakes that gets me the most. The way she free-falls into shock so quickly, her body is a quivering mess of heart-wrenching sobs and bone-crunching wails.

Body weak enough, I retrieve her cell from her hand without a fight, the device falling into my palm with ease.

A gasp escapes my throat before I can school it, the jolt of shock hitting me like a punch to the stomach I was in no way prepared for.

Jesse's face stares up at us from the message. Eyes barely open with how heavily swollen they are. A mixture of dried and fresh blood decorates the lower half of his face like a Halloween mask. He's unconscious, that's obvious enough. The masculine arm in the picture has gripped his hair to tilt his face upward to allow the photograph to be taken.

"Jesse," I whisper. "What? Who?"

"Sarah," she answers me, numbness having claimed her.

"Sarah?" I echo in confusion, but she doesn't respond.

I move to stand, but she grabs onto my leg, holding me hostage.

"I need to call Rocco."

"Please, no. Camryn, you can't."

Hands twisted into my pant leg, she stands on her knees, *begging* me with her life. Face blotchy with the salt of her tears, chin quivering incessantly, her confidence strips away, leaving a young girl pleading with a stranger to help her.

"Hey." I drop back down, pulling her into a hug. "Rocco will fix this."

"No," she cries into my shoulders. "Not when he realizes what's happened. What I've done."

Pushing her shoulders back, I look into her eyes. "What you've done?" I query.

Her head moves up and down quickly. "He'll *hate* me forever."

"That's not possible."

"You don't know what I've done."

Hands gripping her cheeks, my thumbs swipe at her cheeks, attempting to remove the rush of tears silently streaming down her face.

"What did you do?" I ask gently.

"This was all my fault," she declares. "They retaliated."

"Who retaliated?" I question, confusion setting in.

Her chin lifts and drops slowly, her bottom falling to the ground as her body gives up. "They're punishing me."

"Who?" I stress.

"Sarah," she tells me, pausing for a moment before adding, "Jonathan."

My blood runs cold—pure liquid ice coursing through my veins.

"Jonathan?"

Eyes closing in regret, she nods. "I'm so sorry. I'm so so sorry." She repeats herself over and over again. The words are nothing but stuttered sobs that send shockwaves up my spine. Every cry is like the whisper of his name tying itself around my vertebrae, ready to snap at any moment.

Jonathan.

"Talk to me," I beg her, needing to understand how Jonathan became entangled, not only with my *mother* but in something sinister enough to involve the attack of a teenage boy.

"Sarah," she whispers again.

The cogs are turning so quickly in my head that I can't get any to line up and make sense.

"You're talking to Sarah?"

Chin wobbling, she nods.

Click. Fears falling into place like puzzle pieces I didn't even know I was missing.

"Did she send you here?" I breathe. "You coming to Dominic's home… was that *her* idea?"

Her head shakes vehemently, her hand coming up to wipe at her nose, transferring the snot and tears from her face to the bare skin of her arm.

"Blake, I'm so confused. You're going to have to fill me in."

She forces herself to inhale, defeat now defining her. "I fucked up," she tells me. "I really fucked up, Camryn."

"We can fix it," I assure her, not one hundred percent believing my promise.

She drops her head into her hands. Thick, jagged sobs wrack through her body.

I move in closer, sitting on the floor beside her to drag her into an embrace. I made the mistake of forgetting she was a teenage girl. A *child*. Her life has forced her to grow up too quickly, but deep inside, she's a scared little girl needing someone to guide her.

Climbing onto my lap, her face buries into my chest as she cries. My hand rubs up and down her back, a soft *shh* echoing the movement in an attempt to calm her.

It takes a good ten minutes, but she settles, her sobs trailing off into sporadic, stuttered breaths. Eyes, wide and unseeing, stare into nothing.

"Blake," I test softly.

"Sarah was watching Dominic's house," she starts, her eyes still fixated on nothing, her voice utterly devoid of emotion. "She saw us there and approached me."

She sniffs, her palm coming up to graze the upside of her nose. "She offered us cash."

"You and Jesse?"

Finally, she blinks, turning to look at me before she shakes her head. "Yes. No," she corrects. "Just me. She knew Jesse wouldn't give her the time of day. He despises her. She was always around. She got Mom hooked on smack and whatever else she was snorting and injecting."

My hand never ceases its constant track up and down her spine.

"It was a lot of cash," she tells me robotically. "Enough to set us up with a new life."

Her chin wobbles, and she lifts her palm, pressing it against her jaw to stop it. "It was before I knew Rocco. Before I saw that he was a good guy," she begs me to believe her. "Before I knew he gave a damn about us."

I move to speak, but she cuts me off.

"Before I knew you."

"*Me?*"

She swallows audibly. "You have to understand... you were no one to me."

"I—"

"She wanted access to you both. You *and* Rocco."

Understanding hits, and my hand drops away on its own accord.

She bargained with my life. Rocco's daughter, his flesh and blood, negotiated my life like a transaction.

"All I had to do was give her access to you both, and she'd give me five hundred grand."

"Jonathan," I surmise, so many emotions run through me that I can't determine how I feel.

"I assume so," she offers. "I don't know who he is. I hadn't even met him. I texted Sarah last week, telling her the deal was off."

"Jonathan was my ex, Blake."

I don't tell her he's a villain of the highest order. One that feeds on pain and suffering.

"You pissed Sarah off."

She lifts her shoulders in dismissal. "I started seeing my dad for who he was, who he could be for us. No amount of money in the world is worth losing him. I get that now."

I brush at a lock of her blonde hair, moving it away from the wet line of her cheek to tuck it behind her ear.

"Jonathan sent me a text earlier this week asking to meet, but Jesse had taken my phone. He took the meet, told him to fuck off out of our lives."

"He knew?" I ask, their knives of deceit plundering deeper and deeper. "Jesse?"

"Jesse doesn't trust anyone, not even me," she confesses sadly. "I guess he was right not to. He knew something was up with how quickly I wanted to attach myself to Rocco. He was watching me too closely."

Using the collar of her shirt, she wipes her nose.

"He called me out, and I don't lie to my brother."

"What does Sarah want with Rocco?"

"I don't know, revenge for something?"

It doesn't make any sense. Is it self-preservation? Is her plan to hurt Rocco before he does her?

"You were to hurt Dominic. I knew that much."

I bark out a sinister laugh. Mother of the year, that one, bargaining for her daughter's death, all to hurt the man she felt wronged by.

"They've taken Jesse as insurance. They're gonna force my hand, and I'll have to play it, Camryn. He's my brother."

I don't want her to tell me she'd sacrifice Rocco's life for her

227

brother's. I don't want those words to break for her lips, forever out in the wild.

"Hey." I grab her chin. "You don't have to do anything."

Peace settles inside of me. "Sarah Rein wants to hurt my father more than she wants to hurt your dad. *Jonathan.*" I swallow the acid his name brings me. "He wants me, Blake. Not Rocco. I can end this."

"What?" She backs away from me. "No."

I smile. "Yeah."

It's true. This could end with me.

The threat of Jonathan has never left me. He stands behind me always, a ghost readying himself to pounce. To claim what he deems his. I threatened him once upon a time to find my freedom. I took control, which would've haunted him in a way nothing else could. He'll never rest until he has me back. Until I've walked into his castle, a willing prisoner. I think I always knew that. That's where the nightmares stemmed from—the fear of the future that was already planned out.

Rocco was my saving grace for a time. He taught me how to protect myself. He stood behind me, reinforcing my power with the strength within him. Together we were invincible. Only now, to protect him, I need to be seen.

Sarah won't rest until vengeance is hers. Dominic and Rocco went after her, and in her eyes, that kick-started a challenge she'll never back down from. She doesn't want to take his life. That gives her nothing, and she's smarter than that. My demise will force my father to suffer for the rest of his days. Codi and I are his Achilles heel, and she's more than willing to slash it wide open.

It'll be an easy swap. One my mother and monster ex will jump on.

Me for Jesse.

A life lost and one saved.

Rocco finally has something to live for. Something that has fired his will to *love*. His world is happy now, and he deserves to live in that. My beautiful, devoted soul has spent his life protecting others to the detriment of his self-worth. It's time he knew how worthy he was. It's time someone laid down their life for him.

For once in his life, Rocco Shay will be protected. I'm gonna make sure of it.

CHAPTER THIRTY-FIVE

CAMRYN

JONATHAN WAS ALL TOO eager to agree to my terms. So eager, I convinced him to throw in the five hundred grand for the kids as initially promised.

The bus rattles beneath me, the suffocating smell of old tobacco soaked into the seats. I choose to stand, my legs restless enough to move me from handrail to handrail, up and down the vehicle in disquiet.

A bus was the best mode of transport I could think of. The only one that wouldn't sketch Rocco a handwritten map to where I'd be. It also gave Jonathan time to place Jesse somewhere free from harm, as per our agreement.

Blake texted me a minute ago, confirming he was home and safe.

My solo request of Blake was that she didn't call Rocco. That she didn't call him the moment I left and divulge everything.

I don't trust her to adhere to my demand. Not for a single second.

She's a young girl caught between the gratitude she feels for me sacrificing my life to save her brother's and the callous threat she would've found a way to make me do it had I not taken matters into my own hands. Not that I blame her. If Codi were ever in dire straits, I'd throw almost anyone under the metaphorical bus, including myself, to save her.

I'm oddly at peace.

For years I feared Jonathan Waith. A monster of the worst kind. He'd wake me in my sleep and haunt me through my days. The smell of his breath, the feel of his fingertips; they were memories I couldn't erase.

Until Rocco.

Until the man I thought I hated became my road to peace, to freedom.

Maybe I have to accept that every life experience is a teachable moment. You either learn from it or fail, ready to learn in another time and place.

Maybe Rocco was never my happily ever after.

Maybe he was a life lesson.

He taught me strength. Building me up into someone I was proud to be. I no longer feared my dreams. They fucking feared me.

Come at me, motherfucker, I'd scream, *and watch me destroy you.*

He taught me self love. I no longer saw my broken parts as flaws. They were my beauty. The facets of me that made me the woman I am —the woman I *wanted* to be.

He taught me I was loveable. He sought my company over everyone else. He laughed at my jokes and listened to my fears. He smiled when I shared my dreams and encouraged them the only way he could.

He taught me how to *live*. He showed me that even hurting, I didn't have to hide away in my self-inflicted bubble of self-destruction. Even hurt and angry, I could find happiness. In fact, putting myself out there was the exact thing I needed to pull me out of my pain.

He taught me I still had love within. I had it coursing through my veins like blood. For him. For the monster I was certain I despised. For the broken spirit not so different from myself.

Maybe my end goal was to learn these lessons before I died. To allow me to rest in peace.

HE'S SO FUCKING CLICHÉ.

An abandoned warehouse? Corroded metal and smashed windows.

They say life flashes through your eyes before you die. Your whole life played out before you in a blaze of light. Your achievements and failures… your memories all played out in a click of a finger.

I disagree.

Mine hasn't flashed. It's sailed over the last hour.

Memories I've cherished, warming my heart in a way that has eaten away at the fear threatening to creep in.

The love I've felt, brandished on my heart, ensuring I know I was loved completely.

Regrets I refuse to feed.

Should I have said goodbye?

Should I have asked my dad for help?

The answer is no. Easily. I have zero doubt.

The more people involved, the greater the possibility of failure. An outcome that can't be entertained. Too many lives are at stake.

Straightening my spine, I roll my shoulders backward, stepping toward the entrance.

My feet rest on tarnished concrete, the smell of dereliction twisting my lips in distaste. The scrape of a chair echoes as he stands, their presence a blemish in an otherwise empty space.

I thought I'd feel more when I saw her. That some form of feeling, or longing would spike into the deepest crevice of my heart. I thought I would *miss* my mom or the promise of who she should've been.

I can't even say I hate her. The potent realization of *nothing* hits me when our eyes meet. She's a stranger that provokes no concern, ill-toward, or contempt.

"This is a new level of pathetic." She poisons the air with her voice. "Even for you."

"Where's Jesse?" I turn my attention to the man who has played a starring role in my nightmares for the last few years. I know he is safe, but I need Jonathan to say it. To admit that he gave something away. That he's not a master of the universe. That he had to stoop low enough to hurt a child to force my hand.

"Safe," he purrs, strolling toward me at a pace similar to a panther stalking its prey. "I had him dropped off outside your fuck buddy's home with his briefcase full of cash, as promised."

He's close enough that I can smell him. The bite of his aftershave enough to make me dry retch. I don't give him the satisfaction. Instead, I force my breath to enter and leave my body through my mouth.

"Kitty Kat," he whispers. "I've missed you." The barrel of his gun moves upward, caressing my face in a malevolent affection.

A warning. *I could kill you*, he promises.

"Unfortunately, I can't say the same."

He chuckles. A smooth sound that would make most women weep. "Where did that little backbone come from?" he teases, stepping into my body.

It takes everything I hold inside not to step back.

I lift my chin to the side, avoiding the threat of his face touching mine.

"Don't worry," he whispers into my ear. "I'll break it again soon enough."

Wrong answer, asshole, I want to scream. *It's made of fucking steel now.*

He hasn't changed in the years since I escaped his wrath. Your typical Wall Street jerk. Too pretty to be taken seriously by the big boys. Too weak to be accepted by the underworld. He's a wannabe mobster living off his daddy's money because everyone can see him for the flake he is.

His dark hair has grown. Gone is the clean slick-back style. In its place a grown-out mess of wavy locks that cut across the line of his face like a Hollywood heartthrob. Skin a little too pale, lips a little too red. He's uncomfortable to look at. Attractive but minacious.

"Are you going to kill me?" I ask.

Tongue peeking out to wet his lips, he taps his gun against his thigh. "I don't know."

"Of course, he is," Sarah interrupts. "Are you as stupid as you are weak?"

He ignores her, never moving his eyes from mine.

"Imagine how daddy will feel when his precious *Ryn* is stripped from his world."

I close my eyes against her threat, refusing to think of the pain my father and Codi will feel on my death.

She laughs, a horrible sound that resembles a dying hyena. "This is just so much fun. I might have to take away that ungrateful sister of yours as well."

I step toward her. "That wasn't part of the deal."

"*News-fucking-flash, Camryn,*" she roars. "I'm in charge. I say who the fuck dies and when."

The deafening *bang* of Jonathan's gun firing ricochets through the empty warehouse, bouncing off the walls loud enough to make me flinch. It sails past my head with a crack that makes my eyes water. I don't hear it hit her, but I hear the solid thump of her body hitting the dirty concrete floor with a finality she didn't see coming.

Rest in fucking hell, Mother.

Here lives Sarah Rein.

Deceitful wife.

Neglectful mother.

Toxic human.

"Thank fuck," Jonathan groans. "You know how annoying that bitch was. Fuck. I almost shot her so many fucking times."

I don't move my gaze from my mother as he speaks. I watch the blood around her head grow with every second that passes. A puddle of life that is no longer hers. It belongs to the concrete now. Forever stained as an imperfection in this world. A contamination of the world, in both life and death.

I recoil as Jonathan's fingers grip my chin, demanding my attention. "But if I killed her too soon," he murmurs, "I may never have gotten you to come to me. Willingly, like a good little Kitty Kat."

I want to vomit.

"Now." His hand twists into my hair, pulling it roughly to expose the line of my neck. My grunt of pain makes him smile, and my heart flutters with the beginning of panic. Lifting his gun, he trails the barrel —still hot from the murder of my mother—from my chin down to the hollow notch of my jugular. Pushing hard enough to stop my breath, he leans forward, sucking in the choke of air I exhale. "You'll need to be punished," he threatens. "Leaving me the way you did." He *tsks*. "You made me so mad," he grits against my lips, and I pray he can't feel me shaking. "I wanted to *kill* you and your fucking sister, just for the inconvenience."

"Leave Codi out of this." My voice sounds strangled, the barrel of his gun still leaving me with little air.

Anger flashes through his eyes, and he grabs at my jaw, moving to shove his gun into my mouth. "Don't make fucking demands of me, cunt. You should be on your fucking knees *begging* me to spare you for the shit you pulled."

"I'd rather you shoot me," I mumble around the metal.

He takes a step back, throwing his head back to laugh.

"Don't fucking tempt me. A few years away from me, and you think you're s*trong*? I broke you down with ease once; I'll do it a-fucking-gain. Your little warrior act is cute, but best accept you're back with me, Kitty Kat."

Sliding forward, he bends his neck, making sure I can see his eyes.

"Now, get on your fucking knees."

"Go to hell."

"Oh, I'm sure I will. Just not today." He steps into my body, leaning into me harshly. My neck tips back to keep him in focus. "Get. On. Your. Fucking. Knees."

I refuse to move.

Palm to my chest, he shoves me. *Hard.*

I stumble but don't fall.

He moves forward again, gripping my shirt to lift me off my feet. The muscles in his arms bulge in exertion.

This time he throws me.

Hands flailing, I land on my ass. I yelp in pain, a gust of air jumping from my throat on impact.

Crab walking backward, I scurry away.

But he's faster.

He's on me in a flash and lifts me by my hair.

I wince.

Tucking his gun into the waistband of his pants, he slaps me with as much might as he can manage. Pain slices across my face. My eyes water, my cheek stings, and a trickle of blood escapes my mouth.

His chest heaves with anger.

Eyes always up.

Jonathan releases my hair, letting me stand on my own two feet.

Elbows in. Punch with your right hand first, but rotate your arm as you do.

I lift my head, ignoring the pounding in my temple.

My goal is peace.

Closing his eyes to crack his neck, I take my chance. Knees bent, I jab my right arm forward with as much power as possible, just like Rocco showed me.

You're forgetting your reinforcements. Me. At your back. Holding you up.

My fist connects with his jaw with a loud and satisfying crack. He stumbles backward, shock twisting his face in hate. Hand lifting to his jaw, he massages it roughly. Pulling it back, he takes in the smear of blood staining his skin.

"You stupid fucking bitch." He spits at the ground, a mixture of blood and saliva landing beside his Dolce & Gabbana leather shoes.

Pompous prick.

I fake a level of confidence I by no means feel, lifting my eyebrow in challenge. "Only way you'll touch me like that again is when I'm fucking dead."

He smiles, the blood from my right hook smeared across his teeth. "Your wish, Kitty Kat. My fucking command."

I could run. Sprint as fast as I fucking can. But I'm not stupid. That would only delay the inevitable.

I'm not afraid of him. He's a fucking coward who controls others through fear. If Rocco taught me anything, it was to *take* control. If I die doing it, so be it. I'm not afraid of death. I've made peace with it. I'm fucking happy to give my life away to save my family.

Grabbing me by the throat, Jonathan pulls me in, kissing my lips. A kiss of death if I've ever experienced one.

The idiot is so confident in his power he never imagined I'd be strong enough to exert my own.

I take the opportunity of him being so close, biting his lip to draw blood. My knee lifts at the same time, slamming into his tiny fucking balls.

He drops me, hand grabbing his crotch as he roars in pain.

A second later, his gun is pointed in my direction, fury like fire in his eyes.

"Too scared to fight a girl?" I taunt, throwing gasoline on the flames of his ego.

"That piece of shit Shay poisoned you."

I laugh in his face. "Rocco Shay breathed life into me. He woke the fucking fighter within me."

Licking the blood from his lip, a wretched grin spreads over his face. "Better hope he comes to your rescue, bitch."

"I don't need a hero to save me. I'm my own fucking savior."

"Your savior is gonna let you die."

I shrug, a smile on my face. "At least I'll do it with my fucking dignity intact. Unlike you, having to shoot me because you're afraid I could kill you."

Pulling his arm out of aim, he looks at his gun before dropping it to the ground. Eyes on me, he kicks it as far away as possible.

I watch it slide across the floor, coming to an abrupt stop at my mother's lifeless body.

"I'm gonna kill you," he promises. "But before I do, I'm gonna stare into your eyes as I bury my cock inside you, knowing the last thing you felt wasn't just physical pain but the death of your fucking soul."

CHAPTER THIRTY-SIX

ROCCO

I RUN INTO THE LOFT, my heart pounding like a fist against a maize bag.

Jesse stands in my kitchen, a bag of frozen peas against his eye, dried blood decorating his face.

An open briefcase lies on my counter, with hundred-dollar bills spilling out.

BLAKE

You need to come home.

The text that alerted me to the fact that something was going hideously wrong.

I move toward my son, trying to hide my panic.

Fuck. It doesn't even look *that* bad. I've been bruised up much worse in my time. But he's my boy, and no one is allowed to touch what is my fucking mine.

"Explain."

"It was me." Blake's hesitant voice sounds from my living room, and I glance away from Jesse's face, staring at her tear-filled eyes in confusion.

"What was you?"

"This," she whispers.

"You hit him?"

Jesse grunts out an unamused laugh.

"I made a deal, Rocco," Blake confesses. "With Sarah Rein. For you and Camryn."

Boom. Out here like a grenade explosion no one was ready for.

Talk about ripping a bandaid off. No prelude. No lube.

Just a simple, *hey, guess what… I fucked you.*

My gaze turns back to the briefcase.

"I tried to back out," she tells me, pulling my attention again.

"When? Is that why you came into my life? To offer me up to Sarah on a silver platter? Was that the plan all along?" Bile rushes up my throat, wanting to escape.

"No," Jesse answers for her, moving away from me and toward his sister. "We never even knew we'd meet you. We came to thank Dominic for removing a threat from our lives."

"You were both in on this?"

They're expecting my anger.

Hell, *I'm* fucking expecting it.

But it doesn't come.

"No," Blake declares. "This was all me. Sarah approached *me*. Five hundred grand is a new life for us," she explains unnecessarily. "I was trying to give us something we never even dreamed of."

"I get it." My voice is hauntingly quiet. "Five hundred grand for turning on a stranger you never wanted to meet."

They both stare at me, unsure of what to say or do.

The truth is, *I* don't know what to say. I don't know what to do.

Massaging her hand, Blake's eyes never leave mine. She's scared. Hell, that's not even the right word. She's petrified. *Of me.*

"I texted her and told her I wasn't interested, that the deal was off." She moves forward, thinking better of it and stepping back.

"Is this it?" I ask, overcome with grief. "You have your cash." I gesture to the bag. "Which means you held up your end of the bargain." My eyes skate over my loft, searching for the bullet aimed at my heart.

Her head shakes in denial. "Jonathan," she starts.

"Who the fuck is Jonathan?"

Teeth to her lips, she can't bring herself to speak.

"Camryn's ex," Jesse explains.

My blood runs cold. "Sarah is working with Camryn's psychotic ex?" I can't hide the roar in my voice.

A bullet aimed at me I can handle. One in search of Camryn, not a fucking chance.

"Yes," Blake admits regretfully. "Jonathan tried to meet with me, but Jesse went in my place and told him we weren't interested."

"They didn't take that well." I gesture to my son's face. "Do you need a hospital?"

"No. Nothing a little Tylenol and frozen peas can't fix."

"So, if you haven't handed me over? Why the cash, and where's Camryn?"

It's then that Blake's face breaks open. Her tears falling with full force. Throwing herself at me, she wraps her arms around me, desperation clawing out of her. "Please don't hate me."

"Hate you?" I hug her back.

"She was here. I told her everything. She went... to save Jesse."

My arms fall away. "She went where?"

"To Sarah," Jesse answers, knowing his sister wouldn't be able to articulate the words.

My feet stumble backward, and I keep the momentum, moving into my gym to lose myself. To give myself a second of reprieve from the walls closing in.

Fists clenched, I scream into the small space that has always offered me sanctuary. I can see myself in the floor-to-ceiling mirror. I don't recognize the man staring back at me. Not anymore. Energy bursts through me, and I slam my fists against the lone bag hanging from the ceiling. I hit it again and again and again. Until my body gives out, I fall against it, hugging it to keep me upright.

She went, willingly, to a mother that won't protect her and into the arms of a man that is hellbent on hurting her. For what, *me?*

"She loves you."

I startle at Jesse's voice, brushing at the tears that had escaped during my meltdown.

"She wanted to do it."

"She didn't need to." My voice sounds like scrapped metal.

"That's not the point," Jesse argues.

I move toward him, thumb rubbing over the swell of his eye socket. "Are you sure you're okay?"

"Absolutely," he assures me. "Sarah would've come for her eventually, Rocco. All she wants in this world is to cause Dominic heartache."

"Come here." I call out to Blake, standing just outside the space, unsure of her welcome.

She steps toward me tentatively. I pull her into my body, hugging her tightly, hoping I'm reassuring her that I'm not mad. That I understand. That I don't blame them for any of this.

This was all Sarah Rein.

"I gotta make a phone call."

I HAVEN'T EVER FELT HEARTBREAK like this. I haven't ever felt *pain* like this. But then again, unyielding hate lives inside me. It makes sense that it lives within her too. I think that's where most of my pain comes from, knowing I gave her the shittiest parts of who I am.

Tears dripping down her cheeks, and her chin wobbles.

"Hey," I reassure her, forcing a smile. "It's all good, kid. You're a survivor. You did what you needed to. I respect the hell outta you for it."

"It was before I knew you," she sobs, hands rubbing together in front of her, making her look like a lost child.

I step forward, my hand gripping her chin. I can't determine if it's her jaw shaking or my hand. "I get it. You have nothing to explain to me, Blake. You did good."

She attempts to shake her head, but my hand keeps her in place. "Look at me."

Eyes squeezed shut, her tears tumble out in rivers. The lump in my throat grows thicker with every droplet that falls.

"Blake." I wait. "Look at me."

Her eyes open reluctantly.

"Meeting you and Jesse has been the greatest part of my life."

"They'll kill you," she cries.

I swallow the acid of that reality down. "Maybe." I don't lie. She's not stupid. She knew the outcome when she set it in motion.

It's the only way. I'm not leaving Camryn to fight that hell alone.

"There has to be something we can do."

I look at my son, the rush of hysteria blinking back at me. "Just don't go," he urges. "I've seen this guy. He's a fucking loose cannon. He'll shoot you on sight. You're too much of a threat. *We just got you back.*"

That's a knife wound I wasn't ready for.

"I have to," I tell him quietly.

"They'll kill Camryn anyway," Blake attests. "Sarah wants to hurt Dominic. She knows the only way to do that is through the girls."

The air leaves my lungs.

She's not wrong.

I can't even guarantee she's alive right now.

"Camryn wouldn't want you to do this. That's why she left on her own accord. To *save* you."

"It's not her battle to fight," I argue weakly.

"Let's just go," Blake implores. "The three of us. We'll start a new life somewhere else. *A fresh start.*"

"*She'll come for you,*" I yell, startling them both.

Taking a breath, I quiet the beast inside of me. "Sarah won't stop. This is the only way I know you'll be safe. You made a deal with the devil, Blake, and I'm gonna make sure that handshake is honored. It's the only way."

She shakes her head. "No."

"I don't think I've told you, but I love you." My voice cracks. Jesse walks away, his back to me, as his fist breaks the plaster of my wall. "But I do. With everything I have inside me. You've been my reason for almost eighteen years. The moments I've felt like giving up, the promise of you fed my will to live. I owe you my life." I clear my throat, my voice thick with enough emotion I can barely hear myself speak. "And that's what I'm gonna give you."

Grabbing the sides of her head, Blake begins to cry, soft, stuttered whimpers that force me to inhale to save the same sound breaking from my lips.

"I thought you were awful. That you were like him. Like Marcus, that you dying would mean nothing to me. To us."

"Stop," I tell her.

"You're my dad," she wails. "I love you. You're everything we were missing. We need you."

She looks to Jesse, searching for his agreement.

"You don't." I look between them, ignoring the grief painted on their faces. "You're a force, the both of you, and I couldn't be more fucking proud. My kids are fighters."

"I need more time with you," Jesse whispers. "*We* need more time with you."

"I know," I concede. "I'm so sorry I didn't find you sooner. I'm sorry you spent your whole life thinking someone wasn't fighting for you. I was," I assure them, hoping they believe me. "I was fighting so fucking hard to find you."

A soft knock hits my front door, and I take one last look at them before turning away.

A sullen green stare I'll never forget greets me when I open the door. A pair of eyes that once upon a time held the same level of grief and defeat as mine.

"Roc," he says, moving forward to drag me into a hug. "Good to see you, brother. I wish it was under better circumstances."

I glance over his shoulder at the hulk of a man behind him.

"Trey." His friend offers a hand, and I take it firmly.

"Appreciate you helping out."

He shrugs, dismissing my thanks.

"They don't have much shit, but here." I hand him an envelope thick with cash. "That'll cover you until the rest of my shit is sorted. Parker's number is in there too. For when you're ready."

A dip of his chin to acknowledge my words, but nothing more.

A lot passes between us at that moment.

A friendship forged in self-induced cataclysm. We were nineteen when we met—crazed and broken. In search of meaning, of purpose, hungry for destruction and appeased by our own demise. We beat the shit out of one another, neither of us coming up victorious. It was an illegal fight, one we each lost a shit-ton of cash on. But we walked from the ring bloodied, demoralized, but richer for the friendship we'd formed through our fists.

He's sorted his life, married the girl next door, and had a kid. He's settled, and I feel like a piece of shit for dragging him into the shitstorm of my life.

The truth is, friendships aren't high on my list of possessions. Yet, he's one of the few I know I can trust.

I take one last look at him before turning to the two wide-eyed teenagers standing quietly together. "Blake, Jesse, this is Archer Dean. An old friend of mine."

"What's he supposed to be?" Blake bites out. "Our security? He looks like a retired military brat. And who is that?" She points to Trey. "His resident lumberjack?"

Archer grins. "I'm not looking forward to this. Sachi's still a fucking toddler, and I can barely handle her sass."

"They're not security," I tell the twins. "Archer is one of the few people I trust in this world. You're gonna stay with him until he knows you're safe."

Blake shakes her head. "You know it's a suicide mission?" she barks at Archer, trying to camouflage the knot in her throat. "He knows they'll kill him, but he's going anyway."

Archer breaks his gaze from my daughter, eyeing my profile intensely.

"Don't tell me you wouldn't do the same." I turn to him. "Tell me you wouldn't go in for Annabelle, surrendering yourself to make sure Sachi was safe. Even if it meant adios to your life, maybe even Annabelle's."

Nostrils flaring in panic, he swallows down his anger.

"She wants me," I mumble. "Sarah Rein. She wants me," I tell him. "I need this to end. She can't come for my fucking kids."

He pulls in a thick breath, his chest expanding heavily before he blinks in acceptance. "You're gonna come and stay with my wife and me until I know you're safe." He doesn't look at the kids when he speaks to them, his eyes set solely on mine, grief in understanding tipping his lips downward.

Blake pushes forward, even as Jesse attempts to pull her back.

"No!" she yells, pushing Archer's chest. "You're his friend. Tell him *no!*"

He says nothing, letting her small fists hit him.

"He's our dad," she shrieks. "We *just* got him. Not even back because we've never even had him. We've lived our whole shitty lives without a dad. *We just fucking got him.* Help us. Please," she begs, her hands moving from their fists into prayer. "Help us keep him."

"Blake." Jesse steps up beside her, arm sliding over her shoulders to pull her into a hug.

"If you go" —she looks over his shoulder at me, thick sobs shaking her body— "I'll hate you forever."

My throat closes, her words piercing my heart like a knife never could. "If that's the way it has to be. But at least I know I protected you. In the end, I kept you safe, and I'm okay with you hating me for doing that."

Archer's hand grabs at my wrist. "Are you protected?"

"Yeah," I murmur. "I don't know what good it'll do me, but I'm going in unarmed."

Walking forward, I grip the back of Blake's neck. She fights me, trying to pull away, but I pull harder, Jesse between us. The moment my lips touch her forehead, the fight leaves her, her body convulsing with savage sobs that break away a part of my soul that will always be hers.

I kiss Jesse's temple, stepping back before I change my mind.

One last nod, and I move toward the door.

"Dad." Jesse's voice hits my back, and my knees nearly give out.

Dad.

Glancing over my shoulder, I take in my two kids, holding hands and watching me leave. "I love you. *We* love you. You were everything you were supposed to be," he sniffs. "Everything we wanted."

I turn away before I cry in front of them, forcing my feet through the door. I slam it in a violent rage, wanting to kill something.

I just hope I get the chance to rip Sarah Rein's blackened heart from her chest before she puts me down.

CHAPTER THIRTY-SEVEN

CAMRYN

"I suggest you take your hands off my girl before I sever your head from your body." His voice sounds ready to burst into a million and one fatal shards. Fragments of grief, panic, fear, and fury cut through the space like my very own barbarian.

I'm dreaming. *His* voice finding me in my final hour. The darkness has crept in, but the light of my love makes these last few minutes bearable.

I fought, and I fought fucking hard. My battle wounds are a testament to that.

My ribs aren't broken, but they're bruised like a motherfucker. A gift from Jonathan when I fell to the floor after a nasty punch to the face. His foot powered against my mid-section repeatedly until I was coughing up blood.

I can't see out of my left eye. It's swollen shut. The entire left side of my face is numb, closed off from the excruciating pain I'm certain is about to hit me at any moment.

Random scrapes and cuts decorate my weakened body. Blood is smeared along my skin in a potent reminder of failure.

Jonathan doesn't look fabulous, either. Better than me, but still, no fucking oil painting. From what I can see out of my right eye anyway.

That's the thing about fighting for your life. Everything else falls away. Nothing mattered to me in that volcano of violence. We erupted. I knew if I stopped, if I paused, if I gave up... I was dead. I may be ready to die. But I wasn't going without a fight. I wasn't going willingly to his idea of hell.

I took everything Rocco taught me and threw that power into my fists. *Freedom.* I kept reminding myself. I was fighting for freedom.

The knife Jonathan holds at the breast of my shirt—ready to rid me of my clothing and the last glimmer of hope I had for my soul —pauses.

My body is weak and ready to collapse. I'm nothing more than a puppet. Threads of control held at Jonathan's will, manipulated for his enjoyment. Twisting me easily, he slams my back against his chest.

I grunt out in pain.

"Beauty," Rocco's voice sounds as broken as it did moments prior. His restraint is hanging on by the thinnest of threads.

"Safe." I try to smile, working to reassure him that I'm okay.

"Safe," Rocco echoes, trying to tell me that's now where I stand.

I want to reach out and tell him that he doesn't need to look so sad. I did this so *he* could be happy. Sarah is dead. I won. *I fucking won.* I fought, and because I did, he can have his happily ever after.

It would've all been fine if he had stayed away. If he let me offer him this sacrifice for his peace.

Jonathan's laugh startles me, and the heaviness in my head passes enough for me to lift it.

I let myself become lost in the man before me. Standing only a few feet in front of me, I could reach him in six, maybe seven steps. Big and formidable and affectionately *deranged.*

He looks ready to kill. Only, we're at a disadvantage.

"I'm so fucking glad you could join us, Shay. You're just in time," Jonathan laughs maniacally, the sound shooting goosebumps over my cut and bruised skin.

Rocco doesn't speak. His chest heaves with a fury that makes his eyes look black.

"You touched what was mine, asshole," the man holding me as a shield bites out, the disgust in his words palpable.

"How you holding up, Cami?" He speaks to me as though Jonathan doesn't exist. He's a nobody. He's insignificant.

I'd believe it a little more if there wasn't a knife pressed against my abdomen.

"You look real," I whisper, liking that he keeps moving closer. I'm hoping that he's not a figment of my imagination.

"I am real, beauty. Reinforcements, remember?"

My eyes attempt to close, but a hand in my hair pulls my head back, forcing my eyes open on an anguished whimper.

"Put the fucking gun down."

"I'm not carrying."

"Don't fucking lie to me," Jonathan bellows, specks of his spit flying past my face, stinging the open cuts.

The sharp bite of his knife catches my neck, and I stand still, afraid to breathe for fear it'll cut me.

Rocco concedes, hands lifting in surrender before he pulls a gun from the waist of his pants, bending to place it on the ground.

"Kick it away."

He does as he's told.

"You shouldn't have come," I tell him.

"You shouldn't have gone."

"I love you," I tell him, needing him to know, unsure if I'll ever get another chance.

Jonathan's tongue touches my neck, mocking my declaration.

Rocco surges forward, but the knife against my neck pushes harder, forcing his feet to stop.

Pulling the blade along the delicate skin, he rips at my skin, letting blood trickle down my neck.

I whimper in pain, the warmth of my blood making me shake.

"Control." Rocco stares into me.

"Control," I repeat.

Jonathan has no control. He's lost to his need for revenge. He's not fighting *for* anything. He's fighting *with* the hate inside him.

Too consumed with himself, Jonathan lifts the blade from my neck, licking my blood in warning.

"Elbow, beauty."

As tired as my body is, I lift my arm, bending it at the elbow to slam it back as hard as possible.

Jonathan's grip loosens, and I dive away, lunging for the gun discarded at my mother's feet.

He's right on my heels, his heavy footfalls thrumming against the ground. I flip my body, gun aimed straight at his heart.

Jonathan pauses with a wicked smile on his face. He lifts his hands into the air in a mocking surrender. He doesn't think I'm capable. He doesn't think I'm willing.

"Don't come any closer," I scream.

"You wouldn't have the fucking balls." He spits on me.

I resist the urge to wipe his saliva off my face. Gun still aimed, my arm shakes.

"Do it." He steps closer. "I fucking dare you, bitch."

Thick, heavy sobs fall from my mouth. I can't make them stop.

"I HATE YOU!" I shriek. "I HATE YOU!"

Everything he'd put me through pulses my finger on the trigger. The pain he's caused me. The sleepless nights and the way I cut myself to forget. The liberty he took on *everything* in my life. All of it. Every last thing comes crashing down on me like a tsunami I can't escape.

I'm gasping for air.

I can't see. My tears cloud my vision.

I can't move, save for my constant shaking. I've frozen in fear.

I don't hear Rocco's approach. I don't even feel him until his arms are wrapped tightly around me.

"Give me the gun, beauty."

"No," I sob. "He needs to die. I w-want hi-imm t-t-to d-die."

Only, I can't bring myself to do it. He's right. I'm *not* capable. I hate him, but the thought of killing him, of taking his life, is too much for me to comprehend.

"It's not worth the guilt, Cami."

I shift away as he moves his arm along mine. The indecision pulsates through me like a bass drum.

Kill him, it commands.

Don't, it pleads.

"Trust me. Don't let him fuck with you like this. You're stronger than he is. Look at him, Cami. He's at your fucking mercy. *Yours.*" His hand rests atop mine on the gun. He removes it from my grip, and I fall into him.

Hands balled against his muscular chest, my tears soak through his shirt. I can't hear anything except for my erratic breathing.

"The two of you deserve one another," Jonathan—still standing only a few feet from us—spits. "Fucking pathetic. Just know, Shay, you have my sloppy—"

Three bullets penetrate his chest in quick succession.

Bang.

Bang.

Fucking BANG.

I cry out in shock. He falls to the ground, and the thud he makes as he hits the concrete isn't different from the sound my mother made.

"Never said he wasn't gonna die," Rocco murmurs. "Just didn't want you carrying that burden with you for eternity. "

I look up at him through glassy eyes. "What about you?"

"Baby, taking that piece of shit's life isn't a stain on my conscience. It's a gold fucking star."

My hands stretch up to his face. I need to feel him. "You came for me."

"Never a doubt, Cami. I told you, I fucking bleed for you."

"I bleed for you, too."

His eyes scan my face. "I wish that wasn't so fucking literal. Look at you."

His fingers gently trace every cut and bruise across my face.

Unable to take it anymore, I pull his face to mine, needing to feel his lips.

His kiss is hesitant and dictated by fear and restraint.

"Kiss me," I beg.

One hand in my hair, the other grabs my ass, pulling me into him. Still, the kiss is tender. *Too* fucking tender.

Pulling back, I stare into his panic-stricken eyes.

"I almost fucking died. Let me feel alive, Rocco. *Kiss. Me.*"

Something snaps deep within him, and his lips slam against mine.

If he tastes the blood dripping from the split in my lip, it only fires him up more. He can't get enough of me. Lips wide enough to devour me, we become consumed by one another.

Our tongues clash. Our lips collide. And our hearts find a rhythm.

It's done, it beats.

The end, it thumps.

With you, it pounds.

With. You.

Pulling apart reluctantly, we stare at one another.

"I'm so fucking mad that you put yourself in this position."

"I'd do it a hundred times over, Rocco," I whisper, hoping he believes me. "I was not going to let my toxic mother or monster of an ex play with Blake and Jesse's lives like that. If I lost my life to save theirs, I would've died happy."

"If you had…" He trails off, unable to say the words.

"Hey." I grab his hand, placing it over my heart. "I didn't, and I'm not going to. I fought, Rocco." Tears hit my eyes unexpectedly. "I fucking fought, and I *won.*"

"Yeah, you did." His eyes are as glassy as mine, and without a breath between us, he kisses me again.

"How did you find me?" I ask when our kiss ends.

Scratching at his beard, he shrugs. "I may have taken a page outta Dominic's book and linked the find your phone app on your and the twins' phones."

I attempt to raise an eyebrow, but it hurts too much. "You're stalking me."

"Saved your life," he mumbles. "You had no issue with your dad doing it, so, uh…"

"Invasion of privacy, Rocco," I stonewall.

"Are you mad?" he gripes.

I only need a second to think about it. "Well, no, not exactly."

"Then let's stop fucking talking about it. I love you. I need you. I wanted to make sure if anything like this ever went fucking down and the dickhead that took you was as dumb as this cunt and didn't check you, I'd be able to find you."

Reaching up on my tiptoes—holding my ribs because fucking *ouch* —I push my lips against his. "Let's go home."

I don't look back as we leave the warehouse, my heart wrapped up in the man beside me.

My dad was right. If you're looking back at your past, you'll stumble into your future. I wasn't going to do that. I was finally at peace. I was free, and I would embrace that like the love of the man holding me up.

CHAPTER THIRTY-EIGHT

ROCCO

DOMINIC'S GUYS are on their way to do clean-up. I didn't give him too much information—enough for him to know that Sarah and Jonathan are dead and that Camryn and I are alive.

He started yelling at me over the phone, sprouting some shit about me going off half-cocked, but I hung up. I had my girl back, and I was going to enjoy that fact. I also needed to get back to my kids. Which meant I needed to call Archer and ask him to bring them right the fuck back home. A call he was more than happy to receive.

Camryn sits quietly in the passenger seat of my car, dozing in and out. She assured me she didn't have a concussion and that I needed to *calm my farm*. A bit fucking hard to do when your girl is bruised from head to fucking toe.

It makes me sick to think about the things that she went through. The way Jonathan hurt her. But as angry as I am, as fucking raging as I am, I have no urge to *fight*. All that unfiltered rage has returned to my need to be with her. To make sure she's okay.

Even in the warehouse. The way he stood over her when she was aiming to shoot. I could've killed him. I have no doubt I was angry enough to rip his head clean off his fucking body. I wanted to beat his face into the ground until nothing was left but blood and gristle. I craved to tear him apart, limb from limb, and set him on fire.

But *more* than any of that. I needed to get to her. I needed to make sure her finger didn't press down on that trigger. Jonathan was wrong, she definitely had it in her. I have zero doubt, but she didn't *want* to. The fear was painted openly in her eyes. He read it as her fear for him, but it wasn't that. Not at all. It was the fear of taking another person's life that gave her pause.

"Is Jesse okay?" She breaks me from my thoughts.

"The two of you look like twins."

Her right eye—the one not swollen shut—closes in sadness.

"Hey." I lean over, taking her hand in mine. "He's fine."

"Why was my mother so toxic?" she asks, a desperate need for answers dripping along her words in prayer.

"Sarah was messed up, beauty. The same way Marcus was. Same way Kane ended up. Circumstance has a lot to do with it... I'm guessing so, anyway. But I think they had something evil brewing within them to make them turn so fucking nasty."

Unhappy with my answer, she looks out the window with a defeated sigh.

"Kane's evil was power." I pull her attention back to me. "Some people can't handle it. People like him. He craved it like nothing I'd ever seen before. When he had it, something switched in him. His humanity just disappeared."

She watches my profile as I drive, her hand holding onto mine in a delicate urgency.

"Sarah, I don't know. I'm guessing the drugs and alcohol fucked with her enough to strip away her conscience. It's easy to forget all the shitty things you've done when you're blacked out half the time. She took the shitty things that happened in her life and let them rot inside her, Cami. You had far worse shit happen to you, and you built your life on helping others. But, as I said, something evil was pumping through her veins."

"And Marcus?" she tests quietly.

"Should've been swallowed from the get-go. Even that would've been nasty enough for his mother. No rhyme or reason with that cunt, beauty. He was plain fucking evil. Born into an earthside purgatory that never should've existed."

"Thank you for saving me."

Lifting her hand to kiss her knuckles, I smile against her skin. "'Bout time I repaid the favor, don't you think?"

Blake jumps on me the moment I open the door of my loft. Arms and legs wrapping around me like an octopus. She says nothing, not that she needs to. Her actions scream louder than any words could.

Jesse, a little more graceful, hugs my side. But he refuses to lift his head. I feel the wetness of his tears dampen the cotton of my shirt, and I swallow down my need to do the same by squeezing him tighter.

"Could fucking kill you." Parker approaches. "I haven't even begun to deconstruct everything that just went on, but when your two kids aren't attached to you, you better believe I'm gonna beat your ass."

I smile at him, lifting my hand for him to grab hold. "Like to see you try, doll face."

Standing by my side, Cami has been swamped by her sister and dad. Too many arms trying to hug her at the same time.

"Guys," she grits out. "Few bruised ribs here. *Chill.*"

Tears are streaming down Codi's face. "Ryn, oh my God. You're so hurt."

"Physically, I'm a bit of a mess," she agrees. "But I feel great, Codi. I promise."

"I'm so sorry, Ryn." Blake adopts her nickname with an ease that makes my heart thunder in my chest.

"You have nothing to apologize for, sweet girl. I promise. Like I told Codi, I feel great."

Dominic, eyeing me like he's ready to pull a pistol on me any second, steps closer, and I hold a hand up.

"You once told me that when retaliation is taken out in anger and impatience, it's messy and tends to lead to incrimination."

He stares at me blankly.

"So you're welcome."

Glancing at Camryn and then back to me, he swallows heavily enough that we can all hear it. "Thank you." His words are barely audible beyond the lump sitting in his throat.

"Do you need a hospital, Cami?" This comes from my son, standing cautiously against my side, watching her. He feels responsible for the wounds decorating her face.

"Nah, kiddo." She attempts to smile. "Nothing some steri-strips, a bandage, and a large glass of vodka can't fix."

"And frozen peas," he adds with a smile, relief softening the stern look on his face.

She laughs, the movement enough to cause her pain, not that she lets on.

"Not a scratch on you." Archer only makes his approach after our families have swarmed us. "I need to mess your pretty face up for old times' sake."

"Only if your wife is happy to have you go home bruised and broken."

"Absolutely fucking not." A smoking hot brunette moves to stand beside my friend, big brown eyes dancing in curiosity. "Annabelle Dean," she introduces herself. "And I'll kill you if you ruin his pretty face. I'm more than a little fond of it."

I lift my chin in greeting, watching the change in Archer's face when he looks at hers.

Whipped.

For. Fucking. Sure.

"Don't fucking look at me like that," he gripes. "You're so far down the same rabbit hole, you can't even see the fucking light."

"Whatever that means," Annabelle muses, looking at Camryn with a look that bleeds exasperation. "It was nice to meet you guys, even under the shitty circumstances." Grief flashes through her eyes, one of camaraderie and shared feelings. A story of heartache untold. "We should be getting back to Sachi."

"Are you sure?" Jesse steps forward, a pink touch growing on his cheekbones.

Archer hides his smirk under a rough rub of his jaw.

"Kid, you steal her away, and I'll have to kick your dad's ass.."

Jesse looks embarrassed, but it gives way to delight when Annabelle hugs him. "Get your dad and Camryn to come and visit. Jake'll teach you guitar like he promised."

"Don't forget that Luca offered to take me for a ride on his Harley."

I look at Archer in appreciation. My kids were in meltdown, digesting a level of guilt they'd easily drown in, all the while facing the fear of losing their dad, and he gave them the one thing that could distract them.

Family.

He gave them *his* family, letting them know no matter what happened, they had a group of people that would turn up for them.

"Forever in your debt," I murmur.

"No such thing. Just don't be so much of a stranger. Our family would love to meet you." He looks around the room. "All of you."

"YOU SURE YOU don't need a hospital?"

She stands from her position on my bed. "Nurse." She points at her chest. "Civilian." She points at mine. "I'm fine. I promise. I just want a shower to clean his stench off my skin."

She takes two steps before I grab her arm, forcing her to look into my eyes.

"I'm not gonna cut, baby," she assures me, reading me right. "He's gone, and that is in part to me. I don't need to be afraid of him anymore. You built me up, Rocco. I don't need pain to survive the day. I have something more formidable. I have you. I have love. For me. For you."

I search her eyes for a lie, for an untruth that will see blood pouring from a handmade cut on her skin, but I see none.

Leaning forward, I touch my lips to her forehead before letting her go.

I'm spent. Mentally and physically fucking drained. I could sleep for a hundred years and still be tired. I'm sure of it.

We only managed to kick everyone out half an hour ago. Everyone was too scared to leave us for fear they'd never see us again. Ultimately, I had to turn total cunt and tell them to go before I used physical violence.

Jesse and Blake crashed out about an hour before that all went down. They haven't moved an inch. I just checked on them, and they're snoring like two kids who are *comfortable.*

My chest expands in pride. My kids are comfortable. With me. In *my* fucking house. I'm not an idiot. I know we have a long path ahead of us. One that'll be filled with bumps and scrapes and hurt feelings. But for tonight, they're content and warm and safe, and I feel like the greatest fucking dad in the world.

The bathroom door opens, and I turn my head on the pillow.

She's naked.

Completely. Fucking. Naked.

Skin wet.

Droplets of water racing down her body, tasting her skin in a way I'd kill to do.

Her toweled dried hair hangs around her shoulders, the ends tickling the hard cut of her nipples.

"Cami," I warn, sitting up.

Legs thrown over the bed, I rest my elbows on my knees, taking in the sight of her before I make her get dressed.

We can't. Not tonight. Not after what she's been through.

"I'm wet," she tells me quietly.

"There's a towel." My voice cracks as I speak, and I clear my throat, pointing toward the bathroom.

A grin slides across her lips that is full of promises I'm not ready to accept.

"Not that kinda wet, baby." Her hand cups her pussy, sliding back and forth. "*Wet.*"

Head tipped back, I groan. The sound stripped bare, kinda like my control.

"I'm desperate." She steps closer, her hips swaying with too much temptation for me to watch.

I close my eyes.

"I'm *miserable*," she says, kneeling in front of me. "It's all I can think about. All I want. I'm going crazy."

I move to stand.

"Rocco." Her hand pushes against my cock. It's so hard, it's ready to burst through my jeans. Her words pumping blood to it with every whispered syllable. "*Please.*"

I growl, unsure what to say or do.

"I'm ready," she promises.

I move to argue, but her teeth bite into her lip, head shaking to silence me.

"I *need* you. I have *so* much energy coursing through me, and I need a release. I need to *feel* you. I need you to touch me. To taste me," she moans, massaging the crotch of my jeans. "Baby, I'm not just begging. I'm crying for you to fuck me. *Love* me, Rocco. Show me how hard you love me."

"I won't be able to control—"

"I don't want you to," she cuts me off, unbuckling my belt.

I make no move to stop her.

"I don't want you to be gentle." She slides my zipper down.

A soft moan escapes from her lips when she sees the outline of my cock through my boxers.

"I dreamt about you, about *this.*"

"Tell me," I grit out.

"You bent me over my bed."

"Mm," I encourage her to continue as her fingertips trace the line of my dick through the material.

"God," she groans. "You fucked me so hard, Rocco. *So. Hard.*"

I don't know if she's talking about her dream or my cock right now. Either way, I'm a goner.

Her two index fingers slide along the waistline of my boxers, teasing me. "You bit my nipples. You slapped my ass, my *pussy.* Fuck. I came so hard."

Boxers pulled down, the heavy weight of my cock falls out, my crown a breath away from her lips.

"And then I woke up." She looks up at me, tongue poking out to brush along the slit of my dick. "And I was so sad. And horny." She nods, sucking the head of my cock between her beaten-up lips. "So fucking horny," she mumbles.

Unable to take it any longer, I lift her under her arms. My cock hits her stomach, and I step into her, trapping it between us.

"Challenge fucking accepted."

Arms thrown over my shoulders, she kisses my lips.

Hands gripping her hips, I lift her easily. Like her arms, her legs wrap around me until every inch of her body is pressed against mine.

Pushing her back against the closest wall, I grip the base of my cock, my free hand slamming against the wall. She's pinned between me and the plaster, unable to move.

I tease the head of my dick against her clit. Over and over again until she's grinding against me, mewling, and begging for me.

Please, Rocco.

Fuck me.

Inside.

Baby. I can't take it.

Oh God.

Lifting her onto the tip of my cock, I let her balance there.

She shifts, trying to drop down, but I keep her *just* out of reach.

"Tell me you love me."

"I love you," she rushes out at the same time I impale her on my cock.

Hand over her mouth, I muffle the scream that would shatter my fucking windows.

I could come right now. My cock throbs like thunder inside of her. Cracking with the need to split open and spill inside of her.

"Fuck, Cami."

"Yes," she stutters. "Fuck. Now. Me. Fuck me."

Lips attached to her neck, I suck at her skin, grinding my hips, not yet willing to let go of the feel of her pussy clamped down on me.

I need to be gentle, her ribs are bruised, but she seems oblivious to the pain. Too consumed with unadulterated need to know they exist when she has the feel of my cock in her cunt.

Hands to my shoulders, she pushes herself up, and I grin.

"Greedy, bitch."

She laughs. "Fuck me, asshole."

Sliding out of her body, she grips me the entire way.

Just my tip rested inside her, I pull my face from her neck. Our eyes meet. "Ready for freedom, baby?"

"I already am free. Now hurry up and claim me."

I drive inside her, my thrust so hard the wall shakes.

She whimpers—a little bit of pain, a whole lot of pleasure.

I do it again.

She bites my shoulder, and I groan in bliss.

My thrusts come on quicker and quicker, firing inside her in a need to bruise her. I want her to know she belongs to me.

"*Yes,*" she breathes, head tipping back to expose her neck.

I bite it hard enough to leave marks.

Her pulse quickens under my teeth.

The sound of our fucking echoes through my room. The wet slide of my cock in her soaking pussy. The short, sharp breaths that we can taste between open lips. A slap of skin. A thundering heartbeat.

"Rocco," she screams.

"Cami, baby," I choke out. "Grip me harder. Come."

She does.

Violently.

Her entire body tenses, locking solid for a full breath before breaking beneath me. Arms stretched outward, her legs tighten against my hips. Her whole body shakes through her orgasm. A savage quake that clamps her pussy walls so tightly, I blow immediately.

"Fuck. Fuck. Yes. Cami."

Coming down from our climax, I drop my lips to hers. Kissing her in a way I plan to do forever.

Lips separating, she smirks at me. "I think I broke my rib."

Twisting from the wall, I drop her to my bed, the softness of the mattress catching a groan of relief from her.

"I'm so fucking happy right now, beauty," I confess. "I've got you. I've got my kids. I'm just so fucking happy."

I searched for it my whole life. Freedom. Peace. And in the end, that's what I found.

My kids offered me peace—a place for my heart to rest.

Camryn offered me freedom—a place for my heart to find a home.

EPILOGUE
ROCCO

"Rocco," she whines, bucking her hips upward, trying to escape. "The twins will be home from school soon."

"Wife." I grab her hips, pinning them to our bed roughly. "Shut the fuck up and let me eat your fucking pussy."

Rising to her elbows, her blue eyes stare into mine.

"We've been like ships in the night for a week. Let me eat you."

"It's been one night, baby." She laughs at me.

"Same difference," I grumble. "Have I ever told you I hate you working the night shift?"

"Once or twice." She arches up, pushing her pussy into my face.

Temptress.

Bitches. Complains. Still. She needs her cunt licked at least once a day.

My tongue drags heavily against her clit, resting there for a second before continuing. Her eyes roll backward, her head tipped back as she groans loud and long.

I made her marry me about a month after I shot her shithead ex in the heart. She didn't put up a fight, hell, she all but raced us down to the courthouse to have it sorted.

It was small. Zero fanfare. Blake, Jesse, and Parker. Codi and

Dominic. That's it. Our nearest and dearest were there to witness the most important thing we've ever held. *Love.*

Camryn fucking Shay.

My savior.

"Suck," she instructs, and I pull back.

"Who's eating who here? Let me do my thing."

Eyeballing me, she lifts a dark brow. "Rocco, the twins are going to be home any minute. I'd prefer them *not* to walk in on your tongue dragging up and down my pussy. I'm trying to come faster."

I shrug. "Would serve them right for barging in. I don't *want* you to come faster. You're all wet and dripping for me. I want to live down here for hours."

She laughs, the sound morphing into a moan as I suck on her clit.

"I don't have hours," she pants. "Yes, keep going. I have to, oh god, don't stop…"

I pull away. "You were saying?"

"You're evil." She drops to the bed heavily with an irritated sigh. "I wanna make the twins afternoon tea before I have to run to my OB appointment."

I rub the small swell of her stomach with my hand.

My baby.

My. Fucking. Baby.

Growing inside of her.

Five months along, and her belly still hasn't popped. It annoys me that she can hide our baby under her work scrubs. I want it to be visible to everyone.

Back off, I want it to scream. *I have a daddy who'll happily kill you with his bare hands.*

"Two minutes, Rocco," she warns. "I have it timed to perfection. You have one hundred and twenty seconds to make me come."

I laugh against the smooth line of her pussy. "That's not even a challenge, beauty. A finger in your ass, tongue pressed against your clit, and you're done in about five seconds flat."

"Confident," she baits.

Instead of doing as I threatened, I slide two fingers into her pussy. They glide in easily with how heady her excitement is. She pushes into my touch, making me press against the rough spot inside her that makes her weep.

Fingers massaging inside of her, I kiss along her thigh. Then, moving up until I find the scattering of scars that have faded into white cords of yesterday, I lick each one, tasting the beauty of her once broken soul.

She whimpers. Her breaths coming on faster with every tender caress of my tongue.

"So beautiful."

"*Rocco*," she cries.

"Let go, beauty," I murmur.

She groans. "Catch me."

I growl, knowing she's close. The walls of her pussy throb around my fingers. Her body stretches out, muscles like granite, readying themselves to shatter.

Dropping back down to her cunt, I lap at the excitement making her glisten. She shudders. *So close.* Lips latching onto her clit. I suck. *Hard.*

She falls into pieces around me, an orgasm so intense she screams out my name.

And I do exactly as I promised.

Mouth still sucking on her clit, hands gripped to her hips hard enough to leave marks, face buried as far into her pussy as I can be... I catch her.

Not two seconds later, the front door opens, and the sound of two teenagers arguing echoes through the loft.

Pulling back reluctantly, I wipe at my mouth and beard, the excess of her orgasm transferring to my hand. She watches me as I lick at my palm, savoring the last of her taste. "Challenge accepted, fought, and won, baby."

Falling to the bed with a groan, she slams a pillow to her face, screaming into it.

"You're gonna have to wait for me to fuck you."

Throwing the pillow at me, she frowns. "I fucking know, asshole. I'm going to meet my OB with damp panties. Let's hope he doesn't do an internal. I might fucking come."

I snarl. "Codi's not going to this appointment with you. I am. He touches you wrong, and you can visit me for conjugals."

Her laughter rings out around me. "Baby. You've met my OB. *She* is a fifty-year-old woman."

I grumble. "Still."

"I love you, but wash your face and greet your children."

"Why do I need to wash my face?" I lick my beard.

"Are you gonna kiss your son and daughter's face with my cum on your lips?"

"Having kids is a pain in my dick sometimes."

"Go." She kicks at my chest.

"JESSE RECEIVED an award at school today for his reading."

Pride storms through me.

"It's no big deal. Stop talking about it, Blake."

"It is a big fucking deal," I combat. "Did they give you a certificate or something?"

He looks at me, pride in his eyes but the nonchalance of a teenage boy dipping his shoulders. "Yeah, but it's lame."

"Not to me, it isn't. Give it."

Twisting his bag to his front, I watch him unzip the backpack without argument. Pulling the small piece of white card from the depths of the bag, he hands it over.

I can't stop the smile on my face. My boy is coming leaps and fucking bounds with a solid education. He's smart, super fucking smart. He just never had anyone invested in him enough to see it.

Moving toward the fridge, I place it front and center, making sure he knows how fucking proud of him I am. Camryn's arm slides along my waist, and I drop a kiss on the crown of her head, refusing to take my eyes off the fridge.,

"You crying, Cami?" Blake asks.

I look down at her as she swipes her eyes. "Yes," she grumbles. "Pregnancy hormones are killing me. Whenever I'm ridiculously happy, my eyes just start leaking."

Jesse's smile is coy. "Blake almost got suspended today."

"Jesse," she speaks through her teeth. "We're celebrating you, not talking about me."

"What happened?" I ask stonily, turning Camryn and me to look at her.

"Some bitch started talking shit about the fact that my mom was a junkie, so I punched her."

"Makes sense," I agree with a nod.

Camryn *tsks*. "What your dad meant to say is that you can't go around punching everyone that offends you, honey. Your dad was the one who taught me not to let my self-worth be affected by someone else's words."

My daughter shrugs, moving to the muffins that Camryn had made earlier today. "Oh, I didn't care what she said. My mom *was* a junkie. She was annoying me." She takes a bite. "Plus, she needed to know not to disrespect you by telling everyone I didn't have a mom."

The waterworks. Again. "*Jesus.*"

"Come here." I pull my wife into a hug, smiling at the twins in bewilderment.

Blake comes up behind us, moving into our hug, arms wrapped around the crying pregnant woman in my arms. "Jesse, get your ass over here."

Lips finding her temple, Jesse's arms cocoon her even more.

"Aren't you guys just the sweetest?" The rough teasing of Parker's voice has each of our heads turning.

"I am so in on this hug," Codi declares, moving toward us at a speed that tells me she's afraid we'll break the embrace off before she reaches us. "Parker," she calls. "You too."

"I'm good, Sugar. I'm just going to take a photo so I can threaten Roc's man card whenever he tries to beat his chest."

His wife snaps her fingers. "Don't make me threaten you with things you don't wanna lose."

Blake pretends to vomit.

"Jesus, Aunt Codi," Jesse grumbles.

Still, it works, and I grin at my brother triumphantly as he steps up behind his wife, arms stretched as wide as they'll go to surround us. "This is weird."

"You should be used to it by now," Camryn, tears having subsided, tells him.

"It's not weird. It's family," Blake hums, squeezing in tighter.

Family.

Codi and Camryn head off a few minutes later, leaving the four of us in the kitchen.

"The girls are gonna meet us for a bite when they're done. We just need to text them and Dominic where to meet us. We're celebrating this." I point to Jesse's award.

Parker, reading over the certificate, smiles big. "Right on, nephew." He pushes his fist against Jesse's.

"Can we go see Lila and Mira first?" Blake asks.

"Of course," I tell them. "Go change. We'll head out in five."

They race each other to their bedroom. They've finally conceded to a renovation to give one another some privacy. Archer has an architect friend working on the plans as we speak.

"Like this look on you." Parker's hand slaps my back.

"What look?" I turn to him.

"Proud dad."

I bark out a laugh, not willing to deny it. I am a fucking proud dad.

It's been nearly ten months since Cami and I almost lost everything. Ten months of healing and navigating our way through parenting two teenagers who were used to taking care of themselves.

It's been tough, but that hasn't stopped me from taking every day as a blessing. I missed the first sixteen years, so I take every day, even the tough ones, in my stride.

They both jumped at the chance to speak with a therapist. They seem to get a lot out of it, talking out their feelings and thoughts with a stranger. They come back *lighter* after every session. They're healing.

I NO LONGER HAVE TO *FORCE* MYSELF to take each step forward when I visit Mom and Mira. The wet grass is a welcome mat, a familial spot to place my feet.

The flowers no longer scream death and loss to me. They tell a story of love.

The kids get a lot out of coming here. Especially Blake. She'll talk Mom and Mira's ear off for an hour, chatting about life and mind-numbing nonsense like reality TV and social media drama. You'd think they were talking back to her. Maybe in Blake's way, they are.

Hands full of white roses, the twins place a large bunch on my mother's headstone.

I swear I could see them if I looked up. Lila and Mira. Watching the four of us with broad smiles and happiness in their eyes. It's taken me a long time to realize that Lila never wanted nor needed retribution. She needed this. *Love.* She wanted Parker and me to find our place in the world, surrounded by a love she could no longer give us.

It was a bloodied and downright scary road at times, but with her watching over us, we finally found it.

We found them.

Rein and Shay. A battle forged in hate and won through something more powerful than any of us could imagine.

Love.

That was all she ever needed, and now she finally has what I'd been fighting for all my life. *Peace.*

***

THANK you for reading Reining Devotion. We hope you loved Rocco and Ryn!

Not ready to say goodbye?
We have an *extended* epilogue for both Parker and Rocco.
They're available in our newsletter, and you can sign up here.

If you enjoyed Reining Devotion, you'll *love* our mafia series **Lies of the Underworld.** It's dark and dirty, and you can read the first chapter of Virtuous Lies after the acknowledgments.

If you started with Reining Devotion and *need* to go back and read Parker and Codi's story, you can find Tangled Love here.

ROCCO & RYN'S PLAYLIST

Don't Be A Fool, **Shawn Mendes**
Your Song, **Rita Ora**
Fallin', **Jessica Mauboy**
Praying, **Kesha**
Warrior, **Demi Lovato**
Bloodstone, **Guy Sebastian**
Toxic, **Alex & Sierra**
Breaking The Law, **Emeli Sandè**
A Drop In The Ocean, **Ron Pope**
Dear No One, **Tori Kelly**
Blue Blood, **Laurel**
I Found, **Amber Run**
Tequila, **Dan + Shay**
Someone You Loved, **Lewis Capaldi**
Wait, **JP Cooper**
Choose You, **Stan Walker**
If I Lose Myself, **Corey Gray, Madilyn Bailey**
Best Part Of Me (feat. YEBBA), **Ed Sheehan, Yebba**
Nobody But You, **Blake Shelton, Gwen Stefani**
Arms, **Christina Perry**
Darkness, **Eminem**

You Make It Real, **James Morrison**
Kiss Me, **Ed Sheeran**
Intentions, **Justin Bieber, Quavo**
Come And Get Me, **Jay Z**
Don't Get Me Wrong, **Lewis Capaldi**

Listen Here Reining Devotion

ACKNOWLEDGMENTS

We know you babes have been eagerly awaiting Rocco, and we can't thank you enough for sticking with us while we found his voice. From the moment we met him in Tangled Love, we knew he'd have a tumultuous story to tell, and boy was it a ride.

As always, there is a community of people pushing us up and helping us deliver the best possible stories our hearts want to tell.

Ellie McLove. We say this often, but we'll continue to shout it from the rooftops. Thank you so much for honoring our voice. Thank you for always seeing our vision and making sure it comes to life in the most impactful way possible.

Michelle Clay and Annette Brignac, could you please tell us how we survived life without you? Thank you for all that you do for us. We heart the everloving shit outta you both. Your friendship means the absolute world to us both.

To the authors who continually inspire us and lend an ear when we need to chat, we are forever grateful for your love and support.

To our Group Therapy babes. Oh, how we adore thee. Thank you for being our favorite place in the world. You bring a light to our lives we never want to lose. Love you.

To our street team, the bloggers and bookstagrammers who stand up and shout about HJ to the world. We could not, and we stress we *could not* do this without you. From every corner of our hearts, we hope you know how much you all mean to us.

To our readers, the babes that pick up our books and get lost in the worlds we create… THANK YOU. Thank you for taking the chance on us time and time again. Thank you for supporting us and encouraging us to live this amazing life. It's a dream come true.

All our love. Always.

H and J.

P.S. We'll love you forever and a day if you would consider leaving an honest review of this book #NoPressure.

VIRTUOUS LIES
A MAFIA INSPIRED ARRANGED MARRIAGE STORY

BIANCA

HOLDING MY HEAD HIGH, I walk from the apartment. One high-heeled foot in front of the other moves me toward the elevator. The silence is deafening. The plush carpet mutes the sound of my heel. No music plays through the hallway speakers. Even the lift moves silently.

The dress I meticulously chose from my closet—the sexiest one I own—brushes my upper thighs as I step into the elevator. Anxiety rushes over my skin, but I force myself to stop fidgeting. I push my shoulders back in a posture that screams confidence.

My racing heart pounds against my rib cage. I'm convinced I'm only moments away from a heart attack. At eighteen.

My eyes move to the digital read on the elevator, the metal cage moving closer and closer to the ground floor with every second that passes. My body wills to shake, to tremble with dread. I refuse to let it, holding it in. It inverts, my organs rocked by tremors that make me nauseous.

Life changes so fast. You blink, and your world turns inside out. Six weeks ago, I was told I would marry Salvatore Bianchi in a peace deal brokered between our family and the Chicago Outfit. I wasn't surprised, certainly apprehensive, but I hid my hesitation well—as would have been expected. Salvatore was due to arrive in the coming weeks. I was of age, having just celebrated my eighteenth birthday, which meant by my family standard, I was ready to belong to a man I was yet to meet.

I know the basic facts about my future husband. Thirty years old and boss of the Chicago Outfit. Never formally married. Mama assures me he's handsome, but she'd say anything to make me agreeable. Honestly, I couldn't care less if he had two heads. I just wanted to know whether he'd hurt me. Mama tells me that men can't hurt us if we don't let them infiltrate our hearts. I told her I meant physically. She told me to learn to disassociate. Inspiring, no?

On the same day I was told of my union with Salvatore, Caterina was told of hers with Roberto Ferrari. An act to preserve power *within* the family.

Caterina and I knew this was our path. *This* being the accepting mafioso women who we were, we'd accept our fate. Only, I couldn't acquiesce my sister's.

Caterina Rossi would never belong to the consigliere of Cosa Nostra. Not if I had anything to do with it.

I pretend I can't see myself in the reflection of the elevator doors. My lipstick is smeared, but I don't fix it. My hair has lost the neat silk of the wave I'd styled it into, the strains a messy resemblance of what they were a simple hour before.

The elevator comes to a stop with a delicate jerk, and I take a fortifying breath, relaxing my face into what I imagine an eighteen-year-old woman stupidly in love would look like.

I adjust my dress purposely as I step from the open doors, the resounding click of my heel against marble loud enough to steel my nerves. The black Town Car parked curbside is impossible to miss, and I'm both elated and petrified at the sight of it.

My brother, Tony, eyes me warily as I exit the building with balletic strides. He stuffs his hands into his black dress pants. The leather of his gun holster is visible, his jacket haphazardly thrown open, and I eye the concealed weapon with trepidation.

God, if he makes Tony kill me.

My brother dips his chin inconspicuously enough that if you blinked, you would miss it. I return the indecipherable gesture. The success of a scheme coming together without issue passed through silent conversation between siblings.

Tony was surprisingly agreeable when I came to him with my plan. Our sister is naïve and amorous. Traits that wouldn't fare well in the possession of a monster. Our father had no issue with pushing her into the lion's den. Mother would stand by idly and watch the carnage. I would not, and Tony wasn't convinced he could close his eyes to the slaughter of Caterina's soul either.

Tony steps forward when I'm mere steps away from the car, grabbing my upper arm roughly. "Well done," he whispers, his face a contradiction to his praise, twisted in disapproval to make my father believe he's reprimanding me.

He pushes me forward unexpectedly, and I stumble on my stilettos, falling against the car roughly. I scowl at him, my reaction one-hundred-percent real. "*Ow.*"

I straighten myself, retreating onto the sidewalk and adjusting my hair. Normally, a driver would be waiting, car door held open for me to slide into the sanctuary of my father's presence. Not today. Today, I'm forced to remain outside, waiting for a punishment I had hoped for.

Bile twists itself in my stomach, and I'm thankful for the heat New York City slathers my skin with. The sweat grasping my upper lip will be mistaken for the humidity in lieu of what's actually causing it—crippling nerves.

He could kill me.

Men have died for less.

The dishonor I've drenched my father with is a scandal my family has not had to overcome for generations.

I was the golden child.

The swan in a gilded cage.

I was my father's most prized possession.

The key to the expansion in the business.

And I've just fucked it all.

There will be blood on my hands. The loss of life resting heavily on my shoulders for eternity. But I can't find it in me to care. My hands might forever be bathed in red, but I would wear it proudly. If only to myself.

The back door of the Town Car opens slowly, and my heart skips a beat. I avoid Tony's eyes, afraid of the panic my older brother will be unable to hide.

Armando Rossi moves torturously slow, and I consider he does it purposely. I refuse to look at the buffed leather of his loafers as he steps out, my eyes kept forward as my father—all six-foot-two of him—unfolds from the car.

He straightens the cuffs of his pressed shirt.

He adjusts his collar.

He spins his wedding band three times.

He does all this before taking a single step. Before even looking at me.

The fury in his breath coats my face in warmth, and it takes everything within me not to grimace in repulsion.

I want to apologize, but I refrain.

I want to swallow, yet I clench my jaw to abstain.

"Look at me."

My chin longs to wobble, the fear in my throat like acid. But I do as I am told.

The back of his hand scores across my face before I register he's lifted it. The slap is hard enough the metal of his wedding band rips into my skin in a caress of reproach.

"Let it bleed," he grates out when I lift my hand.

Fist clenched, I drop it to my side, my eyes watering unintentionally at the feel of blood trickling down my cheek and onto my neck.

"Tony," he murmurs, refusing to take his eyes from me.

Tony moves toward the glass doors of the building without delay, and I send a prayer to anyone who will listen that he'll be safe.

"No, Daddy," I cry. "Please." I throw myself toward him, grabbing the lapels of his jacket. "Don't hurt him."

He pushes me back with a disregard and disgust that pierces my heart in a way I wasn't expecting.

"Get in the car before I'm forced to kill you."

I swallow. It was always a possibility, but hearing the words fall from my father's mouth with such ease slices me open and makes my heart stutter in pain.

I scramble toward the car, attempting to be seen as a dutiful daughter when, in fact, I'd just blown his entire world apart.

He waits long enough for me to swipe at my tears before following me into the car. His stare burns a hole into the forefront of my head, where a bullet would lodge itself right between my eyes.

"I love him," I lie, massaging my hands in my lap. My eyes are cast downward, afraid my deception will shine through.

He snorts in disgust. "You know *nothing* of love. What of loyalty, Bianca?"

"I'll do anything you ask of me."

"Anything I ask?" he bellows. "It was implied, Bianca. You are *given*. You are promised to another. To the *boss* of the Outfit." The veins in his head pulsate so fiercely that I fear his head will explode.

"And I will remain dutiful to him."

"He will not want you," he sneers. "You are no longer pure. What will Lorenzo tell him? The disrespect is unforgivable."

My father is a beautiful man. Tall and muscular. A strong jawline and thick lips. Brown eyes the color of cognac. Women throw themselves at him. I'd love to say that he only has eyes for my mother —as beautiful as she is—but I'd be lying. He takes advantage of his beauty.

While he remains respectful of my mother, which is the Cosa Nostra way, he's kept a *goomah* for many years. Even then, he enjoys the women the family has on the payroll when it suits him.

I want to hate him for it. It's not uncommon for made men to cheat on their wives, and it's not frowned upon. The women accept it. My mother tells me my father does it respectfully. How does one *respectfully* commit adultery? He does it discreetly, yes. But respectfully? There is no such thing.

My father is a capo, and while he has never outwardly vocalized his charge, I know he's responsible for the underworld prostitution ring run by the family. It should make me sick, but I've met some of the women under his charge, and they're happy. As happy as you can be sucking cock for money. But their vocation lets them live a life they're comfortable with. They're protected, to a degree, by the family, and I can't begrudge them that.

"Why is it okay for you to have mistresses but not okay for women to live the same?" I stupidly spit. "Were you a virgin when you married Mama?"

"Watch your mouth." His mouth doesn't open as he threatens me. The clench in his teeth so tight, the words are scarcely audible. "You honor and you respect the old ways, Bianca. I am a capo, for fuck's sake. What do I tell Lorenzo? Huh? His key to peace with the Outfit has been blown up because you fucked his *consigliere*? His closest advisor?" he screams, shaking the windows of his Town Car.

I can't swallow. I try, but my throat has tightened. An invisible palm having closed itself around my neck. I didn't think about what Lorenzo would do.

Tony jumps into the passenger seat, startling us both. "*Go,*" he urges my father's driver.

Twisting in his seat, Tony looks ready to combust. "Did you fucking kill him?"

"What?" My mouth falls open.

"Did. You. Kill. Him?" he snarls, his face twisted with unease.

"Wh—No. Of course, not."

Looking at our father, he shakes his head. "Roberto already had a serious fucking headache when I got up there."

"A headache?" I repeat dumbly.

"A gunshot wound to the *goddamn* head, B."

"Who else was with you?" My father grabs my wrist, and I cry out from the pain.

"No one. I swear. It was just Berto and me."

You want more don't you? Don't worry, you can download your copy of VIRTUOUS LIES here.

ABOUT THE AUTHOR

A blonde. A brunette. A tea lover. A coffee addict. Two people. One pen name. Haley Jenner is made up of friends, H and J. They're pals, besties if you will, maybe even soulmates. Consider them the ultimate in split personality, exactly the same, but completely different.

They reside on the Gold Coast in Australia's sunshine state, Queensland. They lead ultra-busy lives as working mums, but wouldn't want it any other way.

Books are a large part of their lives. Always have been and they're firm believers that reading is an essential part of living. Escaping with a good story is one of their most favorite things, even to the detriment of sleep.

They love a good laugh, a strong, dominating alpha, but most importantly, know that friendships, the fierce ones, are the key to lifelong sanity and fulfillment.

ALSO BY HALEY JENNER

Stand-alones

Impact

Impact

Cross your Heart

Cross your Heart

FOR KEEPS. FOR ALWAYS.

For Keeps. For Always.

UNTAMED (a short story)

Untamed.

Series

The Chaotic Rein Series

Tangled Love (#1)

Reining Devotion (#2)

Lies of the Underworld

Virtuous Lies (#1)

Fractured Secrets (#2)

Made in United States
Cleveland, OH
08 May 2025

16739893R00164